THE SPLINTERED BEAM

INKLINGS OF A DIFFERENT KING

Book 2 of The New Seed Series

CHARLES ANTHONY SOLORIO

Printed in the United States of America

ISBN: 978-1-956019-70-4 (paperback)
ISBN: 978-1-956019-71-1 (ebook)

Canoe Tree
Press

4697 Main Street
Manchester Center, VT 05255

Canoe Tree Press is a division of DartFrog Books

"Where are you?"
—God

THE SPLINTERED BEAM

He planted the splintered beam of the cross
as seed into the shore.
Flawed, he claimed the land for God,
but did he lust for more?
Which would be the currency
used by created hand—
Right or might, love or lust,
that would soften or harden the beautiful land?
Spilled blood cries out for liberty,
for victory . . . who shall heed?
Those rich in gold or rich in love,
the thorns or the planted Seed?

Chapter 1

ABRAHAM

Southampton, England
1620

The wind of a new day moved the old torn veil covering the window.

A light from outside flashed through the window. Abraham awoke with a gasp, lying on the ground in a pool of his own vomit. He wept as he held the box containing the knife on his chest.

Jonathan was in the back of the house ending his life.

A fist pounded on the front door and echoed through the small house. "Abraham! You must open up!"

The single voice outside drowned in the war of screaming voices inside Abraham's head. A chorus of pleading voices within the recurring nightmare still cried for help. Abraham opened his eyes farther and set the cube-shaped box next to him on the ground.

Birds, free from terminal guilt, sang outside in the aftermath of the dream that assaulted him. That nightmare had burst through whatever barrier he had erected in his mind and returned six months ago and remained. It appeared whenever his defenses were down.

He closed his eyes and turned his head away from the empty bottles scattered on the ground and standing on the table. The covering over the window fluttered toward him.

Abraham smeared his long hair out of his eyes. He wiped his mouth and his thick, unkempt beard. A strange odor above him burned inside his nose. He tugged on his long, matted hair like pulling on a rope. His trembling hand pushed on his forehead as he tried to breathe through his sobbing.

Make it go away! I cannot do this!

The pounding on the front door came again. "Abraham! Open the door!"

Jonathan and Abraham were born on the same day, and they were to die on the same day. Jonathan was dead by now, and Abraham was to follow.

But Abraham was not alone. Something else moved in the room.

Like a fear-ridden obedient child, Abraham opened the box. He adjusted his wedding ring and studied the knife inside. What would be his family's destiny?

He watched his shaking left hand take out the weapon. The veins on the back of his hand pulsated. The light skin of his fingers turned lighter.

With honor demanding for him to pay the rightful price of justice, he watched his grip tighten around the knife, like the invisible grip around his throat.

No more guilt. No more regret. No more fighting. He pressed the cold blade against his neck. He winced with the anticipation of pain. His hand prepared him to soon join his best friend, Jonathan.

He closed his eyes. He tried to breathe as the cold blade pressed harder.

Fully awake, a new scene from the recurring nightmare flashed before his eyes. A bloodied hand reached down toward him. A different voice whispered above the storm in his head.

"Abraham!"

A sliver of light flashed away from him. He opened his eyes fully. The covering over the window hung still. Like a newly delivered infant, he gasped for an unexpected breath of air.

Who is calling me?

Abraham flexed his left hand. The knife was as if held by fingers that belonged to someone else. With a gasp, he dropped it into the box.

He stared at the back of his pulsating hand and crawled away from the knife. Through the dim light, behind empty bottles, legs from a tall, lean body lay in a bedroom doorway, with the rest of the body behind the wall.

Jonathan, I failed you. I could not kill myself. I betrayed you.

They had vowed to die and settle their insurmountable sin debts together. It was to be their last day on earth and first day in hell. What happened? Now they could not pay for their mistakes together.

Wiping the blurriness from his eyes, fighting weakness on his left side, Abraham staggered toward his best friend's body.

Jonathan sat up with a clean knife beside him.

Jonathan?

Abraham shook his head, trying to fully awake. "What happened?"

Opening his eyes wider, Jonathan looked at his hands. "Something stopped me."

"Abraham!" cried the voice from outside. "He stayed your hand. But you don't have much time."

Abraham's arms and legs moved easier. He now lifted them with ease. He shook his head.

How can this be? I am still alive. Jonathan is still alive. The man outside my door saw something. Maybe he can tell me what happened here.

He crossed the room to the front door and opened it. With his head bent down, he shielded his eyes from the bright light of the new dawn.

The silhouette of a man of medium build and bent spine stood in his doorway. Avoiding eye contact after a glance, Abraham recognized the man. Cuts, bruises, and gashes streaked across his face.

He hadn't seen Edmund in months. Edmund followed John Robinson, one of the nonconformist leaders of the Resistance against the king.

The bent man spoke with labored breathing. "I escaped from the king and his men to deliver a message to you." He looked side to side and behind him. His eyes widened, as if he saw someone down the street. He leaned closer to Abraham. "Will you let me in?"

Rubbing his eyes, adjusting to the light, Abraham kicked clothes and garbage aside to clear a path and motioned for him to enter. The man rushed inside and closed the door. Bloodstains covered his shoes.

Had this man killed after convincing others he had a message for them?

"My life is in danger—for I am a danger," the man panted. "Many resist the message I bear. I come to share with you a seed planted within me."

Was this man running from the king, or did he work for the king? Was this a trap to find more rebels in the Resistance? Abraham's heart pounded. Stories of the king hunting his opposition made his chest hurt. Abraham inched closer to the wooden box in case the bloodstained subversive became a murdering madman.

Edmund placed his hands on Abraham's shoulders and guided him to be still, attempting to make eye contact.

Abraham did not want to see what was inside the man committing crimes against—or for—the king.

"Standing outside, I saw a hand moving you to end your life. Then I saw another hand save you." Edmund squeezed Abraham's shoulders.

How could he know that? This man had the eyes of God and knew all Abraham had done! No one else must know what he did.

The call to open the box wrapped its noose around him tighter and pulled him to pick it up. Abraham charged toward the box. He turned toward Edmund.

Jonathan stood paralyzed in his bedroom doorway.

Abraham's chest burned. He dropped the cold box. His knees hit the hard ground beside it.

The madman crouched beside Abraham and leaned toward his left ear. "What if we have believed a lie from the liar hiding within the king? What if the king is not God on earth?"

Abraham tried to breathe as Edmund helped him to his feet. Abraham turned his eyes toward the back door as the man said, "God will soon turn over your hourglass. You will then have seventy-six days left in this life."

A few minutes before, Abraham had prepared to end his life. He'd seen a hand in his dream. He'd heard a different voice above the others inside his head. It was a voice that knew him. It called him by name. And now his life was limited to seventy-six days?

What have I done with my life? I spent the precious gift of time on selfish pursuits. I am now bankrupt.

Like a beggar negotiating with a king, Abraham blurted, "Do not tell others of all my sins. No more nightmares and voices. My family—give me more days to return to my family."

The follower of the rebel John Robinson kept Abraham upright like someone preventing a man from drowning below in an angry sea. "I cannot grant you this. I am but a fallible man."

Jonathan moved from the doorway. He motioned with a matchlock musket for the madman to move away from Abraham. Jonathan aimed it at Edmund, ready to ignite the readied weapon. "I know who you are. You are an enemy of the king. I will not let you put my friend in danger. Leave now, or I will kill you."

The madman raised his hands with open palms. "I came to save your friend."

Abraham yanked the weapon from Jonathan. The weapon burned cold in his hand. "He is not a threat. He has risked his life to share a message with us."

"The blood on him speaks otherwise," Jonathan said as he lunged forward and struck Edmund in the face with his fist. The haunting thud rose with the dust in a low-lying cloud as Abraham stood frozen.

Moaning in pain, the man placed his hand on his bleeding face and wiped his eyes with his darkened sleeve. Abraham cursed Jonathan as Jonathan grabbed the weapon back and pointed it at Edmund's head. "Leave now before you get us all killed."

Abraham shoved Jonathan away. "If you shoot him, you will alert the authorities, and they will come looking for us. Let him have his say."

His friend clenched his fist and mumbled curse words under his breath.

The messenger, with a new cut, rose, took his hand from his face, and looked at his doublet's bloody sleeve. His hand glistened in the available light. He smiled and wiped the side of his mouth again, adding a darker shade to what he was wearing. He adjusted his torn breeches and dusted himself off.

As if nothing had happened, he asked, "Do you know about the City Cubed and the King?"

Abraham raised an eyebrow and looked at Jonathan, who narrowed his eyes.

"There is no other king but King James the First." Jonathan snarled his lip.

The madman paused. "I speak of the King above all kings and His City that He has prepared for us."

He truly is mad—but I need to hear more.

The friends looked at each other. Jonathan locked eyes with Abraham and pointed with his eyes toward the back door. Jonathan appeared to be ready to report the madman to the authorities. He prepared them to run.

The rebel with no sound mind closed his eyes and said, "He seeks those who will resist the adversary lying and deceiving within yet another counterfeit king of this world."

Abraham put his hand on his chest. He looked at Jonathan, and they both shook their heads.

He wants us to commit treason against our king.

"You know what they do to those who oppose the king. I would rather that you meet death before Abraham and I plead for it," Jonathan said as he grabbed Edmund's doublet.

The man did not resist Jonathan and continued, "Today, you have been saved. Now you can save others."

"Not if we are in prison—or dead," Jonathan scoffed.

"A new friend has taught you for the last few months. More will be revealed."

How does he know about Steven and us?

Who else knew their friend Steven had been secretly reading to them from a book that rebelled against the king's book? Abraham refused to look Edmund in the eye, but he could feel him moving closer . . . like a father getting ready to commission his son to care for the family in his absence.

Abraham's mother had expressed a deep love for Abraham the last several months of her life. Eleanor loved him with a love he had never known. But Abraham grew up most of his life without parents to teach him how to navigate life's waters. For most of his thirty-three years, he'd been left alone to sink or swim—and no one had ever taught him how to swim.

The famine in his chest burned as something penetrated through the hard heart ground.

The subversive paused, as if to let Abraham finish his thoughts. "There is only one King, and He is not idle. But there is one who opposes Him, which dwells in many counterfeit kings. The one true King has smuggled contraband from the City Cubed into you and into this world. But the one who dwells in our counterfeit king knows this."

How can I be carrying something when I have nothing? Who dwells in the king other than the king?

Edmund paused and pressed his pointed finger on the left side of Abraham's chest. "The contraband dwells within you. It is living. Breathing. Waiting to receive the command to fully awaken its host. The adversary dwelling within the counterfeit king does not want this to happen."

Abraham rubbed his beard. The clear path still pointed to a door of escape. "How can there be another king?"

The intruder walked and stood between Abraham and the back door and smiled. "Your eyes have not yet seen things as they truly are. Scales will fall from your eyes as you receive more revelation."

The hairs on the back of Abraham's neck stood up. He crossed his arms. The morning felt colder.

The messenger of suicide placed his hand on Abraham's shoulder. "Will you allow Him to carry you so that you may carry to others what He implanted inside you?"

Abraham looked around to see if anyone heard the pounding in his chest. Something within him moved.

Edmund moved his hand from Abraham's shoulder and turned his head toward Jonathan. "I have done what I was appointed to do."

A powerful knock shook the door. They'd found them.

How could a door stop a king? All eyes glanced around the room in preparation for a quick escape.

Jonathan aimed the gun at the front door. Abraham grabbed the gun from Jonathan. Shooting the king's men would result in cruel torture before a welcomed death—or, at the very best, spending the rest of their short lives running.

Muttering on the other side of the door made Abraham's feet feel like lead. The few words he could decipher indicated they were looking for someone at the wrong house.

Footsteps moved away from the door, and the voices carried down the street. Abraham exhaled. The door remained closed, but something within Abraham opened.

"In your last days, whom will you serve?" Edmund asked.

Each word hit Abraham like a large and heavy two-sided coin taken from a bag of coins and thrown at his face. One side was life. The other side was death. Which side would land up?

Edmund walked to their table, where empty bottles lay among tools gathering dust. He took a hammer and nail from the table and pushed several empty bottles onto the ground with a clatter of broken glass. He placed the hammer and nail back onto the table next to a remaining container of water.

He turned to Abraham with wide eyes. "I did what was asked of me. This is in His hands now, as it has always been." He opened the door and ran out.

Abraham and Jonathan bumped into each other heading to the doorway and peeked out the partially open door just enough to see Edmund hiding behind a tree between Abraham and Jonathan's place and a group of men walking toward their house. Edmund locked eyes with Abraham. Abraham diverted his eyes toward the group of men.

Edmund ran toward the group of men. Abraham and Jonathan jerked their heads farther back inside as Edmund tackled one of the men.

Still holding the man's legs, Edmund pulled a second man down. The others kicked him and punched him until he stopped moving. They dragged him away.

Jonathan closed the door.

"What just happened?" Abraham glared at Jonathan. "We have to help him."

"That is what happens to those people who oppose the king. There's nothing we can do."

"We can't just stand here."

"He's gone now."

Through blurry vision, Abraham shook his head and turned to Jonathan. Abraham reached for the door as Jonathan's strong grip pulled Abraham away from it.

"You know I have always been with you. But this . . . this is a matter of life and death. We must choose well." Jonathan ran his fingers through his closely trimmed hair.

Abraham pulled on his own unkempt beard and turned away.

"Abraham, you need to be careful. I don't know whether people should be able to serve whatever king they desire. But what happened to Edmund could happen to you. We have always tried to stay away from the fight between those people and the king and his men."

Abraham sighed and slumped forward. He closed his eyes. "Perhaps that is how we are to end our lives together?"

After navigating through the broken bottles on the ground, they stood and looked at the table and what Edmund left on it.

"We need to seek wise counsel," Abraham said.

"There is no one we can trust."

"I understood some of what Edmund said today, because of my conversations and readings with Steven. We do have one friend we can trust."

Abraham looked out the window and down the barren street. "Maybe Steven can help Edmund . . . if Edmund is still alive."

A shadow fell on the room as the clouds moved. The covering over the window wafted. Abraham sat down and wanted to close his eyes to rest and recover.

But would the nightmare and voices invade him once again?

Proper judgment for the things that I have done.

CHAPTER 2

STEVEN

Southampton, England
1620

Steven awoke in the early morning to the sound of a familiar voice speaking a single word. The same voice and the same word for the last five years. He opened his eyes, but as always, no one was there.

He sat up in bed and sprang to his feet to prepare for the day. The voice summoned him again for a silent breakfast and conversation. Breakfast would include stale bread, old fruit with old cheese, and secrets entrusted to him in preparation for an early morning meeting with a local.

He walked down his narrow hall as shadows flickered on his walls from a short candle he carried as it lived out its last hour. He sat at his table and ate as he read the page left open from his previous day's studies, though he knew the words by heart. With no other sounds, he began his daily silent conversation.

These conversations were more precious to him now than ever. Having lived fifty-six years with deteriorating health, he didn't know how much time he had left. In his last days, he had just two requests.

One, that he could go home. After his mission, he longed to be with family—those who survived the king's men. Though he would miss his friends in Southampton, he was ready to begin the last chapter in his life back home. Before he completed his final mission, he longed to help his friends Abraham and Jonathan affect the nations.

His second request was that his writings, written over the past several years, would be used to change the world so that others could learn of another King. They were words of treason.

Steven tried to cover his nose as something or someone moved in his dining area. An object fell from a shelf behind him, and he jumped when it hit the ground. Something slid behind him.

He grunted and stomped to the item and picked it up. "You can't stop this," Steven said with a smile.

The sliding noise stopped. Still smiling, he placed the item back up high where it belonged. Where it would one day change everything. He returned to the table and continued his silent conversation.

A prompting pushed him to pray for two women in a faraway land. After praying for them, he prayed for their husbands and their children, the entire continent, and for all the brothers and sisters in all lands. Then he prayed for the vision of a future man, dying in prison, who would one day give many the eyes to see.

My King, remove the chains, visible and invisible. Show us You and a hint of your New World, Your new creation, and Your kingdom. Give us a glimpse of Your City.

Things moved in the heavenly realm. He rejoiced that his prayers, like sentences joined with the prayer paragraphs of people in other lands, could fill pages and hearts and nations. And his writings, combined with what others had written, would become part of a living Story.

He cleaned up after his breakfast and thought about the important meeting he had in a few minutes. Many people feared being with him, with rumors growing about his resistance against the king. Yet someone asked to meet with him in secret that early morning.

In preparation, he spent part of the previous day gathering his writings from the last few years. He was a scribe receiving messages. From a Voice in his dreams and prayer conversations, to his hand, onto paper, and into the hands of those who were enemies of the king.

He had to be careful with whom he shared his writings. The king who ruled over England and its church had no tolerance for rebellion. Yet Steven still placed his letters into the hands of the king's enemies. A few days before, he had shared his most recent letters with Abraham and Jonathan.

He divided the stack of writings into four piles and hid each pile in a different location. No one would think of looking in walls, under furniture, and buried in holes.

A knock on the door startled him. His visitor was early. He finished securing some of his writings in their final locations and opened the door.

Steven rubbed his eyes. A silhouette of a large man towered over him. He had gray hair but looked to be about thirty years old. A scar ran along the left side of his face from his eye to his jaw.

"Richard, please come in." Steven looked outside to see if anyone followed him.

With an initial look of fear in his eyes, the man entered, turning his head to look behind him. "Thank you for your time."

"Thank you for coming." Steven closed the door.

"I have been sent here. I believe you are the one I am looking for. I am in need of a miracle. I came here to see if what people say about you is true."

"I have no power in myself. But please, tell me more. Then we can seek the Lord for His direction." Steven shrugged.

He pointed Richard to a well-loved chair as he sat down. Most members of the local rebellion against the king had sat in that chair or knew someone who had. Oh, the secrets that a dirt-stained chair could tell.

"Do you have a family?" Richard asked as he sank into it.

"Yes. They're not too far from here." Steven tried not to let his emotions arise.

Richard touched Steven's hand. "Family is why I

am here. The last few days, I have had nightmares of someone hunting me down for serving another King by killing me in my sleep. I know I should rest in faith that God will protect me. But . . ."

Steven waited for him to continue.

"If I die, who will protect my family? I need to help my wife raise our kids in the admonition of the Lord."

Steven nodded and silently continued the conversation he had started during breakfast.

"We have heard rumors that some from the Resistance who fled to Holland years ago have returned to start a new life. What future do we have here with the king? We want to join them. The Lord has shown us that He plans to send them to the New World. I need to find them before they leave."

Steven closed his eyes and nodded.

Like a man trying not to slip into a pit, Richard grabbed Steven's forearm. "This is no time to sleep, old man!"

"I am not sleeping," Steven replied without opening his eyes.

"I need to find them. I must find them. They can't leave us here. We want freedom to worship our true King." Richard released his grip.

Steven nodded, as if agreeing with a third person sitting with them. Head still bowed, he prayed, "Lord, you know Richard's heart. Use him to further your kingdom. Reveal your power and your love in a new way."

"Pray that the real King would be known," Richard said.

Steven smiled and continued praying for several minutes. When he finished sharing some of the secret words and looked up, Richard was wiping his eyes with the back of his hand.

Richard's eyes widened, as if he had seen a ghost in the room. He fiddled with his hands. His feet shuffled in place. With mouth open, he staggered up, and Steven walked with him the last few steps to the door.

Steven opened the door and turned to Richard. "Are you ready for what the King is going to do with you?"

Richard walked outside, again wiping his eyes.

As Steven stood at the threshold and watched Richard walk away, a group of men dragged a body across the street a few houses down from Abraham's place. Steven gasped as he recognized the body. Edmund. A follower of John Robinson. The rebel pastor defying the king.

Richard walked toward the group of men. "The body you are pulling is not the one." He turned and pointed to Steven. "It's him!"

The leader of the group stopped some of the other men from returning to Abraham's home. He redirected the men toward Steven.

Steven closed his eyes and remained in the doorway. The running footsteps became louder. He closed his eyes and stood his ground.

As the steps pounded louder, Steven heard for the first time the voice he had only heard in his sleep.

It repeated the same word.

"Africa."

CHAPTER 3

PADA

Ndongo, Africa
1619

Pada poked his head out from behind the baobab tree under the moon's revealing light. When would they attack his village?

Just that same morning, his mother, Chinasa, had prayed here. This baobab tree had become her new place of prayer years ago after they'd fled Luanda. He did not understand his mother much of the time, but he understood why she came here every day. A peaceful calm rested here at his mother's prayer tree and in the nearby canyon.

Until the killing that was coming.

His people did not have a prayer.

Where was his love? His Amara? Was she still upset about both their parents missing?

It didn't matter now. The most important thing was that he and Amara would soon be together—free from all that opposed them.

The knife strapped to his side would make sure of that.

Something then tapped his chest. He tilted his head down. Nothing visible touched him. He turned his head in all directions. No one else touched him. Nothing was thrown at him. It seemed like an invisible hand tapped over his heart three times to get his attention.

"Pada!"

No! Not that voice. Why did I come to this tree? I should have known better.

He placed his hand in between whatever touched him and his chest. It was the same voice that periodically spoke to him above the crying voices in his recurring nightmare.

But this time was different. All previous times it hid within his head. This time it was an audible voice.

It followed him. Pada put his hands over his ears and pressed his hands toward each other.

"Stop . . . make it go away . . ." Pada mumbled.

Grimacing upward to the heavens, he shook his head. "You will not stop me from enacting justice. You cannot stop this. I was only a little boy when You did not save our home and everything we had in Luanda. Mother consoled me with tears in her eyes as they burned our home—and many other homes. We had to run away over the bodies of our friends. Where were You *then*?"

He wiped his eyes and studied the shadows hiding and waiting in the canyon. "God, You did not stop our enemies then," Pada said into the night. "You are not stopping them now. You took away everything we had. You took away our friends. Any sense of security. My father was never the same. You took away the father I barely remember. And now, because of You, I did bad things—I will not allow You to take everything away from me again."

Pada pulled out the knife and gazed at the moonlight shine reflected onto his trembling hands. They trembled, but they were strong. The same hands destined to save his future. The same hands soon to serve vengeance against the traitor working with the coming mercenaries of the government. Tonight, one less Judas working with the Imbangala to commit crimes against his people.

Where is Amara? She should have been here already. My time is short.

The sound of something sliding on the ground alerted him. He tightened his grip around the knife. Then a head appeared above the short brush.

"Amara!" Pada exclaimed, forgetting any sense of secrecy.

He ran to her, and they hugged. They kissed. He wiped her eyes as her lips quavered. They kissed again. He lifted her and carried her to hide behind the baobab tree.

"You are okay. I was getting worried. I forgot that it might take you a little longer," Pada said as his hand covered the left side of his chest.

"Something is not right. It feels dangerous out there, and I was worried about you. I went as fast as I could. These legs are slow from all the broken bones—but faithful."

"That doesn't matter. You are here, and I am now complete."

He bent his head down and closed his eyes. "I am sorry I had to leave you alone for a short while. I thought it would be important for you to hide in another part of the canyon and then meet me here at the tree. But I have been worried sick since I let you out of my sight."

Pada held her hand. "Please forgive me. I had to find someone by myself. I ended up not finding him, but I think I now know where he is. I need to find him soon."

She caressed his face. "I love you. But again, please tell me why you are hiding me in different places these last few days. You continue to not tell me what is happening. And today, our parents are gone? What happened to our parents? When are they coming back? They did not even leave a note."

"As I told you, I think we should go away too. I am sure our parents are fine—you and I need to go away to be together."

"I want to be with you. I want our parents to be okay. Maybe, somehow, we can all be together and stay? But we cannot go away today. You have been hiding us for days preparing for our marriage, and now *they* are gone. We need to stay here because our parents are looking for us. That is where they are. They will come back looking for us. We can't move away now."

Just let us leave this place—before it is too late.

"Maybe they went away to make sure they were united in their plans against what we want together. They do not see what we see in each other." Pada kissed her again.

"I know they think we are too young and moving too fast, but does it make any sense they would leave us together as they plotted against us being together? And it is not like them to just leave without telling us. They have never done this before. They must be coming back soon, right?"

Pada shrugged. "Perhaps they went together to prepare a place for both of our families to be safe in the future and did not want to alarm us of the coming threats they have warned us about. Our mothers have told us of a coming evil. But I am eighteen, and you are sixteen. They should treat us as the adults we are. They know that God wants you and me together."

"It is strange to hear you talk about God. You worry me sometimes. You only talk about God to justify us being together. It is not right that you put me above God. I want a man that puts God above me. Then you would be able to protect and serve me as I should serve you."

"I trust you more than God. You didn't let people burn my home when I was a child. You did not force my parents and me to run away for our lives, away from the only home my parents and I knew." Pada shook his head and looked downward. "You are not asking for everything that I have. Enough of that. I want to rule this kingdom with you. What do you think of King Pada and Queen Amara one day? We could rule together and change everything for the better."

"Maybe God allowed those things to bring you to me, for us to stop the injustice—His way? Maybe His plans are bigger than yours?"

"All I know is that I have you now."

Amara placed a hand on his head and studied his eyes. "There is something you want to tell me, isn't there?

"Well . . . yes."

"You are sad. What is wrong?"

Pada grabbed her hands and held them softly. "You have to trust me. I have another part to our plan, and you have to trust me. Can you trust me?"

She narrowed her eyes. "I have trusted you enough to allow you to hide me in different places the last few days. I have always trusted you before. We should be together. But you have been preoccupied the last few days. It started right before we started hiding."

"Will you trust me?"

"Yes."

Pada waved to someone in the distance. A man stood up from behind a large bush and walked toward them. Amara turned her head toward the man and then back toward Pada with her eyebrows raised.

"Pada, what is going on?"

"You have to trust me."

The man walked up to them and smiled a warm smile. "Amara, this is Chizoba. He is a new friend who

I met a few weeks ago. I have come to have faith in him and his family."

Amara turned to Pada with a puzzled look. She then turned her head to the man and shook her head.

Pada sighed. His voice cracked. "Trust me. You need to go with Chizoba. He will take you to a safe place as I look for our parents. Then wait for me with Chizoba's family, and I will come to take you back home. Maybe then we can all figure things out between us and our parents."

Do I move forward with my plan? How can she trust me, when I do not trust myself with what I am about to do? But someone has to stop the traitors of my people and the Imbangala. Or at least one of them.

He had never seen fear like this before in Amara.

"What are you doing? I am scared . . . please hold me."

Pada hugged her and kissed her forehead. He pointed to the base of his mom's baobab tree. "We know our parents will have a good explanation for why they were gone. They are safe. This tree shows us the reminders of many answered prayers. You know that each time people prayed here, they left a little stick under the tree. All those little sticks are reminders of all my mother's prayers. You and I are represented there with many of those sticks. She has prayed for us, and now we will find out what happens with those prayers."

He leaned toward her again and placed his cheek next to hers. "When you have your doubts, remember the prayers said under this tree. If you remember to hold a prayer within you, it will be like a part of me is within you."

Pada bent down and picked something up. He opened his trembling hand and put one of the sticks into her shaking hand. She shook her head and pushed Chizoba as he picked her up over his shoulder and carried her away. "Pada! Pada!"

He wiped his eyes and gripped the knife strapped to himself.

Now it is time.

He stomped back toward their village, fisting and unfisting his hands. The plan was in place. King Pada was moments away from returning to his kingdom with justice in his right hand.

Pada sneered. The Imbangala. Worthless mercenaries working with a corrupt government.

He pulled his knife out and stabbed the air. Justice would find the Judas among many others. Some of the people betrayed their own families and friends by working with the Imbangala.

He put the knife back. He smiled. He raised his fists toward the sky, his hands now steady.

The knife slipped out of its strap in the midst of Pada feeding vengeance another serving.

I will find him.

CHAPTER 4

ABRAHAM

Southampton, England
1620

What had happened to Abraham and Jonathan earlier that morning? A voice above the other voices, and a madman, ruined their death pact. Was Edmund still alive? Abraham and Jonathan could not leave their home that day with the men of the king still roaming the streets.

It was evening, and Abraham lay in bed. Before Edmund pounded on his door, Abraham had been prepared to die to pay for his mistakes—even willing to take his best friend with him in the process. Their debts of sin paid in full with their lives.

Then he was saved to live. But to live out the invitation from Edmund would bring a painful death for treason against the king. In the same day, death to life to death. And what did one do with hearing a voice speak out one's name to stop a planned suicide? It was a voice that pulled him out of the abyss with a claim upon his life.

That voice was barely distinguishable from his own thoughts. But it was different. A previously unknown, peaceful security accompanied its presence.

Before Edmund had knocked on his door, a different voice seduced him into joining Jonathan in a mutual death pact. That voice reminded him of rotting flesh pulling chains tangled around Abraham. Who or what had persuaded them to end their lives? Who or what stayed their hands from executing self-justice for their sins?

Though no one was with him in his bedroom, he knew he was not alone. Something new accompanied him since Edmund had interrupted his impending death earlier that morning. A faithful remnant of the peace and security remained with him.

But there was also the other, familiar, competing presence with him. It was dark. It spoke from a darker-than-night shadow. It shape-shifted as it desired. It hid—and waited. Sometimes cloaked in his own thoughts. It stole sleep. It stole rest. Abraham concluded it stole his health. His hope.

If life could be a book with chapters he'd written with others, it sat on a high shelf, out of view, to gather dust. Like a whisper behind a mirror, the dark voice called him to take it down and look at it.

In the past, he'd tried to drown the voices with liquor. But he'd used up all his alcohol, believing that yesterday was the last day of his life.

He knew little about his family. If there was a book of his life, the early pages of the book were almost blank. Abraham had never met his father. Growing up, he'd learned from other kids that his father was one of the king's leaders. He'd longed to know his father the way his friends knew theirs.

During one ceremonial procession honoring the king, the crowd cheered in adulation. So many people. His mother pointed to the reason they waited hours to have a closer view. From a distance, Abraham's father on his horse rode in stride next to the king. Finally, his father! Next to the king! The beautiful cadence of the horse's hoofbeats were in rhythm with his expectant heart. The procession advanced toward him. Father was coming his way. He squeezed his mother's limp hand. When Father got closer, her hand fisted with his hand in hers. He yelled and refused to let her pull him away from where his father would be in moments. With disappearing distance, Abraham could see the approaching face of his father! Now his eyes! He was so important as people waved and shouted for him and the king. Abraham elbowed others out of the way with his father just a hug away. He reached out for a touch so Father could lift him up and take him home. But he was too small. He could not reach far enough.

His father looked down at them with the corner of his rolling eyes and passed them without a direct glance.

No hug.

No picking him up like a father should.

He rode away. The final image of his father's back,

working hard to sit up straight, burned forever into his memory.

What happened to those eyes?

They were empty.

Abraham would never have a father.

Every day his mother had rested in a back bedroom of their home. She'd said it was to protect him. Because she did not have any close friends, Abraham did not learn his mother's name until later in life. A woman had called her "Eleanor" and shamed his mother because of her matted hair while they shopped for food. As he'd grown older, he understood the taunts and grew to hate them.

In the present, he was still thin in build, as he'd grown up learning to have one meal a day. There were days when his mother could not venture out for food.

A onetime mistress of a leader of the king could never approach the father of her illegitimate child. She could never help Abraham navigate the difficult waters that threatened him daily as she stayed below deck, chained to a ship taking her to another king waiting in an engulfing shadow.

Was Steven right? That rebel book that Steven read to Abraham was a Voice that said there was another Story beyond the king's. Another Author. Another language not Abraham's own, yet somehow familiar. A language that sought to be known. Yet Abraham needed help to make any sense of it. He needed Steven.

He also needed someone else. Lying on his back, Abraham stared out the window into the moonlit darkness. Only one person in his life knew most of his past yet loved him anyway.

Do you still love me, Humility, after what I did?

Humility. Oh, what a name! How he wished he could hear her thoughts now. Perhaps she was gazing at the same sky. Could she be thinking of him? Could she still be waiting for him?

I am sending a message of my love to you tonight. Can you hear it? Will you forgive me? Could you ever take me back?

Would their young children remember any good that might have been in him at one time? He did not always possess such worthless and wishful thinking.

God, please tell Humility that I am a different man this time.

Abraham breathed in the weight of his mistakes and exhaled regret into the night. He could be empty of hope, but he would never be empty of regret.

If there would be a day when his seventy-six days left of life started to countdown, could he overcome his fear of drowning and cross the ocean in time? Face his secrets? Could he see his family one more time? Or was he better off staying with Jonathan and Steven to await a slow death?

Then it hit. Something fell in the dark of his room, like a hammer hitting a nail on a coffin. Abraham sprang up on his bed. The dark voice that used to be only in his head spoke audibly.

"You can't stop this."

Abraham gasped and had difficulty inhaling air, like a large wave that crashed into him in deep waters in which he could not swim.

If there was a book of life recording his mistakes, it was now next to him on the ground. Opened to the page he feared the most. That page. Enticing him to pick it up. The page, like a bird of prey, pecked at him in pieces as he lay rotting, powerless to swat away the hungry birds.

Should he remember? Should he read that page? Abraham stared at the corner next to his bed, where the noise came from. It was darker in that corner.

I can't stop it.

He prayed to the new presence with him during his time with Edmund that morning. The cold on his hand surprised him after he wiped his face. Shivering, he crawled back under his covers. It was quiet.

Steven would be proud of him for praying. His prayers would never be as powerful as Steven's, as people came from miles around for Steven's prayers. They sought anything from God's wisdom to a miraculous healing.

When Abraham had visited Steven two months ago, a father had brought his little boy to him. The father sought prayer for his boy's broken leg, which was not healing straight. He had broken several bones in his young life. He was such a beautiful and strange boy. The boy asked Steven to pray for the lineage of future family members, leading to a little boy who would one day live in a new country.

The strange boy said, "The little boy I speak of will live in a beautiful and flawed country, where a remnant of the people of the light will live with freedoms that will spread to other nations."

The father of the boy had stood with his mouth wide open.

What a strange boy.

What would happen if Abraham prayed to return to his Humility?

Abraham smiled as a fresh hope of returning to her filled his heart. Perhaps someone had spared his life for a reason.

He fell asleep without fear for the first time in several months. Tomorrow was day one of a new life.

A strange dream infiltrated past his defenses.

CHAPTER 5

ABRAHAM

Southampton, England
1620

Abraham opened his eyes to the sounds of birds singing outside. As he crawled out of bed with his usual stiff lower back, something moved with freedom inside.

Even if the king's men still roamed outside, he had to visit Steven and thank him for his friendship and his prayers. Steven's readings and writings helped Abraham see a veiled story he'd not been aware of. Abraham wanted to better understand the Author's language and illegal writings that people died for.

Who was this other King Steven spoke of?

Who breached Abraham's self-made walls and saved him from his own hand?

In between small bites of stale bread for breakfast, which fell out of his thick beard, Abraham told Jonathan of his plans to visit Steven that morning.

Jonathan wiped his mouth. "I heard noises outside in the middle of the night. People were running. I need to go with you for protection."

Abraham and Jonathan had a difficult time finding the energy and desire to work. With Abraham having not worked on a ship for months and Jonathan not being able to utilize his carpentry and metal skills for weeks, they knew Steven would be home on a Tuesday morning, praying with someone or preparing for church on Sunday.

Jonathan opened the door and peeked outside. He insisted on scouting the area before they both departed. After a few minutes, Jonathan returned. "The streets are quiet. No men of the king. A few people moving about, but not as many as usual. I do not know what happened to Edmund."

Like all the other times, people waited for somebody else to find out if it was safe outside. This was life after the king's men went through a neighborhood.

The friends stepped out with wandering eyes. They walked down their street toward Steven's house with the same daily offense assaulting their nostrils. Wastewater and rubbish thrown outside onto the walkways, like subversives under the feet of the king's men.

Old stains covered the scraped ground. It looked like someone had been dragged away.

Jonathan stepped around the dried blood. "I am afraid for all of us right now. I can feel eyes watching us."

A curtain in a nearby home fluttered back into place. Abraham scanned the neighborhood again. Were neighbors the only ones spying on them?

A short distance from the front entrance of Steven's house was another dried pool of blood.

"It looks like somebody wounded ran to Steven's for help. Who would be foolish enough to resist a power stronger than the ocean with but a single prayer for safety? The king is too powerful." Jonathan shook his head.

Steven's front door was partway open. Jonathan pushed it open farther and called out.

Silence.

Calm down. Calm down. Steven is just fine. The thumping in Abraham's chest built in intensity. He pulled on his beard. "He's in the back of the house. He is always praying there."

They crossed the threshold into Steven's brick home. The air inside always felt warmer and more peaceful there, a rare refuge from the refuse.

With the door left partially open, this time it was cold. They called out again. Still no answer.

They found small remnants of stale bread and biscuits, cheese, and dried fruit on his table in the kitchen. Someone had tipped over the heavy oak chairs and tables. Another dried pool of blood on the ground called out to them.

Abraham and Jonathan split up to search the small house. Abraham found shelves tipped over, books strewn on the ground. Nothing seemed to be missing.

Abraham trembled with concern for his friend. Steven was a vocal critic of the king, never cowering in fear for his life. It was a dangerous way to live.

They met back in the dining area without any sign of Steven.

"This was no common burglary." Abraham's voice cracked. "What little he had of value is still here."

Not that Steven didn't own anything valuable. His writings were his most prized possession. He believed his writings would change the world because God had promised they would. He lived for that day. When they'd killed part of his family for their beliefs, those papers were all that kept him alive.

"His letters. Did you see them?" Abraham asked as his hands flexed.

Jonathan shook his head. "I'll search the dining room and kitchen."

"I'll check the bedroom." Avoiding the mirror, Abraham pulled out the drawers of Steven's dresser and bedside table. He lay on the ground to check under the bed. Clusters of dirt had been pushed into the corners. The ground under the bed was flattened, as if someone had been there hours before. Was he too late?

A hole in the wall was now exposed behind the headboard of the bed. A ripped corner of paper clung to a board near it.

Abraham crawled under the bed and reached into the hole. Empty. Other hiding places indoor and outdoor were empty. Gone.

He did not need to ask his friend if he had found Steven. Abraham stood shaking. His chest tightened. He put his hand on his chest to help calm himself. "He's gone. His writings are gone. How did they know he had letters? How did they find out where they were?"

Jonathan hit a wall nearby him. "Somebody found out. It was probably someone he met with." The hit left a mark on the wall. "He told me he was going to meet someone yesterday morning. Someone had approached him for help from the king."

"Why would anyone hurt Steven? He never hurt anyone in his life. He only helped people. He didn't hurt people."

Jonathan grunted. He shook his head and looked at Abraham, concern clear in his eyes.

Oh, God, no. "No sign of theft of anything of value to other people . . . A gentle enemy of the king"—Abraham's voice cracked—"did not fear death."

His friend unclenched his hands and raised them toward Abraham. "Abraham, do you really know what the king's men are capable of? Do we *really* know?"

Abraham looked around. Books were strewn on the ground. Chairs tipped over. Shelves on the ground. Abraham backed up on his heels. "We need to save him . . . so he can write again."

The room appeared empty. Colder. They stared at the door. Abraham closed his eyes and sighed. He knew it was there. That bare spot near the beam in the ceiling where the shelf had been pulled down.

It felt as if someone was looking down at him from that splintered beam.

He moved backward with his hands up, as if ready to flee from a soldier poking at him with a sword. Abraham tripped and fell backward. "We need to get out of here."

Jonathan bent to help him up. "What if they already saw us in here? The king does not want anyone even appearing to side with the rebels resisting his church and power."

Jumping over fallen furniture, Jonathan stumbled and with trembling voice said, "They will draw and quarter us."

They ran toward the door.

They are going to kill us. Abraham tripped over Jonathan. Jonathan helped him up. Abraham pushed him out of the way and jumped over the fallen furniture to get to the door.

Fog had rolled in and covered the streets. They ran for a minute, when Abraham spotted a man with a bowed spine watching them.

Were the men of the king returning? Abraham and Jonathan stopped in their tracks.

They recognized him as a man who lived in the neighborhood. Nobody knew him. He stayed in his home most of the time. Lines filled his face, pointing toward a shut mouth. That trait seemed to make most who lived in England related. It was the brotherhood and sisterhood under the reign of the king.

The man scanned up and down the street as he approached them.

Abraham tightened his right fist. Ready. Was he a man of the king?

The man sighed as his body bent to the weight upon him. He signaled with his bony fingers for them to come closer. He cupped his hands as he leaned toward them with a remnant of the voice of his youth.

"I saw six of the king's men go to your house yesterday morning. They knocked. I expected them to break your door down. Instead, after they attacked someone, they went to Steven's house. He was standing in front of his home as the leader of the king's men was leaving Steven's house. They pushed Steven inside his house and closed the door partway. I heard hitting and kicking. I did not hear a sound from Steven. A few minutes later, they dragged him away after they dragged the other body off the street."

The man walked away more bent forward. Abraham's legs wobbled as Jonathan put his arm around him. Abraham's heart sank like a man spiraling into deep water.

The heart must be transformed. Abraham could hear Steven's words as if he were standing next to him. New feelings pounded in his chest, like someone had awakened in his open coffin.

What is happening to me? I am losing control. What protection does one have when one loves?

Abraham did not know how to control the new feelings in his chest. What used to be asleep was now awake.

On his knees, Abraham remembered the strange dream, different from his nightmare from the previous night. A groom stood waiting for his bride. The bride said she wanted to go to the wedding but was distracted in many directions. Guests from the wedding called her name. She turned her head in every direction toward each of them.

The groom watched competing suitors pull his bride away. Her lovely dress became soiled. Her suitors grabbed at her and pulled on her, and she lay bleeding on the ground with missing limbs as her multiple lovers laughed.

The groom raced to his love. He wept, and as his tears fell upon her, her dress became clean and white.

Her eyes opened. The groom swept her into his arms and lifted her up. Life pulsated in her veins. The groom commanded her limbs to come back into place, and they did. The bride became whole.

Steven had grieved over all the lost sheep separated from their Shepherd. Ripped apart and displaced. Even with Steven torn away, could someone be putting things back into place?

Where is Steven? Is he still alive?

Jonathan put his arm around his friend again and pulled him up. "We need to go."

A wave of thankfulness swept over Abraham as he remembered the many talks they'd had in Steven's home. A slow burn of rebellion began to ember in him.

He was not going to run. Not today.

He arose and wiped his face as he turned to Jonathan. "There's something I need to do first." He walked back into Steven's home as Jonathan waited outside. Abraham crossed to where the shelf had been ripped away, below that beam in the ceiling.

This is for my friend.

He looked up at the ceiling. Behind the beam. Waiting for him. Speaking to him. It wanted to be found.

Abraham did not want to be found.

In Steven's absence, there was a silence. But staring up at the beam, a new yet familiar presence. Like a gentle fist pushing its way out to fight for others. He stood in silence and listened, holding his breath.

Abraham shook his head and walked backward toward the door while staring at the beam. He bumped into a wall. Like a man underwater, he ran outside to breathe again.

As voices screamed inside of Abraham, Abraham and Jonathan walked back home in silence.

CHAPTER 6

JONATHAN

Southampton, England
1594

Young Jonathan stood near his parents, sprawled on the ground in their dining area. He covered his nose as his parents soiled themselves again. Or was it the garbage on the ground between him and his parents that burned his nostrils?

He used his feet to push the garbage to the side. He stopped breathing to make it quieter so he could focus on watching them. Were their chests moving? Could he hear any breathing?

Jonathan closed his eyes. His heart raced. Previous nightmares now screamed of justified abandonment. One day his parents would go away.

Please be alive.

He did not want to open his eyes. "Mother. Father. Is it time to get up?"

His mother opened her eyes and gave him a death stare. His father awoke and said, "Be gone . . . leave us . . ."

They are alive.

Jonathan opened his eyes and resisted his urge to obey and run far away. But was that the way a responsible eight-year-old should act when he had a family to care for?

He shifted his feet in the dirt in a lone open space on the ground. "You have to get up. It's already late morning. You can't spend another day like this. We need to eat. I cannot find Katherine. She ran from me as I was cleaning."

Shaking, he stayed an arm's swing away. At least they were still alive. He summoned all his courage to ask a question.

He closed his eyes. "Mother . . . Father . . . do you want to live?"

His parents had been slowly killing themselves since his father had lost several jobs in the last three years. They hated the king but were subservient to their lord of liquids.

Rebellion would never happen in the king's house. The mighty king ruled over all things. The king would never allow himself to be a slave to desires that would negatively affect his family and kingdom. His parents just did not know any better.

The piles of the discarded were not yet high enough to block the windows. Sometimes fleeing Hope could be grabbed and held on to while looking outside at a better life. At least there was one person within the house who believed in the king. And his little sister Katherine always followed her big brother. At least, most of the time.

Where was Katherine?

Jonathan pulled on their arms. After several minutes, everyone had played their roles, and they sat up.

His father, with his eyes spinning said, "Diiid you finishhh . . . ch . . . chooores?"

"Yes! I am done. I am now starting with both of your duties. But now that you are awake, perhaps this time *you* want to do them?"

His mother stopped rubbing her eyes. She wiped her mouth and looked around. "Where is your sister?"

He stepped back another step. "That is what I was saying . . ." Jonathan closed his eyes as he tilted his head farther away from his mother.

"I don't know where she ran off to . . ."

He could not stop his fluttering eyelids as he shifted his weight backward.

"I am sure she is around here somewhere. Go look some more and tell me when you have found her," his mother said without moving her face.

He shifted his weight forward. His parents tried to stand but looked tired with their red eyes and red faces, and both lay down to get some more rest.

I fear it is exhausting to be a parent with a disobedient son like me. Sometimes it is exhausting to be a parent when their son neglects his duties of caring for his family. I need to be a better son for the king.

It was his fault his sister wandered, and it was up to him to find her. Though it was difficult to care for four people, they needed him, and he was determined to do things right. He lived for his family. He protected his family.

They needed help. Jonathan would lead them.

They had a neighbor who worked for the king. Perhaps he could help him find his sister. How far could a five-year-old go? Jonathan stepped outside and started to run toward the man of the king, and then stopped. Somewhere nearby, someone was singing. His sister Katherine was always singing. Somehow, she could remember the songs that her mother once sang to her when her mother was still young and not as tired.

He recognized the song and the voice. It was his sister. The singing was coming from the backyard. Jonathan stomped his feet as he made a sharp turn back to the house.

He walked toward the backyard and rehearsed the angry words he intended to scream.

You need to listen to your older brother. Do not walk away unless you ask me first. I have to protect you.

He turned the corner and stopped with his mouth wide open. There in the midst of the tall weeds. Katherine had one of her father's knives and was stroking the back of the knife gently across her throat. She moved it back and forth in rhythm to her song. She was playing the violin with a knife and her throat.

"Katherine! What are you doing?"

Startled, Katherine accidentally poked herself. "You scared me."

"Put that knife down. What do you think you are doing?"

"Look, I'm just like Father. I've seen him moving his knife across his throat. Like this. He was in one of his angry moods. He got mad when I saw him, and he sent me away. I was not happy. So this time I am changing things. I am going to be happy today. I am a violin, and I have decided to play a happy song. The last time mother sang this song, she was happy."

He ran toward her and grabbed her hands before she could hurt herself with the knife.

Father will be so angry.

In the most authoritative voice a young boy could muster, like a father should sound, he said, "Let go. Let go."

He grabbed the hand holding the knife and pulled on her fingers to open them. Katherine resisted. "Stop it, Jonathan. It's my toy—Father said I could have it."

Why did she fight what was best for her? His hand slipped at the same time as Katherine used all her strength. She cried out and fell.

Jonathan pulled out the knife and stood above her. Their faces mirrored each other. They both looked at each other, unable to move. Not a sound could be heard in the busy neighborhood. They had never seen blood like that.

While lying on her back, Katherine lifted her head to look down at herself as she held her stomach. She closed her eyes and then let her head down.

What was Jonathan to do? His parents were passed out inside of the house. If he ran to a neighbor, they would find his parents asleep again. His parents would get in trouble. They would take Jonathan away from being able to help his family. Would they think he tried to kill his sister?

He stood still. Blood dripped off his right hand holding the knife.

He put the knife into his left hand and pushed his shaking right hand up against her wound, trying to put the blood back in.

Jonathan continued Katherine's happy song as she tried to smile. He stopped singing. "Katherine . . . the king . . . the king will save you."

CHAPTER 7

ABRAHAM

Southampton, England
1620

The morning fog had lifted. The silence of a new day was fleeing. After returning from Steven's, Abraham went to his bedroom and closed his door. He coughed after he swiped the dust off some books and papers lying undisturbed on a small table, and then collapsed into the dusty chair and coughed again.

He sat without moving. His life had changed so much in the last several hours, the last several months.

As he sat staring at a wall, shadows of a disappearing day moved from one wall to another. In the late afternoon, he wrote a message to his lovely Humility. She needed to know what had happened to him. He was a different man this time.

With a heavy sigh and a sore back from sitting, he plopped onto his bed.

Abraham imagined walking the shoreline of Lepe Beach, his favorite beach, and finding a letter hidden inside a bottle that had landed at his feet. Walking the shoreline always brought such peace. Would he ruin it by reading the message?

Images passed in his mind of that nightmare that almost killed him.

A random dream did not occur almost every night for months. It meant something. He rose and wrote down details on yellow-colored paper to help him understand it. The message he received was not in a bottle but in the rolling tide of thoughts in his head. Perhaps someone delivered the message in the only way he could eventually understand.

Images foretelling in the language of a dream.

He needed direction. A compass to navigate. Without a guiding hand to help him in his previous thirty-four years of life, how could he understand? Someone must be able to help.

Or was he supposed to walk past the bottle with the hidden message and live an uninterrupted life?

He grew exhausted from the day and the internal wrestling. His heart still raced as he returned to bed and fell asleep.

The nightmare did not knock but busted through his door.

In it, he was floating in the ocean. Thunder and lightning. The unforgiving sea tossed him like a leaf blown from a tree in a strong wind. He turned his head to his right and gasped, watching the ship he was on sinking. A multitude of hands from underwater grasped for the floating ship debris. Hands grew tired and disappeared into the ocean.

A beautiful land in the distance lay to his left. He pivoted his head back and forth between the sinking ship and land. In a pause between peals of thunder, Abraham shook his head and cleared some water from his dripping long hair. He was not alone. Someone was behind him. He could feel it. He did not want to turn around. Was the presence behind him good or evil? He began to sink and turned his head and—

"Abraham." Jonathan interrupted his reliving of the dream. He walked closer to Abraham. "I need to go into town. Is that okay with you?"

Abraham rubbed his eyes and sat up. Jonathan never went into town in the evening. "Is everything okay?"

"I sense that things are going to happen soon. I need to warn more people about what is coming. Don't go outside without me."

Jonathan paused.

"Our lives are about to change. The lives of people all over the world will never be the same. Do you feel it too?"

Abraham closed his eyes and sighed. "Yes."

Wanting to hold on to something, Abraham pulled on his beard. He turned to a window with its covering in place.

What is waiting for us out there?

How much safer it would be to stay inside. Nothing good happened when opposing the king and his men. But Abraham and Jonathan needed to *do* something.

"Be careful out there."

Jonathan turned and walked away. Abraham scratched his chin and slumped backward onto his bed. Something was going to change soon. It would not be good.

***

Abraham awoke the following morning and remembered he had not heard Jonathan come home. What was he doing out there?

He jumped out of bed, dressed, and stuck his head out the front door. The usual invasion of the deep morning fog and people missing waited outside. The fog moved through the streets and reminded him of fingers in the night that abducted people from their homes. He exhaled when Jonathan turned a corner down the street.

Jonathan turned his head in each direction for anyone following him.

When he was close enough, Abraham pulled him inside and closed the door. Abraham leaned toward his ear and said, "What were you doing out there? Is everything all right?"

Jonathan put his hand on Abraham's shoulder. "I found a place to rest and I was careful to make sure no one followed me. I needed to let people know what the king did to Edmund and Steven. I asked for help finding them, and people told me to find a William."

They turned their heads toward noises down the street. Abraham opened the door. A small gathering talked in hushed tones in front of Steven's house through a break in the fog.

Abraham forgot all concern with the king.

Steven was back.

His heart jumped like a young son seeing his father return home from war.

Wait till I tell him what happened. I prayed. He can help me.

They laughed as they ran to Steven. As they moved closer, people gathered around someone who had fainted in the excitement. Through the gray fog, Abraham saw Steven bend down and help someone on the ground.

As they approached the gathering, people appeared confused with what to do about the person who'd fainted. Steven would know what to do. Steven always knew what to do.

But it was Steven on the ground.

Abraham and Jonathan knelt to help Steven up. He was not moving. Through blurry vision, Abraham noted the bruises on his beautiful face, like the face of an angel. There were cuts and a deep, large wound at his throat. He was almost decapitated. Cuts from a knife carved upon his forehead reminded Abraham of the letter N.

As he bent farther, Abraham turned his head and vomited. He could not empty himself of the rage. Sorrow. Regret.

Steven was gone. His home was boarded up. They'd taken his life and his home.

With eyes emptying and then refilling, Abraham lifted his head upward for help. Birds flew away in a pocket of clear sky. So far away. With others, Jonathan helped raise Abraham to stand but then guided him back to the ground as his legs buckled.

Jonathan's voice quivered. "Our friend . . . he is gone."

Abraham covered his head with his hands and tried to breathe.

"Abraham, are you all right?" someone asked.

Someone else in the small gathering said, "We are all devastated. He will need some time."

Abraham was still on his knees when he felt it rising in him. It was moving. If he could swim, it was like he was swimming in a raging river emptying into the sea. It rose from his feet, through his chest, into his head, and onto his tongue.

"God! Are You there? Are You asleep? Wake up." His lips trembled. "Get up. Where is this almighty God that Steven told me about? Yes, the One that allows evil to go unpunished. Are You any different from every other king? Yet another was killed because of You. Is Humility dead too? Did You kill my wife? I don't even know You. I don't even know if I want to know You. Am I going to be murdered because of You as well? How can a father stand idle and watch his children murder each other? What kind of father are You?"

As if spiraling down, Abraham tried to raise his hand above the water level. He heaved, and when he was able to catch his breath, he spat on the ground.

His hands pulsated with uncontrolled fire raging through him. Sinking farther, it was as if he were drowning. The veins on the back of his hand moved. How could he swim if his hands remained in fists?

Steven's hands. Always open. For greeting. Comforting. Giving away. Preparing meals. Turning pages of his Bible. Warm. Sometimes hot like a fire when he prayed for me.

And if Steven was right, Steven's God had created Steven. Beautiful Steven.

Would not beautiful creation require a beautiful Creator?

Abraham looked upward into the sky, screamed, and clenched his fists even more and then . . . opened his hands. Maybe there was a truth to what Steven said about his God.

Something pointed on his shirt in front of his chest. Like the tip of a single finger. Through the blurriness though, no one was touching the shirt. It was like someone pointed to his heart. He stood and walked to the boarded front door and kicked it.

"Abraham, he is gone. There is nothing in there. There is nothing you can do. I don't want them to come for *you*," Jonathan said as he reached for Abraham.

Abraham kicked through one of the boards nailed over the front door. He pushed the door open and bent to fit under a broken board. He walked inside and stepped on the dried bloodstain. He walked forward.

Forward.

Forward.

To the beam.

There it was above. The room darkened as clouds moved outside. Abraham ignored a sound that seemed to move from a back room toward him.

His heart ached in anticipation as he picked up one of the chairs and put it upright. He climbed onto the chair and reached above. He winced as he cut himself on the splintered beam and grabbed what was hidden behind it.

He wiped off the blood and turned his head back and forth between what was in his hands and the open door.

The object that killed Steven. It was now in his hands. To hold it still, he pressed it against his chest. He tried to open it, but his hands could not hold it steady.

It feels hot.

He almost dropped it.

It caused blood on his hand and the blood on the ground. It was the reason for the murder of his friend.

He tightened his grip and hid the object that killed inside his oversized coat pocket. He walked outside to Jonathan, the only person outside waiting for Abraham.

"Where is everyone? Where is Steven's body?" Abraham asked.

"We took his body to someone who will prepare it for burial later." Jonathan narrowed his eyes.

"You did that in five minutes? How can that be?" Abraham tilted his head.

His friend shook his head. "Abraham, the late morning should show that you were gone for much longer than five minutes. We did not want to disturb you, so we waited. When you still did not come out, we took care of the body, and then everyone else went home."

Abraham scratched his head. *Time. What happened to my time? How much do I have left?*

Jonathan shrugged, and they began their walk home. Abraham kept his eyes searching throughout the neighborhood, like a soldier smuggling something across enemy lines.

His seventy-six days would soon begin and then end. He thought of the hidden contraband in his coat. The men of the king had not found it. They'd failed this time.

Why do the men of the king want this?

Through gritted teeth, Abraham whispered to himself, "You can't stop this."

CHAPTER 8

ABRAHAM

Southampton, England
1620

Abraham searched his bedroom and closed his curtains. He shut the door and reached inside the large secret lining of his oversized coat. He gripped with his right hand what had killed both Edmund and Steven.

It was an honor to hold a reason for the failure of the men of the king. To protect Jonathan, he did not let him know what he had taken from Steven's house.

Alone, he closed his eyes, confident that for the moment the contraband was safe. He took a deep breath and opened his eyes and looked around one more time. He pulled out what was in his coat, and this time his hands were steady.

He was ready. He opened it and read, "Imprinted at London by the Deputies of Christopher Barker 1599."

There was also a handwritten message from Steven.

Abraham,

The cloaked one has opposed you for your entire life to not hold what is in your hands at this moment. The King summons you as the counterfeit king within kings hunts you.

The movements of two different kingdoms will be influenced by what rests in your hands. The fate of millions from today to hundreds of years into the future will be affected by you and a small group assembled by God.

Which kingdom will you seek?

Whose hand will you take?

Your friend,

Steven.

Abraham slammed it shut. *What is inside of this?*

Shadows from the day moved across his walls as he sat reading and pausing several different times. The events of the last few days had already fragmented in his mind. He had to record what he remembered before the details escaped him. He knocked over a chair and tripped over clothing as he found writing material under other unfinished projects. As he sat, he knew exactly who he needed to write to.

Someone he had not seen in months.

Dearest Humility,

I love you.

I yearn for truth.

I flee from truth.

Though I long to be with you one more time, I will never be with you again. My words are my only substitute. Please receive them, as I know I do not deserve to be received by you.

I miss gazing at you as you prepared for the morning. The feel of your warm hand in mine. I miss reading stories to the children. I long to be next to them under blankets on a cold night when sharing my stories with the children. I want to see the candle flickering and casting shadows of monsters and heroes over the pages. I smile, remembering the children hiding under the blankets when I read something that scared them and jumping on the bed when they were excited.

I will never be able to replace my lost time with the children. Can you please read my words to Caleb and Rebekah so that they can remember me? Please teach them my words so that they may know their father better. Show them who I was. Show them who I am. No more secrets.

Caleb, are you following what I tried to teach you? Protect your mother and sister.

Rebekah, are you being brave and fighting the monsters?

Humility, my prayer is that you would help show us the way home.

As you know, my parents' time together died before I was born. My father abandoned me. My mother hid for me.

You and I married in holy union. I drifted apart from you at sea.

I left you. You wait for me.

You deserve to know the truth of what happened to me. Why would your husband of ten years leave his wife and his children? Children, why would your father leave? I have so much shame that I cannot write words trying to explain why. For this, I yearn to return to you.

Please know that I love you all. I miss you. Please pray for me as I am trying to find my way back home. Humility, if my words find you, please pray to your God to not kill me for all that I have done.

My health has deteriorated these last several months. I have grown weak on one side of my body. It is as if one side, my older self is fighting in futility the new self rising. My old self asks, "Who is usurping my authority? Who is attempting to replace my kingdom within which I have spent a lifetime building?"

You have always had such a strong love for your God, even though I forbade you from learning more about Him. I was wrong. I failed you all. People I know have died for the words of your God. They knew something.

For the first time, I give my blessing for you to read and teach the children the Word. I felt threatened in my old life, and I now desire to undo my censorship. I will learn more about the dangerous Story with you by writing about it in my letters to you and the children. Please read the stories like I used to do. Though apart, we can learn together.

In my final days, I want a new beginning. A new chapter. A new life. I now take my first step with the beginning of the words that kill. My love, my children, here is the beginning of the Story.

In the beginning God created the heavens and the earth.
—Genesis1:1

I do not know what to do with these words.

Even I can see that if these words are true, they are the most important words ever spoken or written. There are

enormous consequences and ramifica-
tions from this very first sentence. If these
first few words are true, these words are
the foundation of all other truths.

There was a beginning. There is a God.
He created all things. This Creator is
greater than His creation. I can see it—the
reason people are killed for having these
words. It is here in the very first sentence!
In the book that threatens the king, there
are notes printed that contradict what
the king wants us to believe in his book! It
is a book of treason!

Do I want to read more, for I know it
will only get worse? These are notes and
words of treason! Sedition! To the king, the
words are an infection attempting to enter
me to then spread to others.

The words of the book of treason say
there is only one King—and that our king,
claiming the divine right of kings, is actually subservient to the will of another one
true King.

For my entire adult life, I have believed
and lived a lie.

I dropped the words as they were burning my hands.

I picked it back up while looking for
surrounding spies.

Before I smuggled the contraband out

of Steven's home, I slept sleepless nights haunted by a nightmare, voices, and the men of the king hunting me down. I fear now that I will be slain by the enemies of yet another King.

I dropped the words on the floor again and kicked them under my bed. I cannot have these! I cannot touch them!

As I lay on the floor, I looked first to my door and then under my bed. I considered running again. Across another ocean. Farther this time so I could never find me.

But this familiar Story that I do not know calls me. How did things go wrong with this other King and His creation?

How you have fallen from heaven, morning star, son of the dawn! You have been cast down to the earth . . .
—Isaiah 14:12

I want you to know this Story as I am learning it. The God in the book created the angels, and Satan was His morning star. His son of the dawn. The most beautiful of His creation. His favored one.

But Satan rebelled against his Creator. Steven told me this is where error crept into creation. He rebelled against his father. Would not the heart of any father have been broken with His own creation deciding to reject and rebel against His love? Who can console a father God?

Satan, and the angels that sided with him, fought against the Creator and His angels in the heavenly realm. In the battle, God cast down Satan, and one-third of the angels, as they failed to overthrow God.

But Satan now roams the earth!

Many have died because of those words. After seeing my friends die, I must ask, where is God? Why did God not spare many future lives and destroy Satan when he rejected God? What chance against Satan do we have here on earth with an absent father? Why would this God, who is love, the King of all creation, our Father who art in heaven, demand that we be without sin? He is the one who implanted needs and desires into us. These needs will cause us to sin to satisfy our needs and wants because of the angel that He created and threw down and is now roaming here on earth.

In my youth, I wandered into a church when I knew it was empty. Desiring a father and a mother, I sat and wept in the empty church. I prayed to what I hoped was God, of whom I did not know, to send someone to me who could help me navigate my difficult storms. Someone who could take me by a hand to lift me and guide me.

I was not alone. I heard, "I am with you." It was not my voice or my thoughts given a voice. I heard it! I looked around me, but the church was empty.

I held on to those words. But over time I forgot the voice and listened to others. I wandered out of the church, never to return.

I thought my friend Steven was my help, but he is now dead. Killed by the men of the king.

Can He speak again? Where is this power of God when His church is without power? Of what use is a man of this God when forced onto his knees before the occupied king, waiting with a sword at his neck?

While I yet have time, O lovely bride of mine, I feel the pull to come back home to you. I am no longer joined to my mistress of alcohol. I now only want you. My lovely Humility, would you take me back again?

Do I live, or die? Do I lose my life trying to return to you, or do I save my life and stay?

If I am ever able to see myself in the mirror, will my eyes reveal a Satan roaming the earth?

> *I do not know if I want to know the truth.*

As Abraham paused his writing, Jonathan opened Abraham's door.

"I am sorry for disturbing you. You have been in your room for so long today. Come, for you must see . . ."

They ran to their front window. Through the evening air outside, two groups of people fought. One group was much larger and more prepared for battle. The other group was ill equipped and broken.

A storm cloud of shouting lifted into the air. Someone lay motionless on the ground. After another wave of fury hit the shore, the smaller group broke up like a small boat hitting rocks and breaking into several different directions.

"Put out the light!" Abraham said with his voice shaking as he moved the curtain back into place.

Jonathan blew out the candles, and they stood silent. Footsteps moved outside, running for safety. Like a single fist hitting the outside of an ark, a heavy knock on their door broke the silence.

A voice mumbled, "Abraham, Jonathan, are you there? Open the door!"

They looked at each other in dim lighting. Would the lock hold? If they let him in, they were aiding the Resistance. Should they ignore a plea for help?

"Should we do something?" Jonathan whispered as he reached for his weapon.

"Open the door!" the voice outside demanded.

Someone dragged the voice away.

Abraham held Jonathan back. Abraham held his chest as it tightened. "There is nothing to be gained at this moment. We could never overtake them. I hope Steven was right when he said that this battle is not fought with earthly weapons."

Only a few men were left outside. Three of the king's men dragged another body from the street.

After several minutes, they relit their candles. Abraham went into his room and brought out the object that killed Steven.

Jonathan stood with his mouth open. "*What* are you doing? Is that Steven's *Bible* you were reading all day? Did you not hear a friend's voice silenced a moment ago? Steven, Edmund—did you forget what happens to people who have that book?"

Abraham did not answer, as he thought he saw a quick flash of a man's face peering in and then away from their front window where the curtain was not closed all the way. Or did he just imagine a scarred face?

"The king uses his book to justify him being God on earth," Jonathan continued. "The subversives that oppose him use their book to say that the king is subservient to the King of *their* book. Do you see how they both can't be right? The king *can kill*. Those who follow that book of treason, that you now hold, *get killed*. Do you see a problem for us?"

Who would agree to suicide? Abraham smiled, remembering their pact not too long ago.

"I can't stay silent any longer. I can understand helping the Resistance to a certain extent. But now you have that book? Everything changes now. That book kills. Will I end up having to pry that away from your corpse and burn it to save other lives?" Jonathan yelled as he shook his head in his hands.

He walked backward as Abraham stepped toward him. Abraham pointed to the opened book. "This is what they were looking for. This is why they came and took Steven. The reason why people hide in secret. I know why the king and his men are living in terror. "

"*They* are living in terror?" Jonathan sneered.

Abraham held the book up toward Jonathan. "Yes. And I know why. They couldn't find this book at Steven's, and I discovered their secret fear. I compared this Bible to another one I remember seeing years ago. They fear this one more because of—"

"You don't know what you're doing." Jonathan stared with narrowed eyes as he backed farther away from Abraham. After bumping into a chair, he gasped out a nervous laugh. He lunged at Abraham and grabbed the book.

Abraham pushed Jonathan away with one hand and held on to the book with the other. "They fear this Geneva translation because of the published notes within it that contradict the king's version."

"Get rid of that!" Jonathan yelled. "I have seen

what the king's men do. They sometimes move at night. They have no fear of the light. I have known fathers—I have seen fathers taken away from their screaming children. They steal people from their families. In the morning, there is no more husband. No more father. They rot in prison. They are forced to renounce their God. With mercy they are killed or slowly die in prison. And for what purpose? So that their widows can die day by day without them?"

He moved closer to Abraham. "They hang seditionists. They sometimes stop killing you just before you die. When you are barely alive, they then cut your stomach and make you look down to see them pull out your insides. They light them on fire! You watch and feel yourself burn in horror." He closed his eyes. "If you read this, if you keep this, you will die crying for mercy."

Jonathan raised an eyebrow. "I see now . . . that *is* what you want to happen. Have you given up again? You didn't have the courage to kill yourself before, so now you are going to have someone else do it for you?"

Abraham was surprised that he did not want to hit Jonathan. He loved Jonathan as a brother. Abraham lifted the book higher. "I now think this could lead us back home—the Author of this book is calling! We need to talk about this."

"Abraham, this will kill you. If you go forward with this, I cannot save you this time."

"You gave me a home here. I thank you. But I want to go home. I don't have much time." Abraham turned toward the window. The fighting outside had stopped, but the fighting inside had to continue. He asked Jonathan to prepare dinner to give them both time to think.

What am I doing?

In silence they stared at their food with the book between them. It was another day of bread, cheese, onion, and pottage with vegetables. Tired of the same tasteless food and tired of the silence, Abraham touched the book as Jonathan raised an eyebrow.

"If the words of this book are true, the king and his men have reason to be afraid. It says that the king should be a servant of a greater King—just like the rest of us. Do we want to know more of what is in this book?" Abraham asked.

After waiting for an answer, Abraham continued. "People will refuse to open their doors to help *us*. I know you are right. I know there will be no turning back to who we used to be if we open this book."

More silence. Abraham waited until Jonathan moved his eyes from the front door. "Edmund and Steven gave us invitations signed with their blood." Abraham extended his trembling arms onto the table toward Jonathan. One hand was open, and the other was closed in a fist. "Do we accept it?"

Jonathan crossed his arms and bit his lip as he looked away.

Abraham kept his hands on the table. One open, one closed.

Something roamed outside, seeking the source of a threat.

CHAPTER 9

PADA

What am I doing?

Pada left Amara with a friend and stepped into his village, looking for the Judas betraying his people. The one who knew Pada's secret. The one who made Pada do a terrible thing.

An unease moved through the late night, infiltrating many in the village and causing restless sleep. It moved like a poison of slow-acting fear, penetrating through all things, foretelling a dreaded arrival. That night it felt even more potent than previous days.

Time was running out. The light of the moon guided his steps. His chest pounded, like someone trying to break into him or stop him. He ran past the familiar huts of his neighborhood and turned to his right, the section where the Judas probably lived. Pada anticipated that at some point the traitor would gather his belongings in preparation for a quick escape before the attack arrived.

When would it come?

There he is. I see him. Probably stepping out of a hut with someone else's belongings while those in the hut sleep.

The Judas narrowed his eyes at Pada. He dropped the belongings and stomped toward Pada. "You came to your senses. Do you have what belongs to me?"

"No. You failed. Your plan failed. Now you will not have the promised protection from the Imabangala when they come to attack. And they cannot protect you from this—"

Pada reached for his knife—it was gone.

Where is it? How can I eliminate this Judas and save my future with Amara?

Pada stood still. Stunned. Nothing in his trembling hand.

The Judas punched him in the face. Pada fell back and collapsed onto the ground. The traitor sat on his chest. "I gave you your chance. I never told you I have another plan. I have not failed, and the Imbangala will kill everything here and save me. They tell me I will even prosper from the selling of people I don't even like. I hate everyone in this village. Why should I not live and make money off those I hate?"

He pulled out a knife and placed the cold blade next to Pada's neck. Pada winced in anticipation of his final moments. The traitor's eyes glowed in the night. "Moments ago someone told me a new friend of yours is hiding someone important to you."

His laugh cut through Pada as the blade pressed in slightly further. "I have a dilemma. Do I kill you now and just get it over with? Or do I keep you alive long enough to see everything you love here burn to the ground? Do I let you live long enough to see your girlfriend crying for help?"

He leaned closer to Pada's face. "I think I will—"

They both stopped as screaming and rumbling approached from the distance. Pada could not make sense of this new sound. The Judas' eyes widened to their maximum, and he mumbled, "They are here already. They told me they would not come for a few more days."

The Judas jumped off Pada and ran from where the screaming was approaching. While still lying on his back, Pada propped himself onto his elbows and turned toward the gathering storm of noise coming his way.

Amara! Will she be okay? What do I do now? Home.

Could his parents have returned looking for him? He rose and ran. He turned a corner too quickly and fell. His forehead ached. The moonlight reflected off his fingers after he rubbed his forehead. It was only a superficial cut.

Where did that big rock come from? In my years here, I have never noticed this rock before.

He pushed off the stone with his right foot and jumped back onto his feet. Though he did not know his final destination, he did know he had to get out of there.

He needed to get away from the terror now just moments away. Away from the horror waiting behind his daily thoughts by day and scurrying about hidden in the dark of his dreams at night, stealing rest and peace in their wake.

As he ran along the packed-dirt path, images and voices from the recurring nightmare stabbed at him like a persistent arrow finding its mark over and over again, leaving its poison inside his head.

In that dream, a familiar dark spirit cast spells against all people. It used dark magic to take away the ability to see good drinking water. Dying of thirst, the people became desperate enough to drink ocean water, even blood from dead animals . . . and humans. Then the dark spirit came, like a cloud of fog, and abducted many from their homes, ripping them from the embraces of loved ones. The village, bereft of life-giving water, also became bereft of life. And what about the ships?

Pada refused to ponder any more of the nightmare. He had to focus on getting back to Amara.

As he reached the eastern part of his village, he heard Bantu voices speaking Kimbundu and Kikongo. They spoke of the fingers of a dark fog taking people from their homes toward the ocean.

Did they have the same dream?

Evil alerted all in the village as people awoke in the middle of the night. Something roamed the land and was now coming their way. What was dreaded for months had arrived. Like a closing grip between the Cuanza and Lucala rivers, something, or someone, was crushing the throat of his village.

He slid in the dirt as he ran into his empty hut. Screams from afar moved toward him. He flared his nostrils as something wafted nearby. He remembered living by the ocean in his younger years, and he now imagined a wave of sound gaining strength and volume as it approached him.

With his heartbeat throbbing in his ears, Pada ran to the back of the hut. The available light of the night limited a clear view inside the hut. He sat and curled up, holding his knees against his chest. He rocked back and forth to help him decide what to do next.

Can I find the Judas? Can I find our parents? Do I run to take Amara away?

Someone had to fight the Imbangala. In the distance the screams closed in and were now accompanied by running footsteps. He put his hands on the ground next to him. Was the ground trembling?

Rumors said the Imbangala, a mercenary group working with the government, gained power and pillaged and plundered wherever they decided. Not even the Sobas, or any political authority, could save someone from the Imbangala.

Scanning inside his hut, piles of clothes and food spread across the ground. Signs that someone had searched his family's hut. Portions of rice, meat, black-eyed beans, and baobab leaves appeared to be missing, yet the thief had left valuable cowrie shells behind.

He covered his nose. Whatever wafted through the air gained in strength. It came from outside, now closer. The ground trembled. Screaming women and children made his heart jump. He turned toward the mass of people in the closing distance. People of all ages running. The old left behind shuffled to catch up with the others. Something followed behind them.

Amara! Please, God. Not the Imbangala. Not now.

He wanted to run, but his legs felt like trees stuck in hard ground. With every fragment of remaining strength, Pada crawled back to the farthest side of the hut from the entrance.

On the ground he hugged his knees and rocked back and forth. He covered his ears in vain to block out the voices in this head. The first time he remembered the voices invading his head, he was a little boy. His mother's arms saved him. She could not save him today.

He wiped his eyes. *Is this where I am judged and killed?*

The screaming came to a peak outside, then faded.

A single pair of footsteps approached the entrance of the hut. Pada wiped his forehead and hands and prepared to attack.

Did they find him? Did the Judas find him? Did he find Amara?

"Pada."

A silhouette stood waiting at the doorway. Small in frame but muscular and strong. Pada relaxed his sore hands when he recognized his friend Goel.

"What are you doing here?" Pada asked as he resumed breathing.

"I know you're in there. I saw a hand protecting

you. It took away a knife. But you don't have much time." Heavy breaths punctuated his words, as if this fellow eighteen-year-old had run a great distance.

"Come in or run."

Goel entered and squatted, trembling, next to Pada. He extended his hand to help Pada up.

Pada ignored his offer and pushed himself up. "Of all times, why are you here?"

"I now know where you are, but where is Amara?"

He looked away from Goel and stared into the darkest part of the hut. He wiped his eyes and shook his head. "I did something bad."

His friend's mouth dropped open. "What did you do?"

Pada moved to the entrance of the hut, wishing he could run away from the question. He tried to brush the dirt off himself. "I . . . I left her with someone."

His friend raised his hands up. "I have been telling you for months you needed to really watch over her. You know we need both of you. You know what God told me about *both* of you."

With one foot outside the hut and the other foot inside, Pada tightened his grip holding on to the hut. Even through the dim moonlight, Goel's eyes narrowed and glared.

Pada loosened his grip as his feet prepared to run. He straightened as tall as he could. "My father said the Imbangala were ridding our country of our enemies. My mother said the Imbangala *were* the enemy. I could not hold on to one side without rejecting the other. So I tried to stay out of this war for both me and Amara."

More screaming and running outside filled Pada's mind with images of his fellow villagers.

Is Amara okay?

The recollection of his life mistakes, and love for Amara, rose within. With one hand in a fist and the other pointing outside, he said, "I will one day die for all I have done."

"The rumors are true, you know. Throughout all history, the groups may change, but the strategy doesn't. The Imbangala make up their own laws. They kill the unborn and newly born babies. They train the youth to fight for them. I have seen them eat their enemies—while they're still screaming."

Goel peered at his friend. He moved his face close to Pada's. "They enslave others and then sell for profit. But something owns them. Someone *owns* them."

Pada had heard such claims before but always discounted them. "Why would they do such things?"

"They believe they gain more power when they eat human flesh. They prosper, with the government, from the ones they choose to capture and sell."

A fire burned in Pada's chest as he put his hand on his own chest.

Breathe. Breathe. Breathe.

He squinted and opened his eyes more fully. His friend moved closer to Pada's face.

I need to run. I will not be owned.

He put his hand on Pada's shoulder. "Your mother told me something years ago. What roams our land now once dwelled in a man, and he stabbed your mother. He killed your unborn brother trying to get to you. Today, they still want you. They know about you and Amara. They know God marked you, and therefore you both are a threat to them and their plans."

Pada's friend shook his head. "Did you talk with one of the Judases working with the Imbangala?"

Pada did not blink.

Goel shook him as if to awaken him. "He may still yet try and trap you and everything important to you. They threatened my life unless I cooperated with them. I will not betray our friendship."

The two friends locked eyes. Pada remembered him and Goel running together in the canyon. They were young once, so long ago.

"Do not worry. They do not own me. We must go separate ways for a little while. Get Amara and then head north. I will go south. We will then meet east. You know where to meet me." Goel smiled.

East of the canyon. Remote. The canyon was their childhood playground where they knew every tree and bush. They would be safe east of there.

His friend opened his hand with a piece of paper with small writing on it. "Will you take it *now*?"

Pada rolled his eyes and pushed Goel's hand away.

His friend let out a deep sigh. "Even in this time of approaching evil, He is still here. He has a plan for the nations and for you."

They had been friends since Pada and his family moved here. Goel always had strong beliefs. Pada did not want to hear what was coming next.

"You cannot put God into chains."

Goel sounded like Pada's mom. The faith of his mother, Chinasa, was legendary in their community. A weight too heavy on his shoulders to bear. Pada clenched his fists and turned again from the outstretched hand.

Goel was not finished. "God cannot be put into chains. He breaks them."

Will I betray what I believe is right? Somebody has to pay for what the Imbangala are doing. I will make them pay.

"I don't know what happened to your parents. I heard them talk in secret because they did not want to alarm you. They talked of leaving with Amara's parents to prepare a hidden place for both of your families before the attack they believed was to come. They may have already returned and are now looking for both of you. Find them. Your mother intercedes for you daily. Chinasa's prayers move hearts and affect nations."

The residual love of a brother pushed Pada's heart. As if an unseen hand moved his, Pada grabbed the small piece of paper, folded it, and slid it into a slit in his sandal.

"We need to go. You are right. I need to find them." Pada nodded.

They strode outside, their eyes moving up and down the village. Stepping out of a shadow, a large, strong man waited for them. He snarled like an animal on the hunt. His eyes glowed in the disappearing light as several other men flanked him.

"Run!" Goel yelled.

Being skinny, Pada could not fight the strong man. He could outrun him but was not sure he could outrun all the other men with him. He ran for his life. The air of the night cooled his face as he sprinted past others running in the same direction. Concerned about being herded into a trap, he turned to a side path. He raced like a future king who needed to live to one day execute justice for all. Then he stopped.

Aside from the screams a distance away, relative silence stood near him.

What happened to the footsteps behind him?

His heartbeat echoed into his throat. He turned behind him, and no one was there. Pockets of fires in the village lit the cool night.

Not again. Where is Goel?

In the distance he saw the strong man with the other men. And Goel. None of them had moved.

An ache moved inside Pada's stomach. Fluids accumulated in his mouth like when he was sick.

What is Goel doing? We are to run as we did as children.

His heart plummeted to the ground, as if struck by a large fist. The strong man howled.

If Pada ran, he could one day return and kill the Imbangala. He might one day grow old with Amara and their children's children.

But my friend.

He caught Goel's eye, like when they'd raced growing up.

The strong man took a step toward Goel.

CHAPTER 10

ABRAHAM

Southampton, England
1620

That same night they argued about the Bible and what to do, Abraham and Jonathan hid in the dark outside their home without a word between them. Something roamed the streets, and Abraham wanted to see it. Various individuals tried to organize into a group to fight as the evening hours passed. Each time they attempted to assemble near the king's men, they ran in separate directions.

The two best friends had yet to confront the question between them. They were both hungry as they returned to sit with their untouched food. It was time for them to say the difficult. Abraham looked skyward as Jonathan buried his head in his hands.

Will Jonathan leave me if I want to know this book?

As Abraham moved to the window, a shot pierced the neighborhood, and another dying life hit the ground. Abraham ran to the door. People ran away. Abraham stood at the door with one hand on the door. His feet did not want to stay.

Abraham looked back, and Jonathan rocked himself back and forth. He turned his head from side to side, as if trying to convince himself of something but was not succeeding.

Abraham's heart ached for his friend. "Jonathan, are you all right?

"I remember my sister . . . and I fear for you. I don't want your death to be my fault."

Abraham returned to the table and placed his hand on Jonathan's shoulder. Abraham sat down and coughed to prepare for what he would say. He cleared his throat. "Should we pray?"

Surprised when his friend nodded, Abraham pushed aside his food. "God, ... thank . . . I thank You for . . . You . . . Yes, I thank You for You . . . and Jonathan. He is a good friend. I think You are good. I thank You for our food to eat . . . but I don't thank You for vegetables. Amen."

Jonathan burst out laughing. Abraham felt his face turn red, and he smiled.

"You need practice," Jonathan said as he wiped his eyes. Still laughing, he walked toward his liquor to complete his meal. He reached for the shelf and retracted his hand. Abraham laughed, holding on to his stomach as Jonathan returned to the table.

"Not quite the same, are you?" Abraham asked as he laughed and wiped his eyes.

"Very funny." Jonathan smiled. "Things are not the same."

The laughing and smiling disappeared. Jonathan

turned his head toward the door. "I have a fear I have not had before."

Each was delaying the inevitable. A decision had to be made. Jonathan kept his head turned toward the front door as Abraham waited.

Jonathan's eyes opened wide. He stood and moved away from him.

Abraham rose. "What is wrong, Jonathan?"

Jonathan kept his back to him. "I know you have already decided to follow that book. But that book reminds me of a voice I heard."

Jonathan turned and stared right into Abraham. "I heard the voice just one time . . . one time when I was with my sister . . . before she died . . ."

He paused, then asked, "What do we do?"

"We are both attempting to remain afloat between choices. If we do nothing, we will sink. We have to move. We should choose together."

"I just don't want to hear that bad voice again." Jonathan's voice cracked as he crossed his arms.

"Maybe the words in this book are the words of a different voice?"

Both nodded. Abraham closed his eyes. *This will be payback for what they did to Steven.*

They wanted to read the words of treason.

Both sat down as Abraham pointed to the book. "I remember Steven told me about this Geneva translation of the Bible. He said it came with a great cost."

He picked up the book and turned it, studying every angle as if holding a hundred-year-old battle-tested sword. He did not want to cut himself with it.

Abraham turned it each way, observing it in the light and shadow. "He told me it was translated not just for the educated elite at the government puppet pulpits, but also for the uneducated commoners seated in the pews and those outside the church. The king outlawed the printing of this Bible because it rebels against his beliefs and his power and his version of the Bible. Steven said they created the Geneva Bible translation so all people could know the contents within for themselves, without a king and his church telling them what was inside and not inside it."

Abraham stroked his beard. "I compared this Geneva Bible to the king's version. This Bible has printed notes in the margins that the king's Bible does not have. In the marginal notes it says things that contradicts what the king has taught us about following him and *his* church. But words snuck past even the king's censors. The first sentence in *both* Bibles contradicts kings being greater than God." Abraham laughed.

Abraham talked about reading the first book in the Bible and the creation pattern from the simple to the complex. And a beautiful garden named Eden.

"From the most simple to the most complex. So is that why the woman was created last?" Jonathan asked as he raised his arms up in surrender.

Abraham nodded with a smile.

"Us men, from the very beginning, we never had a chance," Jonathan said while shaking his head.

"We never had a chance—and I would not want it any other way," Abraham said with a laugh.

He pointed his finger at the book. "In the opening chapters, I read something very mysterious. These words describe God in both the singular and the plural! Later we find out there is the Father, Son, and Spirit. Yet they are supposed to be one?"

"You are starting to believe this. You don't think kings wrote this to control people, do you?"

"Would I ever invent a religion to control people by inventing a God who is one and plural at the same time? In a way that cannot be explained? In a way that I cannot control?" Abraham shrugged. "Would it not be easier for me to invent a religion that gives kings more power over the people? This book is the opposite. This book gives fear to the powerful and hope to the weak."

He tugged on his beard again. "If the powerful made this book to control people, why would the powerful try to stop these words, and why would the persecuted choose to die for these words throughout history? All I know is, this book is different. It reads more like a history book and not just a collection of stories. There is a strong and subtle love, and yet it also mentions names, cities, countries, events, things that people can check to see if it is true or false."

He set the book closer to Jonathan. "It speaks and asks to be tested."

A silence permeated the room as Abraham pondered his next words. "But it is even more than just a historical account of people and events. I thought . . . I thought I could sense a voice that I did not hear . . . I believe probably different from the voice you heard. It was like the Author was letting me know He was reading me as I read His book. I think He was . . . conversing with me." Abraham picked up the book and then let it drop onto the table as he moved his hands away from it. "This book is different."

He handed the open book to Jonathan as he pointed to a few sentences. Jonathan leaned away with his hands partway up, as if avoiding a fight.

Abraham pushed it closer to Jonathan. "I would not be surprised if this book started to throb with a heartbeat of the Author. The powerful are trying to shut the mouth of the Author."

Abraham pointed to sentences while turning pages. "Here He created all things. But now look here at what happened on the sixth day of creation."

Trying not to touch the book, Jonathan arched, leaned over, and read in mid-bite. He spit out his vegetables and looked at Abraham with his eyebrows raised. "Adam and Eve were made in the image of God?"

"Yes. In the other previous days, God did not create anything in His own image. Why would God create differently with Adam and Eve?" Abraham pointed his finger at Jonathan.

Jonathan closed his eyes and rubbed his groomed hair and chin. Then his eyes and mouth opened at the same time. "He wanted children. Like a good father, he wanted relationships with his children."

Abraham pointed his finger upward. "Yes! That is it. He wanted offspring. A good father wants relationship. A father who would not turn his back on his children and leave them behind. And his children were naked in the garden."

"I believe Eve was beautiful. She had no clothes—now that is heaven," Jonathan said as if he'd received a great gift.

"They were made in the image of God and without clothing, and that was a very good thing. He made all parts to function as he saw honorable, proper, and good, and they were not ashamed."

"Why does it seem that throughout history, we, both men and women, have tried to take away the true beauty of the woman and replace it with something that we try to control?" Jonathan asked with a look of sadness.

Another musket shot outside nearby. They remained still. Then another voice with more banging on their door.

"Abraham, Jonathan, let me in."

They looked at each other with open eyes and open mouths. Both mouthed, *Was that Steven?*

Abraham looked down at his shirt, and his shirt moved to the rhythm of his heart. He leaned toward Jonathan's ear. "That is Steven!"

They ran to the door, when Jonathan stopped Abraham from opening it. "That cannot be Steven.

He died. We cannot listen to a voice because we want it to be true."

"Someone needs our help."

"As much as I hate to say this, your time to help will come."

Voices outside echoed through the house as they walked back to the table. Abraham tried to continue. He shared with Jonathan that after Adam and Eve were created in the image of their Creator, God was so near to Adam and Eve that they could hear his footsteps in the garden. God walked with them.

"Adam and Eve first believed God." Abraham wiped his forehead. "Then they believed Satan."

Jonathan glanced at the door as the banging stopped. "I never shared with you that my first wife, Elizabeth, died after the birth of our son. My second wife convinced herself that she could never remove the memories that I would always have of my first wife. She hated my son and seduced him to believe her lies that I killed his mother. She hated me. It drove her into madness."

With his head still looking down, he paused, as if gathering strength. "Maybe Satan thought that though he failed to rule over God, he could rule over the hearts of His children."

"How could Satan accomplish this? How could he possibly deceive those living in paradise, living with the love of God and without the need for anything?"

"Maybe Adam and Eve were deceived into thinking they could have even more. Like rich children believing their wealthy parents were holding back on their inheritance," Jonathan said.

"They had everything. They had a garden of paradise. God was with them. They were given each other. No tyrant was ruling in the garden of Eden, killing those who opposed Him. There was no war. There was no slavery or oppression. There was no poverty in the garden," Abraham said as he turned some pages.

As if an invisible hand continued to protect the front of the house, they heard more footsteps in front of the door running away.

"So what happened? What went wrong?" Jonathan raised his hands upward.

"There were two trees in the garden. There was the tree of life and the tree of the knowledge of good and evil. God told them there was only one thing they should not do in the entire garden. If they ate from the tree of the knowledge of good and evil, they would die,"

Another musket fired into the night.

Abraham turned his head from the door to his friend. "God cast Satan down from heaven. In the form of a serpent, Satan told Adam and Eve that God had lied. That God was a liar. Satan told them that they could eat from the tree of knowledge of good and evil, and they could have even more than what God gave them."

He leaned forward closer to Jonathan. "They could be like God."

More footsteps ran outside their door. Abraham recognized the yelling commands of the men of the king.

"Am I not like the king? Are you not like the king? If I could look into a mirror, would I not see my own self-monarchy? Have I not made up my own laws? Have I not created my own laws according to what is convenient for me? Because my authority was threatened, I forbid my family from reading this book!" Abraham said.

"They ate the fruit. They chose the rule and reign of a liar over their father?" Jonathan asked as he pulled the book out of Abraham's loose grip.

Jonathan shook his head in puzzlement. "How was it that God said they would die if they ate from the tree of knowledge of good and evil, and yet they still lived after? Wait. Don't answer. I know this. They did not have the presence of God with them anymore, like before. Their human spirits lost their main form of communication. The children lost their previous connection with their Father. The result was a spiritual death and eventual physical death," Jonathan exclaimed.

Pain seared Abraham's heart as Jonathan read about the aftermath of Adam and Eve's decision to eat from the tree of knowledge of good and evil. With a sliver of light falling on the remains of the fruit dropped in panic-stricken haste, a voice cried out in a soon-to-be dark and cursed forest.

Were the words from the Creator to His children,

"Where are you?" cracked in sorrow, bleeding from a gaping chest wound?

"What was God to do now? If he does nothing, are not his children now blind and powerless under the rule of a lying counterfeit king cloaked as King?" Jonathan asked.

Jonathan paused and continued. "Does not love require choice? If God eliminated their choice between God or Satan, that would not be love. Having only one choice is not liberty. If he killed Satan, would that not eliminate choice for Adam and Eve?"

Jonathan raised his hands. "Does he disown them and leave them to themselves? Does he destroy them all?"

Abraham closed his eyes. "I do not know where I am or where to go. I do not know who I am. I do not know this God, if such a God exists. Why do I want to live or even care, if I am going to die soon? All I know is that I should have died hours ago, and now I want to live."

Jonathan darted from the table toward the door. "Seventy-six days. Are you any different from any-one else? I will one day die, but I do not know exactly when. You need to truly live with whatever days you have left."

Jonathan covered his eyes with his hands and then uncovered them. "Our eyes are now more open, and we see life better. I have learned much tonight. Is it all right if I go? I will take my chances, as I need to warn others that the wrath of the king is approaching."

Abraham nodded and walked with Jonathan to the door. A distance away, Jonathan turned his head one more time toward Abraham and then continued down the street.

Facing outside at the doorway, Abraham had his back toward it.

It waited behind him on the table. It called him.

A sound implanted into his mind.

A sword unsheathed.

His concern wasn't the book itself. It wasn't even the words in the book.

It was the dangerous Author nearby summoning those to commit treason.

That book cuts.

Something smells blood.

Satan is roaming the earth.

Chapter 11

JAMES

England
1620

God on earth, now nearing his mid-fifties, did not know how much time he had left. The Dark Light told him a boy was coming to kill him. That was fifteen years ago. James had consulted with the experts of his day and had commanded his men to find the assassin.

A little over ten years ago, rebels fled England to Holland and printed their book of propaganda, and from afar smuggled their acts of treason back to the homeland. The king's archbishop had outlawed the printing of the rebels' book that differed from his own King James Bible.

And now James received word that the group of treasonists who'd escaped him before, now hid in the homeland. They prepared for another move.

Though the Dark Light still empowered and pro-tected James, the voice was usually silent. No bright star in the sky told him where to find the assassin. Had his men already rid the land of the boy in the last fifteen years? Was the Dark Light's prophecy a general warning of a little boy at some time in the future coming to kill him, or was the boy now at least fifteen years of age?

He needed the Dark Light to placate the religious fanatics and parliament, and he savored the power when it surged through his limbs. The veins on the back of his hands pulsated. It even tasted good. The new power flowed into God's Shepherd to replace that wasted on helping the weak and lost sheep.

James was the most powerful man on earth. The most skilled of hunters. The only one who could fix what was wrong.

If he had to live with the mystery of not knowing the presence but gaining more power, he could live with that. He would not question the source of the manna. But still, he wondered, what was that slithering sound?

It was late on that unusually warm and sticky night. Something slid across his bedroom floor and stopped underneath his bed. He ignored it again. Over the years, he'd tired of looking for the source of the sound in vain.

Years ago religious teachers had offered to pray for him and examine his room. He'd refused to let hypocritical Bible zealots ever enter his bedroom. His bed, his life, was his own.

He left his ill sleeping wife in bed, though he suspected—no, he knew she was awake. He grabbed his favorite oranges and apples picked earlier from his favorite tree. He took several bites as he walked down the well-worn path in his garden to his meeting. Even if the clouds tried to block the light and enemies tried to stop him, his time in his beautiful garden awaited him.

Failed plots to kill him demonstrated he exercised life or death over those as he pleased. Who could be ignorant enough to believe that malcontents could blow up God and the country's leaders in 1605?

He walked with a smile into the darkness of the familiar path, a hidden area under the light of the moon in his garden.

His paradise.

Where are they?

He usually made them wait for his entrance. He stood and scanned his nature birthed, pruned, and soon to be consumed by its creator. All the fruit trees. The lovely flowers.

But where were they?

He enjoyed staring into the eyes of his trembling lovers when he was in a foul mood. It was similar to the eyes of one of his cornered animals moments before the skilled hunter ended the hunt.

But this time was different. Gritting his teeth and clenching his fists, he thought of those who rejected him. With a voice like that of a young boy whose friends had abandoned him in a remote part of a dark and cursed forest, he cried out, "Where are you?"

No answer. Something moved in the back of his garden. Noises scurrying in that back corner.

Behind two trees. He knew they heard his footsteps approaching.

Through a shadow, the fingertips of a shaking hand wrapped around the trunk of one of his trees. As his footsteps echoed through his garden, the hand retracted behind the trunk.

He smiled and exhaled. He'd found them. The smile then fled against his wishes. Not only were they hiding from him, but they were fully clothed. He bit the last of his fruit and dropped it as his heart sank.

His enemies had infiltrated them. There was a new and different fear on their faces. He approached his two trembling lovers.

They covered their faces with their shaking hands. "We hid ourselves. We listened to them, and they told us that what we are doing is wrong. We cannot stay here—we must leave."

James' cracked voice pierced the night. "Who told you this? You believed them? Who told you to clothe yourselves?"

James squeezed his fists as the last remnant of his dripping fruit fell to the ground. He opened a fist for a moment and clamped down on one of his lover's wrists. The lover whimpered like wounded prey as juice dripped from the talons of the predator. With wide eyes, the lover looked at the strangled juice of the fruit on the master's wrist.

The master retracted his hands back and rubbed his hands together. He eliminated enemies but could never eliminate the stains on his hands.

Ignoring his hands but aware of his trembling voice, he said, "Please do not leave . . . I . . . I beg of you to stay."

As the lovers walked away, he raised his fist. "I command you to believe in me. You must listen to me. Do not listen to my enemies. Please come back."

For a fleeting moment he thought of the wife he'd left behind on his bed. A cloud moved and covered the moon in the sky. As the lovers ran away from the hunt, the hunter stood shaking, divided by a line of moonlight on one side of him and a dark shadow on the other. His knees buckled, and he collapsed into the shadow.

Why do you torment me, God? This is your doing. You gave me my power and my desires. Yet you torment me when I exercise that which you gave me as I attempt to feed and protect my people?

With his lovers out of his sight, he could not command through the gnashing of teeth. His cry disappeared like his lovers, and he replaced it with animal-like noises. The hunter plotted against his prey.

The slithering sound had followed him from the bedroom to the garden and empowered him to speak. He raised his hands. The power coursed through his veins with value worthy of life itself. No more mumbling. His words were clear, and like a well-used encrusted and rusty blade, cut through the night.

"How dare the self-righteous religious fools oppose me? They refuse to see what I can see. What I can do."

With the light of the moon behind him, he paused and admired his hands in the dark light.

"I used to fear looking into the mirror, but I now see the reflection of the spirit of God's will in the flesh, gazing back at me. I see the culmination of previous generations of power bleeding into me. Your power flowing through me is timeless, and it is time to now enact the full authority of the God who created me for such a time as this."

Evil tried to prevent him from apprehending the power even before he was born. They'd murdered his father when James was about eight months old. They'd imprisoned his mother when James was one and eventually beheaded her for plotting against the queen.

But the cloaked one, the Dark Light, within him trained him to be a gifted intellectual. There was not a subject he could not excel in. He grew in wisdom, rejected the radical teachings of some in the church, and created his own church.

But even as he grew in power, the boy assassin was still hidden from his eyes. Did the murderer, with the other subversives, still roam hidden by the hand covering them? What evil the rebels were capable of! They'd attempted to blow up the Lord in the House of Lords in 1605! They refused to submit to the very same God that they claimed to worship.

After all these years, where was that boy? The wandering sheep rejected the love of their Shepherd. They left him. They spoke lies to his lovers, who then left him. How could this small, weak, ignorant remnant, with their weak Bible, learn?

His appetite was constant, but the objects to feed his desire were replaceable. He reached for another low-hanging fruit from a tree next to him. The apple was sweet. It dripped from his mouth onto the garden soil.

What would happen to his people if he did not find that boy? What would happen if he did not intervene for their lives? The religious leaders were always bickering among themselves. They could never decide what God wanted. The sheep who followed them needed to be taught God's morality. They were thieves, drunkards, adulterers. Their children learned their parents' ways of immoral life. What would happen to his kingdom if they grew older without the proper education?

Like his garden, they required order and pruning. They also needed to be instructed. They needed someone to act for them. For their own good. Pain, torture, persuasion, and death were the most effective schoolmasters. Many had learned this valuable life lesson.

But that small remnant still resisted their patient master.

Obedience to James was obedience to God.

Born to be King James I of England.

On his knees behind the moving line of shadow, the Dark Light shined on him.

King James arose with his appetite.

His lovers were gone. King James wanted more. He needed more. He could not stay partway in the light and partway in the shadow. Could he give away more of himself to gain more power from the Dark Light?

He needed to stay alive to save his people.

To save the peace between the religious fanatics and the rabid parliament.

Where was the boy coming to assassinate him?

CHAPTER 12

AMARA AND HUMILITY

Ndongo, Africa
1609

Someone said Amara's name in the middle of the night. Was it the voice, or was she awakened another night with her stomach's demand for food? There was only so much that a six-year-old could do.

Other than her stomach's pleas, quiet rested in her family's hut. Earlier, she'd gathered food for hiding after her parents fell asleep. Along with the secret Bible verse. Father and Mother could not understand her capabilities of delivering the secret goods that were good for both body and spirit.

She could not walk as well as other children. The result of what her mother, Abeni, said was "God's Grace." But that did not mean she had to stay home feeling sorry for herself.

She gathered all that she needed. Her parents slept, as she was extra careful not to disturb anyone in their small, crowded hut. Mom and Dad would be furious if they knew she was leaving. But they worried too much.

Amara concentrated with an extra-powerful effort. She made sure to lift each foot off the ground to be quieter than usual with her walking. Now was not the time to do her typical foot dragging if she could help it. Sometimes, with trying really hard, she could accomplish just about anything. God would help her.

God told her she would make an important delivery, and she was going to make God smile. She liked it when He smiled. He smiled a lot. How did His face not get tired? *That's right . . . He's God.*

She could not get that family out of her mind. Okoro, Chinasa, and their son, Pada, were their names. They were poor. They'd had to move away from near the ocean in Luanda into Amara's village a few weeks ago. She liked the little boy Pada. He was nice and about her age. Well, maybe he was a little older. She liked him, and he liked her. He didn't care that she didn't walk like other girls.

This food is special. It has power because I put it together from all the small pieces made from my other meals just for them. Just for him.

They would smile when they read her Bible verse for them. Like God did.

Could she slip into the night, past her parents and all the neighbors, who worried too much about her? Outside at night was not as dangerous for a little girl as the adults who worried too much thought. All the bad people outside were much taller than her, and they would look right above her and not see the tiny deliverer.

No one else was outside. She walked about ten huts away from home with just a few more to go. She still had strong legs, and she was not dragging her feet too much. She memorized the way to get there from their previous visits with the family. She tricked them. Though she did like playing with Pada, she was really memorizing how to get to their house so she could one day complete God's adventure.

When she was two huts away from Pada's, a big boy saw her. She forgot she was only invisible to adults and that other children might still be awake. His eyes ignored her and, without blinking, focused on what she was carrying.

"Little lame girl, is that food?"

"I have no time for you. I am listening to God."

"I am hungry. Give me your food."

"What I carry may help others to then be able to help your children one day in the future."

The big boy went up to Amara and pushed her down.

"Let me go!" Amara yelled.

The big boy looked from side to side, as the little girl had a big voice.

"Shut up. You will wake people up."

He grabbed the food with Amara still holding on. He ripped it away from her and ran.

She could not run. She could only watch the thief disappear into the night with the gift entrusted to her. She cried, and neighbors came out.

"Amara, what are you doing by yourself out at

night? You can't be by yourself. You need adults with you at all times."

A man and woman picked her up to carry her home. The woman said to the man, "Abeni will not be happy when she finds out Amara was outside at night on her own. This is her and Chinasa's worst fear. You know how they both protect their kids."

Amara reached out to an invisible hand behind her.

Pada would be hungry again tonight.

The couple awoke her parents and handed Amara over to them. They thanked them and waited until they left.

Should she tell her father what God had told her? Should she tell him about the boy who'd attacked her and stolen the delivery?

Her father looked down at her with angry eyes and angry hands on his hips. "Amara, what were you doing?"

"I was carrying . . . I was taking some food for Pada and his family. They need food."

Amara's parents looked at each other. How could they be angry? Amara's mother stepped between Amara and her father. Abeni picked her up and turned her back to her husband, as if protecting Amara from a strong, cold wind.

Amara's father rolled his eyes and went back to his warm spot on the ground.

Abeni took Amara to her spot and lay her down.

It was a cool evening, and mother settled an extra blanket over Amara.

Her mother smiled with sad eyes. "Your father loves you. He wants you to be safe at home. Amara, we are all hungry."

She bent down and kissed Amara on her forehead. "I am so proud of you for thinking of others. You made God smile. But you have to be smart about how you give. We have talked before. You are different from others, and some people are not good people. There are traps out there, and bad people will try to take advantage of good people. Next time I will go with you. You don't want to fall into a trap, right?"

"But, Mom, people need help. I am good. You are good. God is good. What happens if good people do nothing?"

Amara's mother gasped with her mouth stuck wide open. She smiled and bent down to kiss her again. They said a prayer and then good night.

After her mother returned to her own mat, Amara could not stop her eyes from crying, as she knew others would be hungry tonight. She'd failed with her mission. She'd tried to resist crying with a trembling smile as the tears dripped down. She reached down and felt the Bible verse she had written and hidden.

The big boy had taken the food, but he had not taken the secret that she would deliver.

***

Plymouth, England
1603

Was today the day all prayers would be answered? Mother would be whole again. Little brother would have a father again. And little Humility would have her father to hold her as he did before.

He was the perfect father. He used to tell her there was a wonderful future for her if she was patient. With faith to change the world, God would reward her. She could not wait to tell him of how much she had grown up and how well she had taken care of her mother and brother.

The routine was the same for the last several months. After completing the dinner cleanup, she sat just outside the front door, waiting for father to return. When the conditions were severe outside, beyond the hot evening, rain, or cold, she would be allowed to stay outside for just a few minutes.

This night was different.

Most evenings she waited outside by herself. Away from an indifferent mother and a very different brother. Different in the most annoying ways. But this night Humility imagined the entire town population sitting on the porch next to her, sharing their wisdom the best way they knew how to a seven-year-old. She could hear them now, with their voices adding to whatever the temperature was outside.

"My young child, your father is not coming home."

"Your father is a drunk, enslaved to alcohol. He first has to return to himself before he could ever come home. In my experience, that never happens. He's gone."

"He rebelled against God, and he ran away. Prodigal sons usually only happen in the Bible."

He is coming home.

She knew what everyone was thinking. She stared ahead toward the bend of the path leading to her house. Behind her, the creaky door opened. The creaking and bending of the yielding wood of the porch floor told her what was coming next. She heard her younger brother screaming for attention far away inside the house, just like every other evening. It was no surprise who was coming outside. The door creaked until it closed. Her brother was silenced. She knew who stood beside her.

Through the corner of her eye, Mother tried to get comfortable with extra layers of sweaters. She offered a sweater and some blankets to Humility. Humility did not take them. Her mother wasted no time in using them for herself.

Being outside was still better than being lonely and warm in front of a fire and on the wrong side of a closed door, stuck with a screaming brother.

She kept her head straight in line with the bend of the empty road. Maybe he was about to round the bend? Mother would remain next to her until Humility turned her head toward her. After a few minutes, Humility turned. Her mother's eyes were beautiful. Red. Swollen. Silent.

Her mother's lips trembled as she spoke. "My dearest one . . ." She wiped her eyes. "I have cried out all my tears for your father. Within me a drought has overtaken the heart land. There is no more water. But yet I would still cross the ocean of tears I still have for you. I would cross the ocean if it would save you from the wasted waiting. I still pray, for your sake, that he would sail back into your life. For me, he sank to the bottom of his last drink and drowned a long time ago. The piece of my heart belonging to him broke off years ago and drifted away, never to be seen again."

Humility's mother looked off into the distance and closed her eyes. "I have nothing left for him. I don't feel anymore where the piece broke off."

Tears fell from her mother's eyes as she tried to speak again. "But the other part of my heart that still remains, the part for you, is still cracking. It hurts. It hurts to see your heart waiting for what will never come."

"Mother, I just know if I wait for him, if I believe he will come, he will come."

"My dear, learn from me and marry a man who puts you above the chains that pull at us."

"He's going to come back," Humility said with a firm voice.

Humility did not cry a tear. Love was hard work, and there was no time to cry. Humility's mom cried. She wiped her tears again and hugged Humility. She walked away. Humility heard the creak of the door, exposing even more screaming inside. It then creaked surrender and shut.

How long could Humility keep her secret to herself?

The dream.

What do I do with the dream?

She remembered the dream that had been awaking her off and on for the last year. It was the same dream each time. In the dream, there were many voices. She saw people in two ships, with fingers wrapped around their throats. There were men, women, children, the rich, the poor, religious, and nonreligious. Some had dark skin, some had light skin, and others with every other shade in between. Something, or someone, was killing them. Everywhere in the world, the different groups of people were tricked into the trap of fighting each other. But a small and influential number on the ships did not fall for the trap. They believed that because God was their Father, then all were brothers and sisters.

But something happened to the ships. The people on the ships were now in the water. Drowning. God told Humility to pray for them.

My father is one of them.

Her heart was in one piece and still intact for her

father. She felt that some, not all in the water, would come home.

Should she tell her mother of the dream? Could she handle the pain of seeing her mother, despite the hope of the dream, still trying not to care? Did a careless word from Humility push her father away?

She remembered the Bible saying that all were slaves to sin.

The cold wind howled. It whispered and bit her ear. She grew tired of covering her ear. She was unable to lift her chin up. Humility narrowed her eyes. She thought of those in the water in her dream.

She prayed for her father and all the rest trying to get home.

CHAPTER 13

PADA

Ndongo, Africa
1619

Pada bent over and struggled for his next breath. His body ached with the short run away from the strong man who was after Pada and Goel. His heart pounded in his chest, like feet pounding on dirt while running from a monster.

Through the night, and fires set to parts of his village, Pada stared at his friend Goel. Goel and the strong man stood staring at each other. Pada wanted to run away to save Amara. But he wanted to save his friend. Even if he could save his friend, more Imbangala would replace the strong man. What good would it do to have both of them captured and then sold and traded?

His friend deserved to live another day. Pada crouched close enough and caught the eyes of Goel. If Goel's eyes could speak, they said, "Run!"

Pada turned his head back and forth between Goel and the path ahead leading to Amara.

If Goel's eyes could speak again, they said, "Then I will make you run like I did when we were younger."

He looked at Pada, smiled, and ran full speed toward the strong man's legs. He hit the strong man and wrapped his arms around his legs, but it was like a small child's arms wrapped around a thick tree trunk. When the strong man did not move, Goel pushed with his legs again, trying to topple him. Goel screamed as every part of him tried to force the strong man down. The strong man twitched. Goel pushed again, and the strong man overreacted in trying to maintain his balance and fell with Goel's arms still wrapped around his legs.

The two men wrestled on the ground, with Goel on top. A flash of metal in the strong man's hand reflected the moonlit sky. It appeared and then disappeared into Goel.

Many footsteps pounded and jumped around the men wrestling, which echoed in Pada's ears. None of the men noticed Pada in the distance—except for one.

While holding his side, Goel reached forward with his other hand and utilized every inch of his reach. He grabbed the foot of the only man who saw Pada in the distance.

Pada ran as he had never run before. Like their races in his youth, Pada almost felt Goel's touch to then continue the run after Goel had finished his leg of the race. He did not look back to see Goel, as he could not afford to lose one step. He ran between huts and broke free into the canyon. He looked back after several minutes. No one was behind him. He ran farther into the canyon.

Exhausted, he dropped to his knees. Why did Goel give his life for him? What possessed him? Pada wondered where Amara's parents and his own parents were. For the moment, he doubted the merit of his girlfriend's blind trust in him.

With secrets and burdens too heavy to bear, he relented and let his head drop into his hands as he heaved for air. Something foreign rose within him, as if from a deep ocean floor, and now surfaced above an ocean of grief. He rocked back and forth and put his hands over his mouth to drown the sorrow and rage. He could wipe his eyes, but he could not wipe away what was happening to his country, family, and friends.

Where can we be free? Does such a country exist? Where can I run from my mistakes?

His best chance of escape was to run while it was still dark. He had to go to the family protecting Amara and steal her away from the approaching Imbangala. But he could not go farther without resting. For the moment, he didn't care about being captured.

Baobab trees. Life-giving trees so different yet so beautiful compared to other trees. It was life-giving water. Life-sustaining fruit and leaves. Bark for clothing. Hope during drought. Pada hid behind an extra-wide baobab tree and wiped his eyes, thinking of his mother.

Thoughts about the recurring nightmare also chased him. If one could hear the approaching footsteps of a nightmare, that night he was not alone. And if a nightmare could speak, it spoke with a distant voice of a hunter closing in on its prey.

Though safe and hidden in the canyon, the nightmare found its exhausted target and infiltrated with Pada's defenses down.

In the repeating nightmare, the one of divination cast spells upon the people and the land again. The blinded eyes of the people could not see water that was present and created for them. They believed that drought had spread across the land. Who or what could satisfy the parched mouths? Who could bring peace to the warring groups competing for water? In their desperate search for power and help, the generations turned to the one of divination.

The one of divination taught the people about a liquid that could satisfy them. Over time, drinking the liquid multiplied their thirst. The people came to the one of divination for more. Soon, answering their growing appetite was all they knew.

But a small number questioned what they had been taught.

The one of divination was concerned with those questioning their education. It feared the resistant remnant—and the one that was on the sea. There were two ships. There was someone escaping on the sea. Voices cried out. Someone was fleeing to a land of growing resistance to the one of divination.

Pada awoke from his nightmare hidden under the baobab tree. With the bright light of the sunrise, he forced himself to open his eyes. The clear morning left him exposed and vulnerable. He had to get to Amara.

Scanning the canyon, he breathed easier with no one in sight hunting him. His heart pounded harder, remembering the rumors of the last few years. Did the Imbangala capture his people and sell and trade them as slaves?

Rumors said the Portuguese leaders sought more control and worked with the Imbangala, using them to fight for them. Pada trembled thinking about the horror stories of what the Imbangala did. What madness, what spirit, could enter into a man to cause him to kill his own children? To replenish their numbers by kidnapping children and training them to fight and kill for them? They forced the children to eat the men they killed. The children wore a collar, and the leaders did not remove it until they killed a man in battle.

One day Pada would rule over Ndongo or all of Africa. He vowed to rise above all rulers. He would rule and destroy the corrupt and power-hungry rulers—and those of his countrymen who traded their own brothers and sisters into slavery. He intended to torture the Imbangala, enacting righteous vengeance. Those he allowed to live, he would imprison without food and leave them to gorge on themselves.

King Pada would one day bring justice for all his people. Queen Amara would rule with him . . . if she was still alive.

King Pada was going to feed the strong man to the

rest of the Imbangala. The strong man would pay for killing the king's friend.

He wiped his eyes as he remembered what he hid in the slit in his sandal. He pulled out the small piece of paper to read the last remaining item he owned, other than what he was wearing.

"In the beginning, God created the heavens and the earth."

Why did he give me this message? History tells us these words are from that book that eventually kills those who read it. Goel died living that book's beliefs, and those beliefs killed him.

He crouched down as he reread the words and remembered Goel and his beliefs. He should have thought only of himself, and he would still be alive today. If only there was a Creator who created and ruled above all things. If only these words were true.

He folded it and put it back into his sandal. He shook his head and stood. He turned to his right and left and moved one step closer to Amara in the East.

A hand rose up with him from behind a tree and wrapped around his throat.

Somehow, he recognized the grip.

The strong man.

It was like a living nightmare escaped out of his mind and inhabited a willing body now standing behind him.

The nightmare had a voice.

"Have you ever traveled on the ocean? Hmmm . . . how I envy the travels you will experience. I wish I could accompany you so that at least one person you know, still alive, that is, could enjoy it with you. You do have one friend—I am sorry. I forgot the unfortunate accident that took your friend's life."

He shoved Pada's face to the ground of the rich farming region. Rich with reminders of the local goats, cattle, and chickens.

Pada turned his head to breathe, while the beast held his hands behind his back. He spat to get the taste of the local animal residents out of his mouth. Though the ground looked out of focus, drops of his blood spotted it. If one could smell something else above the odors of the local residents, he smelled old bloodstains from the fist wrapped around his throat.

"I'm sure you can help us with what you are worth. Maybe a single old chicken?" the strong man said with a laugh.

He lifted Pada and slammed him down onto his feet. Pada's foot came partway out of his sandal. The same sandal with the folded paper.

Pada used his foot to try to push the folded edge of the paper back into the sandal. His heart raced. His head spun.

I will not die because of those words on that paper.

The strong man moved closer to his face and looked into his eyes.

I will not let those words kill me.

Something dwelled inside the strong man. Could an emptiness hide behind the dark? It reminded him of what moved through the air in his village when his people were running. The eyes before him did not blink. Like the eyes of an unknown animal staring back at him.

Why didn't I bury those words when I had the chance?

The right hand of King Pada clinched and prepared to enact justice.

The grip around his throat tightened.

CHAPTER 14

ABRAHAM

Southampton, England
1620

"I can't swim!"

Abraham flailed his arms and grasped for anything that could keep him afloat.

The voices. So many voices.

The sea and its hands of justice reached toward him from the depths of the abyss, enacting its law, which Abraham could not contest. He raised his arms and screamed for help as one of many hands from below pulled harder on one of his legs. The water of hell opened its mouth. His arms stiffened. He was unable to grasp the floating ship debris, with the loss of feeling in his stiffening hands. Another hand from below pulled on his other leg as payment past due, the water no longer cold as he sank. Under the surface of the water, with seconds of life left, the legs of three people kicked and tried to stay afloat . . .

Abraham awoke in the morning, shivering and gasping for air. *Where is Jonathan?*

Jonathan had left the previous night, and Abraham had not heard him return home. Jonathan was the only way he could get back to his family. He rose and dressed.

He entered the kitchen area and noticed things were out of place. The book was gone. Some of its pages were torn and left in haste.

Where was the book? *Do not let Steven's death be a waste. Do not let them have what he died for.*

He gathered the torn pages from Steven's book and letters, along with his own notes. For the first time, he found additional notes of Steven's that must have been hidden in the book. He tried to flatten the crumpled pages against his chest. He ignored his untouched coins on the table. Abraham froze when he discovered what else was missing—a list of people whom he thought could give him counsel. Most of the names belonged to the local underground church.

The man with the scarred eye.

Something hid in his room.

I am not alone.

It was a different presence than the one he'd sensed when he was reading Steven's book earlier. He wiped his forehead and then his hands. In the cool early morning, there was an even colder sensation crawling up his back. Like fingers running up his spine on the way to his throat.

What if a man of the king is still here?

He set the items down. Slowly, with fists engaged, he turned. He wiped his forehead with his sleeve. He unclenched his fists to wipe his hands. His home was small, so he would know soon enough if he needed to fight for his life. Step by step through the rest of the house. Room by room, though, nothing else was out of place or missing. But Abraham needed to check one more place.

The closet with their shared weapon, and the box with the knife. Somebody would soon pay for taking what was Steven's.

He walked softly on the ground, but no other noises sounded in the cold dawn hours. He conceded with his racing heart that he would not surprise anyone hiding in the closet. The front door next to the closet was left slightly ajar. He placed one hand on the handle and began to open the closet door.

Through the crack of the front door, Abraham saw part of a stranger's hand opening the front door.

The thief is coming back for me this time.

Abraham tried to slam the front door shut with his foot. The person on the other side pushed back. With his foot pressing the door to close it, Abraham opened the closet door with a free hand and grabbed the weapon from the nearby corner of the closet, where he anticipated another hand grabbing the weapon from him.

"Is that you, Abraham?" said a voice on the other side of the front door.

The person outside stopped pushing the door. "I thought someone was inside your house, and I was concerned for you."

The voice sounded familiar. Abraham opened the door farther, and though he did not know the person's name, he recognized the man as a friend of Jonathan.

The man had a relieved look on his face. "It's me, Francis. Thank God you are safe. We have Jonathan. He is safe. He wanted me to check on you and to get you out of the house. Your door was open. The king's men started taking people away again this morning. It is as if somebody found out about some members of the church. It slowed down when they got Steven, but they are now looking for somebody else."

Should he admit that someone took his list with some members of the underground church? Would someone die because of him?

He remembered years ago in his youth when his best friend was severely beaten. The thief was a much larger boy and stole Abraham's friend's only money. As others were helping his friend, Abraham ran in the direction of where the thief went. He found the thief counting the stolen money. Abraham attacked him. He walked away with his friend's money and pieces of teeth embedded in his right fist. Abraham held his painful left arm against his body. It was an honor that his left arm was broken for his friend . . . who did not survive the beating.

And now another friend had been killed, and Abraham needed to steal back something much more valuable than money. Abraham held on to vengeance and let go of the weapon as he wiped his hands on his stained breeches. Francis had wide eyes as he looked up and down the street. He cupped his hand and leaned toward Abraham. "They killed some of us. Some are missing in the last few hours. We thank God that they did not take you away. We heard a report that someone entered your home. We thought they had taken you away. Come into town so you can hide until they pass through your neighborhood. We have our own spies, and we can tell you when you can return home."

"What do you think is happening?" Abraham asked as he grabbed his coat, Steven's letters, and some dried cheese. He stepped outside.

"Someone is watching us. Have you seen anyone you are suspicious of?" asked the tall and lean Francis with shifting eyes.

Abraham shrugged. "Have you seen a book? It was taken. We must find it. It is more important than me at this point."

Francis looked surprised. "No. I have not seen a book. Have you seen anyone you are suspicious of?"

We need the book.

"I have seen a man with a scarred face. He disappears into the night," Abraham said as he looked from side to side.

Francis sneered. "I think they are after Jonathan. They know his connections, and his skills are valuable. There are not too many highly skilled with wood and metal and willing to risk their lives in the Resistance. Jonathan has no fear for himself, but fears for your life. That is why he sent me here while he is warning and protecting others. We will find this man you are concerned with. He will pay with his life for serving a false king."

"Kings will always kill. That is history. Is this yet another wave of the king's wrath? He is not always consistent. Sometimes he allows us some freedom, and sometimes he pulls the leash tighter."

Francis paused. "Do you know what you are getting involved with?"

Abraham looked at him with a blank stare. "We need that book. It was Steven's book."

Jonathan's friend's jaw opened and remained open. "There is much more at stake here than a book. Like our lives. How do we navigate away from the king and his followers? Do you know what is happening?" He shook his head. "It is already difficult to know who you can believe. It is only going to get worse. His spies are everywhere. The king feels threatened and will protect his power at any cost. Drawn and quartered. He will make you beg for death if you are not careful."

He shook his head again. "His men work in the light and the dark. They have infiltrated somewhere within our people, but we do not know where. Do you hear what I am saying? They hide in the light *and* the dark."

Francis stepped closer to Abraham. "Do you realize what you are getting involved with?"

Could he trust the man who was warning him of people he could not trust?

"Go into town, avoid the central neighborhoods as much as you can," the man continued. "Some are waiting for you, as they want to help you. I must go elsewhere and warn others, as Jonathan sent me. We will find the one watching us. God be with you."

He walked in the opposite direction of town, acting as if he had not stopped to talk to Abraham. Abraham's left arm ached as he looked down the street.

Where is it? Is God protecting me, and that is why they have not killed me yet? Are you okay, Jonathan?

A burning rose up inside him. He stomped toward Southampton's heart, eager to unleash his fist on the thief's face.

Someone will pay for taking Steven's life. I will get that book back.

All was quiet in the early dark dawn hours. Only a handful of people out and about would witness justice on the man of the king holding the book.

As he passed in front of a house, a hand came out from behind a tree and grabbed Abraham's wrist, pulling him to the ground.

***

Abraham rolled to his left side, and his right fist stopped in midair. "Jonathan?"

"I don't know if someone followed me. I prayed that you would be okay," Jonathan said as he let go of Abraham's wrist.

"Are you all right?" Abraham exhaled.

Jonathan's eyes were brimming with tears on the edge of falling. "I do not know who to trust. I needed to test the loyalty of an old acquaintance. I needed to see if I could trust him to warn you. I waited here and watched him. I saw the men of the king enter into at least ten homes during the night. People have died tonight. They are looking for someone or something."

His friend placed a hand on Abraham's shoulder. "Do you remember the body on the street during the fighting? They went to that man's house and took his family. They took away a grieving widow and children. We believe they learned more information about the church opposing the king."

He put both his hands on Abraham's shoulders. "They took away the dead man's wife and three young children. They took one of the subterranean church leaders."

Abraham shook his head and looked at his own feet as they began to shift.

"I cannot believe how deeply I am involved now," Jonathan said. "Seeing Steven's body changed something in me. Whether we know it or not, we look like we have chosen sides. I do not know how much they know, but it will be too late if we are not careful. They will know of our treason."

They looked around as they walked toward town. Though it was early dawn, they were vulnerable out in the open. Abraham kept his eyes away from Jonathan. He was not sure how Jonathan would react.

Abraham cleared his throat. "Somebody was inside of our home . . . they took the book . . . they took a few of the names of the church . . ."

Jonathan stopped. Abraham twisted toward Jonathan but avoided direct eye contact.

Jonathan buried his face in his hand. He pulled his hand away and looked around them. "What were you thinking? You had names written down?"

"I did not want to forget. We need help, and I wanted to write down names that may save us in the end." Abraham stepped away.

"I am in danger. You are in danger. How will I ever get you home to your family if they know who you are associating with?"

"How will I get home if I don't associate with them?"

"That cursed book, like a sword, is going to kill you yet. Those printed words are worse than you being in the presence of the king and pulling out a hidden sword and lunging at the king in the presence of his trembling servants. With the previously failed assassination plots, he sees that sword as a threat of violent death to the king already haunted by fear of a violent death. I just . . . I don't want you to be on your knees before the men of the king waiting for their bloody hands to . . ." Jonathan bowed his head.

Silence. How could Abraham argue with the only friend he had left? How could he tell him that might be exactly what the God of justice wanted?

Jonathan shook his head, as if waking up. "We

need to go into town. I will let the others know that they are not safe today. But I must first get you into town safely."

As they walked, Jonathan appeared to need to say something but clearly did not want to.

"You know something. What is it? Say what you need to say," Abraham said.

Like someone torn between burdensome options, Jonathan seemed confused. Then he snarled his upper lip. He reached down into a large bush near him and pulled out something. "I found this."

"You found the book!" Abraham grabbed the book and held it with both hands near his chest. "The idiot thief did not know what he had. He failed his king and doesn't even know it. We are hiding, but it appears this book wants to be found."

"Or taken somewhere." Jonathan narrowed his eyes. "It was underneath a bush I hid behind. I could not decide whether to leave it or throw it away and save lives. I almost threw it away because these words are cursed. Everyone who has this book and lives those words, in every part of the world, they suffer and are then killed. Or people misuse the book to kill others who disagree with them."

Abraham looked closer at the book. He put the torn pages he had with him back into order as they strode.

Jonathan shook his head again. "We should already be dead because of that book. I will not say it is because of protection from this God they talk about, but it seems someone is looking after us. We will soon find out what the consequences are from the names of the Resistance out in the open."

Abraham held the book up. "People have willingly given their lives for these words."

"Put it away! You have already endangered lives today, including ours." Jonathan pushed Abraham's hands down and spat to the side. "People have willingly killed those who willingly want to die for those words. I would rather we live and let others die for those words. I only kept it for you because it was Steven's. No other reason."

"There are few things in life worth being killed for," Abraham said as he pondered his life. "I hid some of my letters in the secret spot in the closet last night. If something ever happens to me, can you make sure my writings get to Humility? I have so many words to say and no chance to say them. This is as close as I can come."

"Yes. But I will do everything I can to get you back home. I will never see my son again, so I will do what I can to get you to your family," Jonathan said.

Abraham placed the contraband into his oversized coat and surveyed the surroundings with each step.

They recognized a blacksmith and a cooper approaching as they turned a corner in a narrow alleyway. Abraham and Jonathan knew James and John from work in the past. Abraham and Jonathan froze when more men came out of nowhere behind the two men to approach them as well.

The cooper and blacksmith looked puzzled with the arrival of the different group of men. When the other group caught up, John, the cooper, drew what looked like a letter C in the dirt. The leader of the other group drew what looked like a number 3 in the dirt, along with other things Abraham could not see. Each of the men from the two groups then appeared to be at peace.

Other men appeared out of the dawn and encircled all the men and stood guard. They all surveyed the surroundings with eyes going to and fro.

One man whispered to Abraham and Jonathan that some men, to remain nameless, desired to meet with Jonathan at a designated home later in the evening. Jonathan agreed to meet with them. All the men dispersed with haste into different directions.

Abraham tried to convince Jonathan that he needed Abraham at the meeting. A look of recognition appeared in Jonathan's eyes as he focused behind Abraham.

"Don't look behind you. I recognize a man of the king behind a tree," Jonathan said as he covered his lips and leaned toward Abraham. "He is watching us. He may be the one following us. You need to find the William we have been told to talk to. I believe he is a pastor. Find him for both of us, and I will distract the man of the king. Get us answers. Go now. This man of the king will not follow you if I come to him. I will not allow it. I will kill him in the open before he touches you. I need to warn others of what is to come, and we need to change the location of any future meetings."

Abraham held on tighter to the hidden contraband and also wanted to get rid of it. With his hands out of his pockets, Abraham stepped in the opposite direction of where he thought he could find William. He expected to hear footsteps following, but only the silence of the early morning followed him. Abraham worried about Jonathan.

He stopped and turned to find out why footsteps were not following him. Jonathan walked toward the man of the king.

Would the man attack Jonathan? Would Jonathan attack the man of the king? Jonathan continued to walk toward the man.

A familiar taste of nausea arose within Abraham. *Please, not Jonathan.*

Jonathan stood before the man and distracted him. He was right. Abraham took advantage of the extra time and turned toward town when he was out of their sight.

Even with the man distracted, Abraham waited for someone to stop him or attack him. But no one was following him. The few who were out appeared to be carrying on with their daily duties.

A part of Abraham wished that the man of the king would have followed him, as his fist ached for broken teeth.

He turned back again. *Someone is following me. Someone is hunting me.*

He shrugged his shoulders. *Why would they want me?*

He remembered what he was carrying.

I know I am not safe. But I must carry this for Steven.

He looked for a hiding place. He took a step to his left to hide the contraband and then escape.

Is this book worth the risk? Is it worth dying for?

Abraham made sure the book was still well hidden in his coat and took a step toward the heart of town.

A man with a scar on the left side of his face watched Abraham as he walked.

CHAPTER 15

JAMES

England
1620

King James' wife was dying.

The religious fanatics caused James' lovers to flee.

Alexander was the most loyal of his subjects. Perhaps even a friend. Alexander set himself apart, as he did not crave the Crown. He possessed a pure religious zeal to defend and extend the rule of God through his king James. The Bible zealots did not deter Alexander.

Rebels lost their lives when they stepped between the divine right of the king and God. The king could always rest in Alexander's presence, as Alexander also fought to control and protect the vulnerable masses. The sheep needed to be controlled. They wanted to be controlled.

New sensations filled James' chest as he stood above his friend on his deathbed.

The shadowed remains of another day descended in his friend's bedroom. For James, this sunset differed from any previous sunset.

New sensations pricked at his heart. Like the love he should have for his ill wife, Anne. But the feelings fell underneath the burden of trying to rule over a land for God. He envisioned two kings fighting for the same piece of heart land.

The king exercised his rule and did not allow tears to escape. But his most loyal friend lay dying before him. And he could not stop the invasion of the dream in his head. That nightmare.

The same nightmare that Alexander told him about. The same nightmare that hunted Alexander before he became ill. The same nightmare that kept both Alexander and James awake at night.

Alexander struggled to open his eyes as he looked at his king with concern. With a trembling jaw, he said, "I will serve you until death. I know it was only a dream, but it seemed to be very real. Someone gave me a warning to give to you. The ships. The people in the water . . . but there was one who was after you. My Lord, he is coming after *you*." He paused to catch his breath.

The king did not even blink. "I have already been warned of him. He will fail like all the others."

"But in the dream, he was protected, shielded from my eyes, shielded from your eyes. I am sorry . . . I did not tell you the rest." Alexander closed his eyes to rest.

"There is *more*? Do not keep this from your friend."

Alexander sighed and opened his eyes. He turned his head away from James. He paused and then said,

"The one who threatens you. I think I know who he is."

The king stood more upright and felt his heart race. "You *know* who he is? Tell me, and you can rest in peace knowing I will end the threat."

He shook his head. "He is coming after you."

The king waited, for he knew there was more. Alexander closed his eyes and turned his head farther away from James. "He is my son."

"Your *son* . . . you don't have a son. You are not married."

"I have had many women . . . many children . . . I do not know where they are . . . I do not know any of them."

The master grabbed his servant's shoulders and pulled and shook him. "You must know which one of them is trying to kill me."

Alexander's eyes widened, and his mouth opened. He appeared unable to speak. He inhaled deeply. "I do not know where any of them are . . . there are too many."

The king looked at what his hands were doing and let go of his friend. A momentary apology came and went through his mind. His hands. He almost did not stop them.

His voice lowered to a whisper. "Can you tell me any names of any of the women?"

The weak friend sighed, closed his eyes, and shook his head.

It did not matter. It was only a nightmare of ships and people in the water.

But how can two different people have the same recurring nightmare?

His friend was dying, and he was going to die with the only knowledge of his son, the assassin. The Catholics. The Protestants. The Separatists. The Puritans. All these groups wanted power over their king. How could he keep the conflicting powers at bay in relative peace? And now, was this confirmation that the assassin still roamed his kingdom?

Alexander looked at James as if he could tell what he was thinking. He mumbled, "Continue to pursue the religious zealots . . . but it is my son's throat . . . that you need to cut. Can you . . . kill him?"

Can I kill my best friend's son?

His friend's last moments were disappearing like the sand plummeting down an hourglass. He looked down at Alexander, in obvious pain, waiting to die with one last request from his king.

"Know this, my friend—my people will be protected. I cannot trust their religion. I will rule, and I will find the coming assassin. I will find him. I will find him," James said.

James took Alexander's hand and held it. "We both know what happened to us in our childhoods. We both know. Though we never talked about it. The men of religion—who betrayed us—they did things to us and made us do things that were not right. They forced the Dark Light on us with the cutting rituals. We were too young to fight. They cannot have that kind of control over us again. They have to be ruled over."

Alexander struggled to turn his head toward his king. He opened his eyes and said, "My only lord . . . my only king . . ."

James thought of the murderer. "Though he be shielded, my sword shall slay."

Do I tell Alexander that my men followed him? That I know the places where he has been?

I will find Satan's assassin.

I will find him.

To protect the Crown.

To protect the seed in me, to my son, to my grandchildren.

Alexander was gone.

James felt an escapee tear run free.

King James knew the murderer would not.

CHAPTER 16

ABRAHAM

Southampton, England
1620

Abraham entered into town confident that no one had followed him. But did it even matter if he was only allowed a longer invisible leash? Several others wandered in Southampton's morning hours with invisible chains that only became visible if they moved too far.

Anyone who helped Abraham would be at risk of imprisonment. Or worse. Where could he go to find a leader planning an escape from a prison that enclosed all? He needed to find Pastor William, though Abraham was told he was not a pastor. The people in hiding considered him even more than a pastor.

Where was the most likely place to find the good pastor?

Abraham entered into the Single Northern Star Tavern, where the good Pastor William was seated in the bad company of about a dozen of Southampton's finest town drunks. All strangely sober this time.

In the unusual quiet for a tavern, he approached their table in the darkest corner near the back door. William looked up with eyes that glowed and lit up the room.

With a childlike joy, William stood up and exclaimed, "You must be Abraham! It is an encouraging blessing from God to see you this morning."

He approached and ignored Abraham's extended hand and embraced him.

Embarrassed and avoiding the light in his eyes, Abraham said, "I am sorry about our brother. Edmund saved Jonathan and me while also trying to save Steven. I am sorry that someone stole my list of names in the church."

With a quick glance upward, Abraham noticed a smile with sad eyes. William stood in the midst of the odd assortment of lost souls at the table and pointed toward Abraham.

He patted Abraham's stomach as he laughed. "Our Story is pregnant with a grand adventure ahead for Abraham that he does not yet realize. Labor can be a difficult time. We have prayed for your delivery."

He put his arm around Abraham. "Abraham, I am sorry for your loss of Steven. We have been mourning and celebrating what God did through him and Edmund. We are dwindling in number. We are part of the last remnant. Nowhere in the world are people free, as God desires. We pray to God to fulfill His will. May He use us to change the generations. The nations."

They bowed their heads as two members of the group went in different directions. One went to stand near the entrance, and the other at the back door. It was still morning, and the tavern was not open for business yet.

Where better else to have church?

Curtains covered the closed windows. The new day was growing in strength, and the dark inside the tavern was losing to the light. There was no fear in the room. There was a joy that illuminated and cut through the darkened corner of one of Southampton's finest.

The guard at the front entrance warned those inside of someone approaching. An older and burly man stomped toward the tavern. The guard allowed him to burst into the tavern, bearing heavy footsteps and a scowl upon his face. The burly man wiped his hand on his bare scalp and walked to the men gathered at the table and interrupted their prayer.

"You cannot stay here. I have seen the men of the king roaming, and I cannot have them come here. I cannot have my family affected by this."

He turned and stomped toward the young man who was serving the men at the front.

"Did anyone see these men come in here?"

The young man put down the glass he was cleaning. "Father, everything is all right. They mean no harm. No one else has been here. We are safe."

The burly man relaxed his shoulders and spoke to the gathering. "Know that I am with you. They can come and take me away. I have no concern for myself. But they take away their enemies *and* their families."

He looked at the young man and closed his eyes. "I cannot lose my family. It is all I have left."

The man's son crossed the room to his father. "God is here. We will be okay."

The man stiffly turned to the gathering. "Please watch yourselves. No one is safe with the men of the king roaming the streets. You have a few more hours, but then you must leave when we open."

He walked out the door. The church gathered in the tavern was not good for business. They spent hours reading Scripture, praying, and laughing about their coming adventures. Some of the locals left when they realized there was a church in their favorite tavern. A few stayed and moved closer to hear the forbidden.

William, usually bent over in a fixed position, propped up full of life as he taught them of God. All the scars and bruises on his line-filled face seemed to point to the mouth that proclaimed that after the remission of their sins, those in the gathering henceforward were now free.

A different presence gathered in strength in the room. Some said it was the presence of God. There was new life in the air. Indifference was not an option. Those in the tavern who sought their familiar spirits were different. They drew closer to a different Spirit. Abraham had not touched any alcohol since his encounter with Edmund. Sitting in the tavern, he had no desire to drink.

It was gone.

He was free to drink but preferred not to hinder those who had a weakness for alcohol. It was good to desire what was best for others.

When the others saw that Abraham—yes, Abraham—was not drinking, they too pushed their drinks to the side. A strange liberty wafted in the air. Freedom to drink without judgment from the others, but there was a chosen consensus of not wanting to drink.

After William informed them that another of the church leaders was missing for two days, they asked what happened with one voice.

Though he knew the men of the king could be just outside of the tavern, Abraham pounded his fist onto the table and stood up and proclaimed, "Revolution!"

The others sprang to their feet and pounded on the table. Brothers in arms permeated the air.

William calmed the men and asked them to sit down. He did not whisper when he said, "I too desire revolution. But this battle is the Lord's and not ours. This is to be fought with the weapons that God has already planted within us. It will not be won with our own hands. Your hand cannot save you. We will only succeed with the power of our God and not through our means. Are you with me?"

Pounding his fist onto the table, Abraham stood again and yelled, "Yes—but I want to hit somebody!"

The men all laughed as they pushed and shoved one another.

Pastor William, while holding one of the men in a headlock and with his other hand in a clenched fist, said, "I want to hit somebody too. I want vengeance for what they did to my family, my brothers, my sisters. I want vengeance!"

The man in the headlock with a red face attempted to get the attention of someone for help. William kept his attention on the surrounding men, as he did not see the man in the headlock with rolling eyes waving his hands behind him.

William looked upward. "But vengeance is not mine. It is the Lord's. For if it were mine, I would turn into the king. We fight His way."

He released the head and stood as straight as his stooped spine allowed. The man who'd been in the headlock collapsed onto the ground. William looked reluctant to utter the next words. A reverence silenced the room, as no one noticed the shaking arm from the ground asking for help up. Something took over William as he prepared like a cannon. Loaded, positioned, angled, and aimed. The words shot out of his mouth and exploded into the room.

"We need to pray for the king."

All heads swiveled side to side. All voices united to say, "The king?"

Silence.

William stood with eyes locked on the book in the center of the table. After one or two grunts, everyone closed their eyes. Heads nodded. The ex-drunks lifted empty earthenware mugs and prayed for God's intoxicating love to fill them—for the king.

After the prayer, William clenched his right fist. He raised it in the air with a smile. "They will know us by our love. Only the love of God can subvert the strategies of Satan."

After the meeting, he approached Abraham. "Abraham, here are some verses to further your understanding of the Story. Study these. They will help you with what is coming."

Abraham reached out his hand. "As a result of you and Steven, things already look different to me."

William put him in a gentle headlock. Abraham pretended to heave for air. William whispered into Abraham's ear the new time and location for the next meeting, turned away, and said goodbye. Abraham had time to write another letter and remained in the tavern for a few more hours. He opened the book and studied the verses given to him. He finalized putting all of Steven's pages and the pages of the book back into order. He read some more and took more notes.

There was a new spirit that dwelled within the men in the tavern. Though he'd learned enough to know that God did not need forgiveness, he let go and forgave God for taking Steven.

He felt courted by two different individuals. Like he had to choose between a parent who'd raised him and someone new claiming to be his father. The home where he was raised was all that he knew.

As other men entered the tavern that evening, Abraham remembered the secret meeting and stepped outside. A pain stabbed him in his chest when, up ahead, two men in the distance walked toward the tavern. The men were pointing in different directions as they discussed options for their next search. They moved like they sought a specific person.

Abraham held fast to his book and notes and hid behind a tree. The two men moved forward past Abraham and surveyed the area near the tavern. Abraham moved to the other side of the tree out of their vision. After a minute, he looked back. The two men stood talking to the owner's son. The young man shook his head and shrugged. Abraham waited out of view. What could he do?

That is enough. Good men must do something.

He took a step to enforce his rule of law over the men of the king. He sensed a stop in his spirit. Abraham remembered Steven and his belief that God's weapons were different.

After a few minutes, they took the young man away.

The young man's eyes opened wide, and he scanned the area for help. Would he tell of the location of the coming meeting and the names of the men in the tavern, whom he'd overheard?

Abraham's heart broke in a new place. Did he just witness the owner of the tavern losing his son?

Chapter 17

ABRAHAM

Southampton, England
1620

Abraham hid behind another tree far from the tavern. Buried in thoughts about how life had changed in the last few days, he lost track of time. Another person disappeared. He had no concern for his own safety as he walked. His new broken piece of heart had a burden for Jonathan and the coming secret gathering. There was nothing he could do about the young man taken away at the tavern.

Fewer people than usual rambled around town as fear of the king's men still permeated. Tension in the air hung above all as any semblance of peace could snap at any moment. Half a block from the meeting location, he spotted the first group of men hiding in the shadows. After the guards recognized Abraham as Jonathan's friend, they allowed him to pass. The second group of men closer to the meeting site searched him for weapons or signs of the king and asked him questions again before they escorted him to a back room of a small house.

Just as Abraham joined the men, another guard ran inside and reported that one of the guards broke ranks.

"He left us and went to two men of the king roaming in the area," the guard said.

A collective gasp filled the room, and many turned to find the best way to escape.

"The two men of the king attacked him, just short of death," the guard continued. "They pulled him up off the ground and commanded him to lead them to the others." The guard wept. "He led them in the opposite direction of the meeting."

Someone in the group yelled, "He knew they'd found out the location. He gave his life to give us time to leave."

The leaders consulted each other and decided on a plan. They were not running this time. They had a few minutes to finish their meeting.

There were twenty-odd in number, and no one left the room. Abraham did not know most of the people but felt secure with Jonathan and the courage in the air.

Jonathan embraced Abraham. They were in this together.

The meeting in whispers started with an older gentleman. He said that a group from Scrooby escaped the clutches of the king, like the ancient Hebrews escaping Egypt, and secretly immigrated to Holland a few years before. Another representative for the group stood as all whispers stopped. Several people leaned forward to hear how their world was going to change.

"Holland was the only place we could go to worship our God freely. But we were like a small vessel surrounded by an ocean of people who did not share our beliefs. Our children began to resemble them and not God."

Whispering spread in the small room as he continued. "Holland may soon be at war with Spain. If Spain were to overcome, they would kill all of us who have different beliefs than they. The king and his men were already hunting us for our press printing words of treason against the king."

Another man stood. "We cannot stay here in England for the same reasons. We only have one choice."

The group from Scrooby shared more about their travails, both in England and in Holland, and their vision for the future. A move of the Spirit of God upon their hearts returned them back to England to begin a new great work of God.

The group consisted of outcast outlawed individuals. They sought to walk their faith by living their Scriptures.

The older man stood again. "We remember the ancient Hebrews escaping Pharaoh and his slavery. We are going to the new promised land."

A silence joined with the proposal. *God is not replacing Israel. But they are going to sail to the other side of the Atlantic to become like a new Israel. Like a new Israel!*

Abraham looked down at his moving shirt. The pounding in his chest showed a desire to dance with a new partner in response to the rhythm of a new song.

The group from Scrooby turned to Jonathan. "Will you join us? Will you use your skills and connections to help us?"

Jonathan and Abraham had many discussions about Jonathan's wood and metal skills. The group would need to build when they arrived in the promised land. Jonathan wanted to start a business in a new location. But he had never moved beyond serving his king.

Even with the skills of Jonathan and others, this plan of madness is suicide. It is scandalous. Could we even raise enough funds? Could we escape the king? Could we survive the trip on the Atlantic with women and children too?

Abraham could use his influence, coupled with Jonathan's sense of guilt, to convince Jonathan to ask the leaders if he could go.

One of the men sprang out of his chair and pushed men out of the way as he cursed while running out the door. All looked stunned, and no one moved.

"He has been angrier every day as he learned more about our plans," a woman said. "He will report us all to the men of the king."

"They are already on their way here. Should we abort this plan so that we can still live?" a man asked.

"Even with life, we have not been alive," someone responded.

"Should we move quicker than originally planned to escape?" a man in the back of the room asked.

Another stood and asked, "Should I run after him?"

"If this man would have deserted the king," William said, "he would soon be dead. But with us, he is free to leave under his own free will. He lives long enough to have the chance to choose rightly later."

The meeting concluded with a decision not to meet again until it was safe. They departed without any goodbyes. Abraham and Jonathan made their way into the shadows and marched in an indirect path home.

From a distance, Abraham saw that the man who'd left the meeting had returned with two other men.

"Quick. Let's turn this way out of sight," Abraham said. "The men of the king went into the house."

Jonathan looked back and pointed to his right. "Let's go this way."

Every few steps they made sure no one followed them. Several townspeople looked at Abraham and Jonathan with suspicion as they walked with their heads down. Who could be trusted?

They discussed the meeting with a whisper in the night. Abraham, no longer able to contain himself in a whisper, readied himself to swim the Atlantic to return home if necessary.

"You can't swim," Jonathan said with a laugh. "You were a captain of a ship with many Atlantic journeys, survived many storms, and yet you fear drowning. And you assume I will talk to them to let you go?"

"Well, of course. You need me."

"I need *you*? I know you have a lot of experience on the open sea, but I did not know you then. I only know you now as a man weighed down with guilt like an anchor—unable to swim and with a fear of water."

They stopped walking. Abraham shook his head and put his hands over his ears. "I spent most of my adult life working on the ocean. I never wasted my time learning how to swim. I did not always have a fear of drowning."

"I do not know if you are capable of making this trip—and this is a journey of suicide. I do not want this on me." Jonathan wiped his hands on his breeches.

When they arrived at the front door of their home, Abraham reminded Jonathan that someone had entered their home earlier. Who could be waiting for them? Jonathan had Abraham wait outside as he searched the house.

Jonathan signaled all was clear.

Abraham entered. "My papers are all here, but someone moved them." *Is someone here?*

A questioning look covered Jonathan's face. Abraham, with frustration, denied any creative imagination on his part.

Amid his frustration, Abraham felt a sharp pain on the right side of his head. Out of precaution, he reached out his shaking left arm and collapsed into a nearby chair. He could not move his left leg and left arm. His head pounded more, and he moaned as he grabbed his head with his right hand.

Jonathan stood trembling as he watched Abraham. He trembled so much he reached for the nearest chair.

"I am sorry. I promise to believe you next time. If you say someone was here and moved your papers, then I believe you." Jonathan labored to remain standing.

He shifted his weight alternately away from and toward Abraham. He raised his hands toward his face and wiped them, as if something was dripping off his hands. With trembling hands and a shaking voice, he sounded like a scared child. "I will find a doctor."

Abraham motioned that he wanted him to stay.

It knows we are here.

Two sides fought inside Abraham's head. One side said to swim in one direction, and the other side said to go in the opposite direction. His chest felt a pull on both sides, as if caught between opposing grips pulling in opposite directions.

Jonathan remained leaning toward the front door. After a few minutes, the control of Abraham's arm and leg improved. Jonathan let out a loud sigh of relief.

Abraham lifted his left arm and leg. *They came and took away the tavern owner's son. The guard sacrificed himself to save us and our meeting. My body betrayed me. Is someone or something hunting me? How much longer do I have?*

Abraham turned toward his friend. "I don't know what to do. I am dying following the king, and I will be killed if I listen to the other King. They both kill. Yet, as my head hurt, I think I heard God tell me, 'I am with you.'"

He got up and limped to get a drink of water and returned to the chair next to the table, dragging his leg. He pulled out the book. "We need to seek counsel on whether we should leave our home."

He put his head in his hands and prayed. *I do not know if I believe in You. Yet, I need You to confront my fear of death at the bottom of the sea, and I need to return home.*

Through the corner of his eye, Abraham saw Jonathan rise, using the wall to help stay upright. He shifted his weight between moving toward and away from Abraham.

As Abraham began to read Scripture aloud, it was clear a relief came upon his friend. Abraham shared that with that simple sentence that he heard from God, perhaps there was a promise they could trust.

I think I heard Your voice.

They knew they were leaving.

Chapter 18

ABRAHAM

Southampton, England
1620

Standing near a wall for balance, Abraham jumped in place several times the following morning. He squatted then rose up multiple times. Some of Abraham's strength had returned. Jonathan was still asleep, snoring louder than usual. He had told Jonathan that he would meet with Pastor William for prayer and counsel in the morning.

He prepared for the day, and at the door, he turned back one more time. So much had happened in that room the last few days. From months of death, waiting for its moment, to death interrupted in its moment. Edmund's knock on Abraham's door. The invitation given to Abraham and Jonathan. Friends murdered. The illegal contraband.

He left the book hidden behind a wall.

I just want to go home.

Many avoided walking the street in the early morning fog. Abraham could no longer outrun anyone with his left-sided weakness.

As he trekked to the secret location, a man who'd been present with those in the tavern the previous day joined him. The men called him Big John.

Big John, the former towering, sad, and quiet figure most of the time, filled the early morning air with renewed energy. "Abraham, I have not had a drink since our time with Pastor William in the tavern. I feel new. I can feel Jesus inside me. I am no longer alone. I am clean now."

He smiled. "I am trying to figure out how everything fits. How does who I used to be fit with the new man I am now? I am thankful for another chance to live. I used to be a dead man with a beating heart, waiting to die. I was slowly killing myself, thinking that was life."

They both looked up and down the street. Big John paused again, as if trying to locate words hidden in him so well that he had not known of them before. "I do have regrets. Regrets about how I wasted my years. I guess I will have that with me as a reminder of my first life. I do not fear for my safety—yet I want revenge for another leader of the church taken last night."

"Do you think someone within the church is betraying us?"

"I think it is someone watching us. I will find him. Revenge will spill *his* blood on the street," Big John said as he clenched his right fist. "No one will stop me from going to the promised land to make more money than our king,"

Abraham turned his head away from Big John, as he did with all things that reflected. *What riches can one find in the promised land? What evil lurks there?*

The stories of what had happened across the Atlantic reminded him of the lost colony of Roanoke. Abraham remembered hearing about an entire English colony that just disappeared about thirty years ago. No one knew what happened to the people. Where did they go? And what about Jamestown just about ten years ago? Could it be true that only about sixty of an entire town survived the starving time? There were rumors that they did not properly prepare to survive. Many were too lazy to work the land ahead of time to have food for the future. Diseases ravaged them. They attacked and were attacked, by their only hope, the Indians.

There was little food. Many died. Some turned to cannibalism to survive.

Cannibalism.

Abraham waited for an opportunity to separate from Big John and walk alone. Disagreements grew in the fertile soil of the desire for power among all people, even in the church. Even if they survived to step forth on a ship, escaped, overcame the sea, and lived God's will in establishing a new Israel, would they be prepared to survive without devouring each other?

They took a different route to their meeting with William and the others as a precaution. "From everything that you know, can we trust the Separatists?"

Abraham asked. "The religion of the love of gold has a long history of taking over the mission of many explorers in the past. Do they have the interests of God above their own?"

"Does it matter? What other choice do we have? Who else is trying to be free from the king? I know of people here in this neighborhood who turned against their own family and friends and reported them to the king and his men. Many watched their own loved ones taken away. Some who betrayed us tried to save themselves by giving away their loved ones to satiate the king's hunger. There must be another way. There must be another King. Do we remain and do nothing? Who else can we trust? Good people must do something."

Big John sighed. "Where in the world are people truly free?"

Abraham's silence was his answer.

They arrived at the first set of guards and passed their tests. They walked farther and exchanged passwords with another group of guards.

Then men jumped out from behind trees and bushes. They kicked and threw Abraham to the ground, face up, so he could still see the attack. Big John punched and kicked the men while standing in front of Abraham. He delivered blows to the face of the leader. The leader did not get up. One of the men came from behind and stabbed Big John in his neck. He lay on the ground with his mouth open, struggling to cry out.

The first set of guards Abraham and John encountered had fled and escaped. The men of the king captured the other group of guards and moved them farther away from Abraham. Big John lived his last moments alone on the ground, gasping for air.

Several feet away, the captors asked the captured guards questions. Abraham could just make out their voices. When they tried to answer, the king's men hit them in the face. The captors were not interested in their answers.

Abraham lay next to another friend who'd been killed. He was the last living barrier between the men of the king and those at the secret meeting. Should he try to run away? Or remain to deceive the men from going to the secret meeting and capturing Jonathan and the others?

The choice was made for him, as three of the men hit Abraham as they stood him up.

Why do we kill each other?

"You need to let me go. I can give you the information you want, but you must first let me go." Abraham staggered between blows.

If they take me away, I will not survive. O God, don't let them kill me—I will do anything for You if You free me . . .

Like a drowning man in the open sea with one last remaining option, he raised a hand for someone or something to grab. "I can tell you where the others are. The men you captured were never told where the meeting is, and you killed the only other person who could have helped you. Let me go, and I can help you please the king."

Someone hit the back of his head, and he cut his knees on the hard ground. His head throbbed, and the world seemed to rock like a ship in a bad storm as they took the captured guards toward the house where the meeting was being held. They yanked Abraham back onto his feet and pushed him in the opposite direction. They'd achieved their goal and did not need Abraham.

His legs were weak as they helped him walk. The men of the king would be at the meeting in just a few minutes if the rebels were not warned. An ache pierced his heart like an older brother watching his younger brother taken as a prisoner of war.

Jonathan! I'm the one who sent you to war.

"Run! They are coming!" he yelled. His last memory was of Jonathan and falling backward.

He dreamed as his heart pounded a new death beat. Someone's hand held an hourglass and turned the hourglass upside down. The sand in the upper half began to empty. Like a bleeding wound that would not heal, the blood and his time spilled. A hand wrapped around his throat and covered his mouth.

He awoke from his dream on cold dirt with a coughing gasp. The stone room was stone cold. The cube-shaped space seemed to be about ten paces in every direction. There was little light as he reached for his head and his ribs. He touched his face like it belonged to someone else. The dried blood on his fingers appeared forever stained in the partial light. Labored breathing brought pain. Four blurry images stood above him.

One whispered to the others that he was awake.

"You are in prison. You have been asleep for several hours. God protected you, as you are still alive."

Abraham mumbled as he spat out part of a tooth. He gagged and coughed up another piece of a tooth.

"Can you tell me where Jonathan is?" Abraham tried to articulate.

The man squinted his eyes and tilted his head to the side. "There is no Jonathan here. He either eluded them for a short time or is no longer with us in this life. These are the only options I am aware of with the king's men."

Abraham spat again. His heart raced.

"Jonathan!"

The four walls enclosed around him as the figures moved. Were human wolves closing in on human prey?

Where am I? Am I being judged for what I did? The hourglass of my seventy-six days has been tipped! I am running out of time!

The apparent leader of the men stopped the others from getting too close. He reached out his hand and touched Abraham on his shoulder. He introduced himself as Christopher. He asked the others to give Abraham space as they started their Bible reading and prayer. One of them pulled out a torn page and read under a sliver of light as they whispered words and prayers. They thanked God for one of the rogue guards who'd given them provisions for reading and recording on paper.

Abraham closed one eye and opened the other to test his vision. He discovered the blurriness was from one swollen eye. His memory was not as sharp. He attempted to stand but fell, and some men helped him to his feet. He shuffled in the cramped quarters, his limp worse than before.

There were fifteen men in the room with no window. What light they had came from windows down a hall containing several guards. One corner was the place to relieve oneself.

There was nothing wrong with his sense of smell.

Christopher pulled Abraham to the side, apart from the other men. Christopher looked around him in the darkened room and appeared to measure his words. "Abraham . . . I believe you are safer here for now. Even with the king using many of his spies to search for his target, he may not think of searching for you inside one of his own prisons. They were just about ready to find you when you were taken away from his eyes. But for how long he may not see you, I do not know. The longer you are here, the greater the chances he will find you."

"Are you saying he is looking for *me*? He is looking for *me* above others?"

Christopher leaned next to Abraham's ear. "Prayers of protection for you is at the top of my prayer list.

We have prayed for you every day for weeks. Will you survive to save many?"

The men were all enemies of the king. In life and in death, there was no division among them. Though he never had a present father, the men adopted Abraham as a brother.

CHAPTER 19

ABRAHAM

Southampton, England
1620

Moment by moment, his remaining time fled from prison. With the hourglass tipped over, his time was spilling out. Abraham lay on the ground in the dark as the morning light tried to break through the walls.

He needed to get back home. But over the course of weeks, Abraham learned to love his brothers behind walls. With the conversing and sharing, praying, and impromptu Bible studies, a liberty existed within the confines of their prison.

The brothers in the dark shared their last remaining days together. His new brothers lived boldly for another King. In the absence of light, their shared stories illuminated their lives. They were broken. It was beautiful.

Each of Abraham's new brothers said another King made himself known and gave them new lives. In the midst of all the voices crying out in his nightmares, Abraham lived with a living remnant of hope's persistent whisper. The heart of life beat faintly—though in chains, it still beat.

As they revealed their stories, their lives became both transparent and reflective. Though Abraham closed his eyes, he knew his life mirrored the depths and dungeons of their lives.

But Abraham could not fully open his eyes. He could not share all his secrets. He would rather die chained to them.

One morning, he lay awake unable to fall back to sleep, as the other men snored in the predawn hours. In the corner used as the place for fluids and excrement, something startled him. Something moved. Toward him.

It slithered. Even in the near dark, it glistened with what light was available. It looked like old, dried blood crawling on the ground. Like a hand opening with extending fingers. With each finger-length piece of ground colonized, it slithered toward him.

It is coming for my throat.

My mother should have killed me when she had the chance.

In the dark, his life coursed down the hourglass. In his final days, could he tell anyone of his chains unseen, before he died in chains seen?

Abraham wrote into the dark.

Dear Humility,

I am sorry.

My dearest love. I had every intention to attend a crucial meeting to show myself worthy to travel across the ocean back to you.

But I failed you once again. I am behind prison walls again because of what I did. I am waiting to die for my secret secrets.

I will never see you again.

My mother failed to end my life before I committed my many sins. I failed to end my life. If we would have not failed, you would not be wondering and waiting for me. Others would not have died trying to help me.

Why do I still live?

Some told me I am to give birth to something of God. Yet I see a bloody hand with stained fingers coming for my throat to reach inside me to rip out the unborn.

O lovely bride of mine, I am sorry for what I did to you. How many times can love forgive?

The king's men captured me. My friends here tell me that if I write, they will try to make sure my words reach you. I want you to know that I died trying to come to you.

Along with a dream that I had, two friends here in prison told me that God had appeared in their sleep and told them that my hourglass had been tipped. It is now day three of seventy-six that I have left to live. I will not leave this prison.

The morning light is approaching, so I will now write about words smuggled for me. Perhaps there is a hope in a story other than my own.

So the Lord God said to the serpent, "Because you have done this, cursed are you above all livestock and all wild animals! You will crawl on your belly and you will eat dust all the days of your life. And I will put enmity between you and the woman, and between your offspring and hers; he will crush your head, and you will strike his heel." Genesis 3:14–15

I am sorry. I am ashamed that I did not allow you and the children to read the Story. I did not want my family to believe in something that threatened me. Tell them my words of the Story. It would make me smile, knowing you are reading to them as I once did. Please allow me to be the teacher I should have been. I could then die knowing it was not too late for you and our children.

I have learned that God honored the heart's desire of Adam and Eve and left his home with them. With God's presence *now lifted, they possessed a heartbeat, but were dead inside. God eased their shame and covered their nakedness with animal skins. An animal must have died to provide the coverings. How shocking it must have been for Adam and Eve to see life ended before their eyes for the first time in paradise.*

The offspring of God chose Satan as ruler. Perhaps like a sudden onset of the night during midday, the new king, a counterfeit king, brought a Dark Light that infiltrated within and outside of Adam and Eve.

How does a father respond to his children who choose to follow another?

God forced Adam and Eve away from their home. He stationed an angel to guard against them taking from the tree of life.

God. Satan. Adam. Eve. And me. Are we all not seeking home?

Children, I want to come home.

I believe the sentences above are the first prophecy of God. When God talked to Satan, there is a "he" and "his" in "he will crush your head, and you will strike his heel." These words seem to be hints of war and someone coming. My eyes are witnessing a prophecy of war between two different families.

A savior is coming from the family of Eve. The other family is of Satan. There would be enmity between both families. In a future conflict, the promised offspring of the woman would suffer an injury but would inflict a fatal injury upon Satan. Satan's head, his authority, would be crushed.

If this is a true story, and if I am occupying the place of Satan, I know that God does not lie. With all power I possess, I will destroy this coming offspring. For I want to determine good and evil instead of God. I want to control God and His children. I want vengeance against my father, who threw me out of my home and occupies my throne.

I want.

Hidden from the light, I would crouch down, lie, and wait. I would learn how to destroy the coming offspring before He destroyed me. Where is the weakness, the vulnerability, in this almighty God? There has to be something. I see it! This knight of armor has a small opening upon his chest! A fatal flaw of vulnerability. The weakness of God is His vulnerability in allowing His children the freedom to choose, or reject His love. Does the almighty God defer to the heart's desire of His offspring? And He plagued His offspring with the same flaw among each other? What kind of father *would willingly create this flaw into His children? Almighty God? What a fool He is to create humans with the same weakness and vulnerability to free will. A rusted handmade sword will fit nicely into that opening. I will exploit this vulnerability of the desire to love and be loved, with errors in the free will exercise of this love. I will exercise true might. I will eliminate the choice and seduce them to make my choice for them. Love is weak. It bows down to the mighty hand that holds the sword at the neck. I will destroy the seed of the coming savior by destroying all possible carriers of this coming seed. For the good of creation, I will eliminate the weak with their pathetic vulnerabilities and leave only the strong. It is merely the survival of the most fit. The strongest survive. Might makes right. This is how I would be God.*

But I am not God.

Where is this coming seed, the coming savior? Eve gave birth to Cain and then to Abel. Satan must have observed that the opening upon Cain's chest was more vulnerable than Abel's, the favored one. The seed! Could this Abel be the seed prophesied to crush Satan's authority? Could this Abel be God's coming savior of the world?

Satan then expanded his reign from

roaming the earth and entered into Cain's willing heart. Satan moved Cain's heart to kill his brother Abel. The woman's promise lay in a pool of blood on the desert floor.

The first killing occurred with the sacrificing of an animal to cover Adam and Eve. The first killing of an offspring of God happened with the murder of Abel. His spilled blood on the ground cried out to God.

Why would an almighty God allow His flaw to cause himself His own suffering? How can man be made good, with free will intact, with Satan roaming the earth?

But God did not stop.

The promise of the savior was not dead. The hope of the seed then continued through another son born, and his name was Seth.

Over many years, Satan exploited what he had gleaned through the generations. After failing in heaven and flung to earth, he expanded his reign from the garden. Into Adam and Eve. Into the heart of Cain. Into the now empty space within every heart. The earth soon became populated with Satan's family. Satan's plan to stop the savior was succeeding. Where is the seed to penetrate the hard ground when only several feet of excrement covers the land?

"But Noah found favor in the eyes of the Lord."

Noah and his family were the last remaining remnant of the family of God. Noah believed in and accepted the invitation from God, and God saved them in the ark to pass on the seed of the coming savior.

My lovely Humility, learn, and tell this story. Listen to my final words as I add my voice to the multitude of voices. Though it is too late for me, listen to my cries from the pit of hell before it is too late for you and our children.

Delayed justice would only be served if I rot in hell and my friends in the ark leave without me. And yet I pound on the outer walls of the ark passing over me, begging those inside to let me in. I can't swim! I want to live! Please take me in! Take me to the new promised land!

As I sink closer to my watery grave, I watch the ark on the horizon leave without me. It is beyond my reach as it disappears and the fist wraps around my throat to pull me down.

My entire life I have been trained to believe that it is only me in my story. It was only me standing in my garden.

Have I believed a cloaked voice hidden

within me? Have I lived the lie of the serpent? Have I tried to advance my own kingdom when, in reality, I was deceived by Satan into advancing his kingdom and my own slavery? I worshiped this king in my pool of vomit, wanting to end my reign without hope.

Was there someone else with me in the garden? Another voice?

I miss you, Humility. I am trying to be different in heart, and I want to be with you above all things.

In the crossfire, I stand between the two different kings. I stand between the heads of two different families. They call to me in the moonlit garden. I have only known the ways of one of them.

What about the other King?

But both kings lead to death.

I should die, but I want to live.

I am not alone.

Both are with me.

Help me.

I want to go home.

Love,

Abraham

CHAPTER 20

ABRAHAM

Southampton, England
1620

Days dripped like blood from a dying hunted animal. Abraham lay wounded another day and waited for the footsteps to come and finish off the hunt. But Abraham wanted to survive another day. With the available morning light, he stared at the same corner. The dried blood had moved closer.

Abraham strained to hear any birds or signs of life outside the prison. From the corner, *I will find you* echoed in his head.

His deteriorating physical condition troubled him, as he sometimes required help with walking. The men supported each other through prayer as the days passed.

A guard struck one of the men blind with blows to the head. Another man lost his hand. Another lost his brother when the men of the king ended his life in the very room they were imprisoned.

The whispered Bible studies were the highlight of each day. At least one of the guards knew of their acts of treason. They whispered and drew in the dirt using a smuggled candle at night.

Though Abraham could not memorize Scripture, and many other things on paper, and therefore did not volunteer to teach, the men marveled at how much of the wisdom of God Abraham displayed considering his limited time and experience with Scripture. They prayed for those removed weekly.

He requested daily prayers for his wife, Humility, his children, and his friends who'd left to sail the Atlantic. Sometimes he asked for prayer for himself.

Leaning against a cold wall, he confessed his heart to his brothers. "This day, I am angry. I am angry with myself for what I have done with my life. I am angry with God, for why did He place desires in me that will remain unrequited? Sometimes I want to go home, and sometimes I want to die alone. Yet I am still alive. I am still here. Why am I possessed with feelings of returning home that will never be answered? I know I am to have faith, but today I do not have faith. Will I have any remaining days to return home to my family? Will the strength of the king prevail? My body is yet deserting me as my time is running out."

A unanimous proclamation of silence followed. Abraham reflected what was in each heart. But that day he did not share everything hidden within himself.

I pray that one of these friends of mine does not betray me. At times I wish to be like the Lord, but I do not want the same experience of a friend betraying me. My heart and my health are too weak to survive that crushing blow.

That night the walls blocked more of the light. The quiet was broken. Someone yelled in the room. Acclimated to life in the dark, the man yelling moved through the room, knowing where each man was. He moved unseen, like a darker shadow on the hunt in the dark. Slurring and with deep guttural and slithering words, he moved with the sliding of feet in the dirt. The man kicked whoever was still on the ground.

Confused, the men hesitated to strike back in the dark. Was a friend having another nightmare? Abraham grasped into the darkness and caught hold of the man with his vest.

"God is great!" the man mumbled.

They knew the voice.

It was a guard.

The slithering words shocked Abraham as he let go of the man. The guard acted as if under the influence of alcohol, yet they could not smell any of that spirit. What would happen if they defended themselves against a guard?

He continued muttering. "God is holy! You will serve the king, or we will slit your throats in your sleep."

He kicked someone who was already wounded. The guard, fully occupied, yelled again, "God is great!" They heard a noise, like a sword sliding out of its sheath, as he pulled something out of his vest. He grabbed one of the men and ignited his rage with knife in hand as it exploded upon another. He then stabbed himself.

Stunned. Silence. No movement. Someone whimpered. Another sobbed. The men felt their way to their brother and knew he was no longer with them. No words. The shrapnel of fear from the attack entered Abraham's heart. Someone walked to the dead guard and kicked the corpse without ceasing. The kicking continued, as if he wanted the guard to return to life to feel the vengeance. One of the men pulled his friend away from the death.

One man spoke. "We must ignore what happened. The guard was already wounded and did not mean any harm. It is our fault. It won't happen again."

"Are you an idiot?" another man asked. "Of course he meant to do harm—and he succeeded. We must strike them when they come looking for him. They must pay."

"What should we do?" another asked. "They will think we killed him. They will seek justice upon us."

Two guards then ran in with their lights and pushed all aside. "What have you done?"

One of the imprisoned men attempted to explain what had occurred, and a guard struck him silent. That guard then yelled with his fist in the air, "Death will come upon all of you." He pointed to each man still alive.

The guards dragged their comrade's body out and left a candle to illuminate the body of the captives' friend.

Moments before, their friend was alive, and now he lay motionless on the ground. Though the rest of the men still possessed a pulse, there was no life left. It fled with Hope the moment the guard invaded what little security they had left.

Life seemed absent in their silenced kingdom. No advocate spoke for them in the courtroom of death. All would in time be found guilty, and all would have the same sentence. The eventual outcome only con-firmed who ruled there.

Who could overrule death?

Within Abraham, a new tension arose between fury, sorrow, and envy for their now departed friend. Where was God?

If a Father had a history of not coming to His children's aide when He could have in the past, why should they believe that same Father would come to theirs in the present?

In the early hours of the following morning, guards burst in. They grabbed Abraham and some of the others and forced them into separate rooms. Pushed onto his knees, echoes of pleading voices in other rooms penetrated through walls.

There was a pleasure in the eyes of the men before him, with smiles and missing teeth in the dimly lit room. A large and encrusted knife was at his throat. He tried not to throw up as an odor of old dried blood from the knife burned his nos-trils. He gagged and then stifled a yelp as the knife superficially cut him.

A man with death emanating in his breath spoke. "The king is searching for a murderer. I will find him—are you a murderer?"

Abraham stood with his head down. "I am not—"

"Enough! You will renounce your weak religion and submit to the king."

"I do have allegiance to a weak religion . . . the king is all I have known."

The man hit Abraham on the side of his head with the handle of the knife. "Do not forget who you serve," he snarled.

Before Abraham passed out, he mumbled, "I do not know . . . whom I serve . . ."

Abraham awoke the following day on the ground and in a different room. He reached for the side of his throat. Dried blood stuck to one side of his neck. A message from the king. The king always signed with the blood of others.

Why . . . why am I still alive?

Abraham shivered. Or was he trembling? Men burst into the room and pulled him outdoors by his hair and what remained of his shirt. Standing outside of the prison walls for the first time, he stood next to all the other men pulled out into the dawn rain. They looked around at their unfamiliar courtyard surroundings as if with open eyes for the first time.

The guards blindfolded them and lined them up with their backs against a wall that poked jagged edges through the remains of their clothing. With sweat running down Abraham's back, the striking cold temperature of the sharp-edged wall caused him to wince.

Abraham yearned for what was on the other side of the wall.

What does life look like on the other side? Is there a place where the God we pray to rules? Where His people can call on their God—and He answers?

A deep heat rose within him. He summoned all possible restraint not to scream out. The heat rose higher, and poisonous words formed on his tongue.

Someone told the guards of our prayers and our plans.

The sounds of men crying for mercy further chilled the rain coming down but could not drown out the sounds of weapons preparing to execute silence. One man denied Jesus, and another gave his life for the service of the king.

The guards pushed Abraham to the side apart from the others. Abraham yelled out and heaved for a breath. "Who betrayed us? You self-serving fool. You killed my chance to see my wife. My children. I will not be able to say that I am sorry. My last breath is dedicated to cursing you for all of us. I will wait for you in hell. I will find you. You will not escape me. With Satan helping me, I will hunt you down as you helped these men hunt me down. I will have my perpetual vengeance upon you . . ."

Abraham cried. "Over and over again . . ." he said as he wept and tried to catch his breath.

A guard laughed and struck Abraham on the side

of his head. Rain mixed with blood dripped off his cheek. Abraham fell to his knees with another wave of weeping. He tried to hold his head to stop the pain, but the chains did not yield. Abraham winced as someone grabbed him by the neck and pulled him back onto his feet. The sound of sliding feet moved near him. The spy among his brothers was sure to have disclosed secrets mentioned in the privacy of prayer.

Abraham knew he was supposed to forgive the spy, but he did not possess the ability to do so. He had no desire to do so.

The guards moved with step-by-step commands. Each of the leader's orders hung in the air. Executed with gradual emphasis. Purposed second by second to kill Hope so she could never return. Words of last-minute panic and pleading reached and grasped for the fleeing hope. The men braced for their last moments with their final prayer.

A single weapon fired. The whistling and then piercing of a projectile surprised Abraham. The vibration made the hair on his arms stand up as it hit its target standing right next to him. He heard the now familiar haunting sounds of life leaving a man with gurgling and a struggle to breathe one final breath. The sickening thud of a lifeless body collapsed to the ground.

The taste of gunpowder was on Abraham's tongue, along with burning in his nose as the smell penetrated through the lower part of his blindfold. They grabbed Abraham by the back of his long hair and dragged him with the other survivors. They threw all of them into the prison room.

***

An unknown number of hours passed before the guards removed the blindfolds and the chains binding their hands. They mourned the death of another friend—Christopher was gone. With each passing day, there were fewer sharing their prayers and Bible readings.

It is day twenty-one of seventy-six. Christopher is with his God. My friends left for the New World. I pray that Jonathan is well. God, save him. I miss you, my brother. Do I give in to accepting my inevitable death or continue fighting with suffering for my inevitable death?

With no hope for the moment, Abraham kept his concerns private. He believed similar thoughts troubled each man.

They encouraged one another to focus on the love they had for each other.

But first, they had to deal with the spy.

CHAPTER 21

PADA

Ndongo, Africa
1619

As more of the Imbangala gathered around Pada, the strong man's grip around Pada's throat tightened. The gathering carnivores laughed, taunted, and encouraged the strong man to end Pada's pathetic last few weak moments. Pada tried to get his foot back into his sandal so he could push the corner of the folded paper back into the slit in his sandal.

His only chance of vengeance would be with his feet still on the ground. He could use leverage and possibly kick, and maybe even wiggle free of the grip. He would gouge out the strong man's empty eyes before the others killed him.

If up in the air again, Pada could not push off anything, as all leverage would be lost along with his life. There were a few more heartbeats left while at the mercy of the strong man and God.

My life will not be left in the control of another.

Pada prepared to unleash the rule and reign of his right fist before the animal-man lifted him up. Still conscious enough to see all parts of the canyon, it reminded him of playing near Luanda when he was younger. He had two remote canyons in his life. One where he played with his father as his mother watched under her baobab tree. And now in this canyon, near the last place he saw Amara before the Imbangala invaded their village.

The strong man lifted Pada up.

It's too late.

Pada swung his arms at the empty air, longing for contact. The men laughed at him. His village lay in the distance, neighbors' huts broken and destroyed on the horizon. Bodies lay at various locations.

Amara!

The surrounding men continued laughing. Whether it was because of the loss of blood flow to his head or something else, things looked different lifted up in the air with death taunting him from below.

Things felt different.

The evil below him and before him became a crushing weight upon him.

They do not know what they are doing. I can see it. I can feel the weight of it upon me. My sins. Their sins. God, why have you forsaken me?

Pada was dying.

The Imbangala continued to yell and howled like animals in anticipation of a meal.

"I want his sandals. They must be worth something because he is trying to save them!"

"He is hiding something. I want what he is hiding. We know he has a young girlfriend, but I want her—if someone else didn't get to her first."

"In our time of hunger, just kill him now and get it over with."

Along with the grip around his throat, he also struggled to breathe as something pressed and weighed him down. Though he did not have memories of going to the beach in his childhood, he wanted to sail away.

I am drowning and being pulled into hell.

Memories flooded his mind. His mother praying at her baobab trees. His mother with a cut on her stomach. What would it have been like to have a little brother? Playing with Amara in the canyon with their mothers watching. Amara's mother, Abeni, praying for him, like he was the son she never had. Abeni carrying Amara when she was younger because Amara did not want to walk. Him and Amara kissing behind the bushes with their parents distracted in prayer.

Amara.

He pushed off of the strong man's arm to raise himself up to take one more breath. As he was dying, his heart pounded harder, along with a strange slowing of his heart. Like a pause before his final judgment, after his last breath.

The ruling was made.

Pada turned his head one last time toward home and then back to the canyon. One final fight for life or accept death. Then the strong man slammed Pada's feet back to the ground, like a large sword piercing the hard ground. All around him things faded into a blur.

Then it was finished.

Chapter 22

ABRAHAM

Southampton, England
1620

Justice in search of a spy permeated the air in the prison of the king.

It summoned the men.

The men appointed Abraham as their new leader to replace Christopher. Abraham gathered the remaining men and asked them to wait for him while sitting in a circle. Off to the side, Abraham spoke with Henry about how they would proceed.

If things got out of hand, Henry could end any threat with ease. Henry stood ready to serve his God. And Henry, though decimated with the absence of food like the others, was still a large man and not afraid to use his strength for God.

Abraham sat down with the others and addressed the group. He closed his eyes and took in a deep breath. "I do not know your God like some of you here do. At times I do not even know if I can believe in your God. Why would He allow the murders of His children while He remains seated in His almighty throne, unwilling or unable to move? 'Stand up! Do something!' That is my cry to Him. I am without faith, but I know you remain strong."

Abraham stood up and opened his eyes. He spread his arms open and pointed to Henry. "I am appointing Henry to pray and ask God for help. We all sense that there may be someone here telling the guards our secrets. We hid from the guards who our leader was, and yet they killed Christopher. They knew he was our leader. And now I am next."

A reverent silence among the men caused Abraham to pause. "I accepted leadership because my days are numbered less than yours—but I yet want to live. If we do not eliminate the spy, Henry and I are next. We will now determine if there is a spy among us. If there is no spy, we will have restored confidence and trust in each other with future secrets."

Henry stood and took control in the middle of the circle. "Men, arise." The men sprang to their feet.

"Holy Spirit, come and show us your truth. Is there someone here who is betraying us? Murderer repent, or murderer be struck dead among us!"

In the partial morning light, he placed his face within inches of each man's face, violating all laws of social practices. "Have you provided any information to the men of the king that has contributed to our lost lives?" He asked the same question and studied each man's eyes one by one.

Each man said no.

Abraham put his hands behind him as they began

to tremble. Henry finished with all the other men and moved toward Abraham as Abraham turned his head away.

My sins! I can no longer hide my sins. I am on trial to answer to God. I am guilty. The hand has found me.

Henry approached Abraham and looked confused, as if he did not know if he should ask Abraham the same question, or disobey God. Henry walked toward Abraham and placed his forehead on Abraham's—

Three guards burst in. They moved their eyes from side to side, looking for someone. The leader of the guards pointed his finger, and the other two men pulled on Abraham's hair and tattered clothes. Then the leader pushed the other guards away and pulled on Abraham. Abraham tried to keep his head down, but they grabbed him by his beard. Abraham complied minus part of his beard. They shredded his shirt into pieces, so the leader pulled on his arms. Abraham attempted to slow down the pull into the pit, but a hard kick into the side of his ribs knocked the care out of him.

In the past Abraham took care of himself with his fists, but once again, his life was in others' hands. Before they neared another room, the cuts and tears in his skin covered his entire back. The sting of the dirt in his open wounds, along with the pain from the kick, made it difficult to breathe.

As he winced, trying to breathe, bloodstains on the ground and sprayed on the walls called out. Some of the stains were old, and some glistened. A pressure weighed on his chest.

Was the hand with fingers of blood moving again?

The lead guard with Abraham's hair in his fist, accompanied by another guard, cursed at Abraham, as if the lead guard was the one imprisoned. As they entered another room with other guards waiting, they flinched when they saw the lead guard in the doorway with Abraham. Their eyes widened as they saw the lead guard walking in. Each sentinel moved at least an arm's length away from the lead guard. Their arms were up, protecting themselves as they fled the room.

The lead guard, and the other guard with him, stood with Abraham. The lead guard hit Abraham and kicked him in the stomach after he collapsed. Abraham wrapped his arms around his head to protect himself on the ground. In between blows, he noticed the other remaining guard with a strange look of concern on his face.

With Abraham pinned to the ground, a strange new strength rose in him. It were as if he were an observer looking down upon himself and his blood spilling on the ground. His body felt light. His arms and legs felt new. Where was his hate and his rage? He had a foreign feeling of compassion for the man killing him. Was this even possible?

He does not know what he is doing.

With the Dark Light of death filling the room, another opposing presence resisted.

A morning sliver of light penetrated through an opening in a wall upon his murderer's face and chest.

It was as if Abraham had new spectacles for his eyes to see his murderer in a different light. Even into his murderer's past. A child beaten by his father. The child growing up to be tormented by a legion of demons. The guard was a prisoner, defender, and guardian of his own internal prison. Fooled into fighting for his own imprisonment. So much anger caged him. Between punches and kicks, strange thoughts grew in Abraham, like a trampled flower among thorns.

How can I love a man who murdered my friends— and now is murdering me?

Movement stirred the air. One presence opposed the other. Abraham was pulled in different directions. In one moment there was love for his murderer, then in another moment a love for vengeance, then a need to die for his many sins.

"I am only a man. I do not know where to go!" Abraham cried out.

His murderer did not even pause as he slithered more curses out of his mouth, "I have found you . . . unveiled! . . . for the king . . ."

Though Abraham had been reading Scripture and learning insights into its principles, his memory was unusually poor with trying to memorize verses. But words formed upon his tongue. Words of fire too hot to remain behind a closed mouth, seated upon his tongue unspoken.

Abraham spit out verses between blows. Though unable to spit out the blood gathering inside of his mouth fast enough to enunciate well, he knew his murderer understood, as the prisoner began to hit Abraham even harder.

He slapped Abraham in the face with the right hand of a strong man and tried to shut Abraham's mouth with his left. He wept as he tired. Abraham continued proclaiming different verses through blood and broken teeth. He winced, breathing with ribs that cracked with pain.

The murderer stopped hitting Abraham.

He slumped forward clutching his chest, like a man in the throes of an attack upon the walls of the heart. He could not fight anymore and sagged to his knees. With his head in his hands, he cried out, "What must I do to be saved?"

Abraham closed his right eye and discovered that his left eye was as dark as a night in prison. With his right eye opened, a guard, a murderer, was on his knees before him. After he spit out the pooling blood and pieces of teeth, Abraham spoke words that Steven had spoken to him weeks before, that he'd rejected.

"Acknowledge and confess your sins to God. Believe that the Lord Jesus Christ died for your sins, and ask Him into your heart. Repent of your sins. Commit your life to the King above all kings."

This is a man of the king. What has become of me to speak such mad and incendiary words? To a guard! A murderer! I am a dead man!

Abraham placed his hand over his eye, trying to distract himself from the pain. His hand reflected the light available.

The guard began to speak in several different alternating and slithering voices.

"Soon, we will tell the king where you are!"

"The king will find you like all the others, as he always has and always will!"

"We will take the other eye as well. You will be blind and on the bottom of the ocean."

"We know what you did. Your death is the only payment."

"We will hunt you and all your ancestors and off-spring. You will not escape us!"

"End your family's suffering. KILL YOURSELF."

"You know you will drown."

The voices spoke as if emanating from an angry serpent thrown into a deep pit. Abraham covered his nose with the smell of rotting and dying flesh, expelled out of the guard's mouth.

What do I do?

Below him was a man on his knees slithering with many tongues. Abraham turned behind himself, expecting to find the other guard, or something else, as the man on his knees had wide eyes, as if he saw a ghost. His mouth opened wide too, and he could only utter the sound of a man having his insides ripped out of him.

The voices coming out of the man changed.

"Do not harm us! We know who you are. Let us be!"

"Do not move your hand!"

"He is our home!"

The voices united into one voice. "We will tell the king who you are. Do not harm us! Leave us alone! Do not torment us. Stop tormenting us!"

Were the voices directed at him or someone else? What was happening? Abraham was not threatening them. If anything, he was the one who was afraid of the voices coming out of this man, and they had no reason to fear Abraham. They had the power to maim him again or kill him, as that was what they were doing before the guard stopped.

With the sliver of light radiating in the room, Abraham suspected the voices feared something as they pleaded for their lives.

Abraham hurled more verses, from which he did not know, and landed them with the sounds of fire searing flesh. The guard hissed with each wave splashing of fire.

Then a new voice from the guard sounded . . . human.

"Please . . . save . . . me!"

"Spirits. Be gone!" Abraham yelled.

The guard wrapped his hands around his own throat and squeezed. He let go, opened his eyes, and gazed at Abraham. The guard murmured something and collapsed to the ground. Abraham bent to see if he was still alive.

Abraham put his hands on his shoulders to help him up but then retracted his hands. If he allowed the guard to continue beating him, the guard would kill him. And if the guard were injured or dead,

Abraham would still be killed by the other guards.

Will I be the cause of them lining us up and killing all of us this time?

The guard opened his eyes. Abraham resisted trying to run and stayed with him to make sure he was recovering. The guard looked down at his own wrists and ankles with wide eyes and a smile on his face.

Then a sound that no one had heard in weeks.

The man laughed. And then laughed again. He laughed as he raised his arms in the air.

Abraham helped him to his feet.

The man was still laughing. When he was able to speak, he spoke in a new voice. "You saved me . . . He saved me."

Who is he talking to?

The man placed a steady hand on Abraham's shoulder. "Forgive me . . . thank you."

Abraham locked eyes with a stranger for the first time in several months. Even if but just a moment. The two men then escorted Abraham, as he bumped into the walls on his left side, until they reached his room. They closed the door behind him.

A new awareness opened inside him. A voice coming from outside penetrated the prison walls. It was the voice of a father, loud enough to hear him telling his children not to cross the street and to return to him. There was a single bird chirping.

The men inside jumped with joy toward Abraham, and they shared many hugs.

"Your eye . . . I am so sorry . . ."

"We thought you were gone."

"Nobody ever comes back after they are taken away like that."

"Now you look as handsome as me," another one said as he smiled with missing teeth. "Women love men without teeth."

Abraham shared a broken smile. He turned behind him, and the guard gave hugs to his puzzled colleagues, said goodbye, and walked out the prison's front door.

Abraham closed his right eye and noticed he could not see at all. He had spent the last several months not looking at himself, and now he could not see himself through his left eye even if he wanted to. Abraham placed his hand where his injury was. The eye was gone.

Death attacked him. That eye used to see his beautiful Humility. It used to gaze at her beauty uncovered. She used to kiss him just above that eye. He cherished his children with that eye. He watched beautiful sunrises and sunsets. That eye used to help him memorize what a good friend like Jonathan looked like.

It saw Steven on the ground.

And now, the last thing he saw out of that eye was a closed fist.

It was gone.

He was going to die in prison, never to return home.

And how could a murderer, a prison guard for the king, be freed?

Abraham shook his head.

What kind of Father are you? If friends of inno-cence are killed and a murderer freed, what will you do with me?

CHAPTER 23

ABRAHAM

Even with part of him gone, Abraham awoke in the morning with hope still beating within him. More light than usual penetrated past the walls. Creation chirped outside the prison again.

Who could have created such beautiful creation outside . . . and murderers inside? And this same Creator freed a murderer?

Abraham remembered a dream from the previous night. In the dream, he was given a few moments of escape from the walls. He walked toward a dimly lit part of a room that he was not familiar with. And there it was. The sand coursing through his hourglass. He tried to tip it over to restart his time with his strong right hand but was unable. To regain total control, he used both hands with all the strength he possessed.

It did not move.

His days were disappearing and out of his control.

Then in the dream, his eyes opened more fully. He stepped back, as he was too close to see the obvious.

"

A hand held the hourglass.

Guards interrupted as they burst through the door and attempted to drag him out of the room. His friends awoke. Henry wrestled both guards to the ground, and his friends pulled Abraham away from the guards. Three of the prisoners acted as a human shield and stood between Abraham and the cursing guards, in a corner of the room.

The unarmed guards' eyes widened, like a powerful fighter punched in the face for the first time. They yelled out for help when they could not get Abraham. Other guards ran into the room and beat down the shield. Fists were flying and curses were landing when Abraham yelled, "Stop it! Take me—leave my friends."

The guards kicked Abraham and blindfolded him. As they took him away, other guards' running feet entered the room to bring out the others. They pulled him a long distance, to a room farther than before. The sores on his back reopened. Pulled into another room, his knees went cold with pain as they crashed against the ground.

Do they blame me for the guard who left?

Will they punish my friends for protecting me?

Someone tore the blindfold off. This was a different room. Darker than the other rooms. No windows. Abraham could see his own breath. In the darkened room, before him the ruling gods. The six leaders of the prison were seated at a table in front of him.

No sounds in the other rooms.

My friends.

Abraham heard someone whisper, "We do not think this is the one. But he could lead us to him."

The leader, seated toward the middle with blood-stained hands, then spoke like an angry father judging his rebellious five-year-old.

"We have decided to let you choose to either die slowly inside or outside of these walls. Will you pledge your allegiance to the king, or death?"

Abraham stood silent.

Someone seated next to the leader said, "If you commit treason against the king again, you, family, and friends will pay for your transgressions."

"We know about your friend Jonathan. Soon enough you will discover his fate," said another one seated on the leader's other side.

Abraham turned his head toward the door and then returned his eye to look at the feet of the men before him.

Another subordinate leaned back in his chair with his hands behind his head. "You have no hope of fighting the king. Whether you die in here or outside, you will display the horrors of these last few weeks to all who see you. Proclaim to others what happens when you betray your only king. Others will see the limping death that you are."

"We have this for you," the leader said.

Abraham raised his head. The leader had a scar on the left side of his face. He tossed a small bag toward Abraham, like someone throwing scraps from the table to a dog with a leash not long enough to reach it. It landed a few feet before Abraham. He knew that glorious sound before it hit the ground. It was a bag full of silver coins. Maybe even gold?

Another thought hurt his chest.

Jonathan.

What had become of Jonathan? His brother not related by blood. Was he killed at the secret meeting? Did he escape to the New World with the others? Were they all killed or imprisoned?

Abraham could start his life over with the money.

But it was stolen silver and gold.

He could pay off debts and start anew.

They took the money away from those who lived and died within these walls.

He could give money to those who needed it.

It was blood money.

The money could help others either here or in the New World if I ever escape from here. Yes. That's right. My strong desire for money could help others. Yes. It could help others.

If he took the money, he would have to do as these murderers wanted. He would be a servant of the king, under the king's control. If he did not take the money and remained in prison, how could a dying man in prison help his friends . . . by praying?

As Abraham reached forward for the bag, his wedding ring slipped off his finger onto the ground. Abraham grabbed the bag like a hungry rabid dog snatched a bone. He then picked up his ring.

After picking up the bag and ring and opening his hand, the dirt from the bag settled onto his hand. As he raised his head partway, the leader looked at Abraham as if Abraham had just signed a contract in his own blood.

Through rotting teeth, another guard said, "We will be in contact with you. We will allow you and the others to leave, but we will be watching you. You are his, as you have always been, and he wants more of his money returned back with interest—when he desires."

Abraham picked up his coins. What would the others think if he left prison with blood money from those inside? Turning his head from side to side, he stuffed the bag into his pocket.

Like the spy his friends were looking for.

He walked ahead before anyone changed their mind as they accompanied him to the prison's entrance. He stopped at the doorway. Was it a trap? Would they change their minds? What was on the other side? He thought of his friends on each side of the wall.

He stepped through the entrance of the prison and into the new day.

After he walked a short distance, he turned back toward the main gate. No footsteps? How far would the leash go?

He shook his head. Though still blind in one eye, his left side felt stronger. He had an illness and was beaten several times, but he was now better?

The bag of money in his hand felt more dirty than his entire unwashed body.

He walked with broken teeth and ribs and many bones poking through his skin. Old blood called out from his clothing. He walked as a new man with new hope away from the prison. A new wave of energy flowed through him. His arms and legs unshackled as he walked with less of a limp for the first time in weeks.

Ignoring the strange looks from the locals, he walked faster and then ran to test out his new limbs. With his coins ringing in his pocket, he ran with all the strength that he possessed, as he did in his youth.

Did his friends leave for the New World? He fell in his weakness and loss of balance but sprang back up onto his feet with no regard to his reputation among the surrounding townspeople. He ran with his arms up in the air like wings of the birds he could now see, with his feet firmly pressed against the ground made of clouds.

He ran as a fully coherent madman. Was he too late? After weeks of delay, were his friends still alive and able to leave their Egypt? What would he find at the dock?

He ran. He limped. There they were?! They were loading supplies unto two ships. Abraham screamed, "Wait! Do not leave me!"

They all stopped and then recognized him under the layers of dirt and with even longer hair and beard. They dropped everything, and several ran to embrace him.

Abraham spotted Jonathan on one of the docked

ships, and Jonathan waved to Abraham from a distance. He reached down toward his feet and raised both of his arms with one hand, holding the box and the other the book!

The book. It wants to be found. Abraham laughed.

His friend dropped everything and ran to him with tears of joy welling and then spilling. His friend was alive!

They shared many tears with many laughs smothered in hugs. Abraham collapsed into their arms and then onto the ground. They helped him back to his feet and supported him as he swayed forward and backward between heavy sobbing.

"You waited for me . . . I want to go home."

As Jonathan held him, he asked, "What did they do to your eye?"

Abraham pointed to his other eye. "They didn't get this one."

"I'm sorry about your eye. But we are glad you are not your eye. You are here. We care about you. You will always still be Abraham to us," Jonathan said with a smile.

Jonathan hugged him again. "We were not sure we would see you again. God has delayed us, as we have been preparing this ship and patching up the other for the last few days. It was leaking, and we needed to repair it before another attempt. God's timing is perfect, as we will be leaving soon."

They shared that they had fasted and prayed for him. Someone shouted the daily fasting was convenient, as they were running out of food. They shared another laugh as they raised joyful hands toward the heavens.

When Abraham stepped back to see what they were loading, he took inventory of what he now had. More knowledge of finding who stayed his hand from his suicide attempt. Hope. Better health. Friends.

And the bag of blood money he would bring onto the *Mayflower*.

CHAPTER 24

JAMES

England
1620

Voices cried out for help.

The holy thread of the divine right of kings ran through the tapestry of history. The ancestral blood of regality flowed from past generations into another new vessel for the cloaked one. As a babe in swaddling royal clothing, he proclaimed to the world that he was born to be King.

One that would save those crying for help.

With blanched knuckles holding his crown in his youth to his adulthood, how should he exercise that which God bestowed upon him? Where was James to find the murderer, the Judas amongst his people? The one who would try to kill God again. No one could blow up God. Not even religious zealots. God would never allow it. And those who would try would suffer the same fate as those who failed before.

He was getting stronger. He knew the day foretold in his youth would come. He remembered what the man of religion said when he cut James' forearms to exchange blood in that ceremony. The ceremony in his youth with that voice that said one day someone would come to kill him. They would try and kill God's son again.

And now, as an adult, some still did not recognize their Shepherd. Was the hidden assassin leading the small number of rebels, blinded with ignorance and envy? Could they not see that the power in this vessel of God, their King, was the only hope for saving them? Could they not see that only he could make all of his subjects into one collective for protection? To bring security, equality, and justice to all. This could only come true if he eliminated those who opposed God.

The sheep needed peace. The sheep needed him. They wanted him to control them. They wanted the skilled hunter to kill the wolves among them.

In his mirror-gazing youth, one of his caretakers thought it would be a good idea for him to spend a few days at a farm so he could know what life was like for the commoner.

The old-man commoner at the farm tried to teach him how to work the land and care for his animals. The youth had never seen darkened fingernails on his hands before.

His most vivid memory was watching the old man with his sheep. The sheep were compliant to power, but the goats often resisted. Some of the man's sheep were smart enough to follow him, and some were not. One of the sheep had wandered, like the goats, away from protection several times and often led others astray with him. The majority of sheep stayed at the shepherd's side and did not follow those prone to wander.

One early morning, some of the sheep were missing. The same sheep that usually followed the wandering one and the goats. James discovered their route over the hillside and found them lying on the ground. They were not alone.

Wolves held three of the sheep in their mouths. James screamed for their lives and scared the wolves away. The sheep had ignored the old-man commoner's authority, but even the wolves knew real authority and complied.

As the wolves disappeared over the horizon, James walked closer to the sheep lying still on the ground. So much blood. James had never seen the results of animal rule like this before.

His heart moved with a new beat. Someone, or something, initiated a new dawn within him. His hands throbbed in rhythm with his heart for the first time. His hands opened and closed over the pieces of sheep in pools of blood.

He took his shoes off and stepped into the blood pooled on the ground. He put his shoes back on and felt new power in his now dark-red hands. The one that wandered was wounded but still alive and stumbled away. Unable to save the other sheep, James stared at his hands. Their lifeblood was on his hands.

The old man came running and yelled at the youth. "The wolves could have turned on you. Do you understand? You would have been defenseless."

The youth opened and closed his glistening hands. His blood vessels pulsated on the back of his hands.

"I am not afraid."

In a fury, the man took the wounded leader of the wandering sheep and slit its throat in the presence of the other sheep.

James' entire body trembled with the last bleating and blood pooling. He needed to get back home. His people needed to know the truth. They needed him to protect them.

As an older adult, how should King James rule? What should he do to the goats and the sheep? The wolves?

The winds and oceans of creation carried his ancestors' charter to conquer many lands and many people. Most never questioned where the source of that life-giving power came from. Those rebelling against his church were like a cancer consuming a limb of the motherland. It should be self-evident that he was the cure. Of course. Only the king could save.

He'd spent a lifetime warning the sheep of what would happen when disobeying the Shepherd. Some still did not listen.

The king would continue to risk his own life by increasing the rituals with the Dark Light.

To create more might to enforce what was right.

CHAPTER 25

ABRAHAM

Southampton, England
1620

In the midst of England's southern coastal fog, the families divided into two on a Southampton dock. With faith, the ones staying behind hugged those leaving, anticipating they would one day be reunited.

Abraham had heard many stories of those assembled and their God's faithfulness while in prison. Now he stood amazed. They readied the much larger *Mayflower* in London, where leaders obtained a land patent to start a new colony in the New World. The smaller *Speedwell* had arrived from the Netherlands. The seaworthiness of the *Speedwell* concerned many, as the *Speedwell* had leaked on the way to Southampton. Though they were advanced money and close to being ready to journey, the *Mayflower*'s seaworthiness also concerned many, as it was an old vessel used primarily to transport commodities like wine and fur for trade, not a large group of humans seeking life away from the king.

The subversives had a history of printing illegal books and pamphlets and smuggling the articles of treason into England. And now, in their minds, they protected one of the most valuable of all commodities on board. Like Moses raised in the house of Pharaoh, they hoped the printing press would continue to print words of treason on the other side of the Atlantic in the king's new territory.

An interesting mix of people prepared to leave, as some were called "saints" and others "strangers." Those who were in the rebellious church and those who were not. This mix seemed consistent with how the God of the Bible did things. Though some members of each group were uncomfortable with members of the other group, they would have to learn how to live together in tight quarters.

The departing gathered together one final time before they separated families and friends. They asked God to intervene for their safety, both for the journey and for those left behind. They wiped tears and gave away the last hugs. After delays with the *Speedwell's* leaking and patching up, they would now go with less food and supplies than they had planned. They would soon sail on the Atlantic at the peak of storm season.

The two ships left Southampton in August of 1620. After a few days, the *Speedwell* leaked again, so the ships returned for repairs. After the work, the two ships departed again. During the beginning of the journey, the *Speedwell* leaked once again. Morale was at low tide and replaced with the rising high tide of frustration.

Frustrated with what was supposed to be God's will for their mission, they returned to Plymouth. Abraham and Jonathan considered, like many others, leaving while the ships were docked. Abraham wondered if God cursed the journey because of him. There was a shared lack of full trust of the master of the *Speedwell*. Perhaps he had an incentive not to have his ship sail?

Leaders decided it was best to leave the *Speedwell* and transfer people and supplies from the *Speedwell* onto the *Mayflower*. Some of the faithful left the venture with doubts that God could prosper the trip.

They were now down to one ship. Overall fewer people. Less space. Less food. Fewer hands to assist. Less good morale. More fear.

Some still believed that God was in their plans.

But others had doubts. Was God trying to save them from death on the open sea? Was He trying to protect Abraham from certain drowning? Did they hear the voice of God correctly?

As they neared final preparation to leave one more time, a man stopped to observe. The man paced back and forth, toward and then away, from the dock. After several minutes he returned and walked up to William.

"William, I am supposed to speak with you. Can I have a word with you?"

William set down a heavy bag of seeds and turned toward him. "Certainly."

They walked to a private area where William could still observe the preparations. Abraham moved closer to listen.

"My name is Bartholomew. I know Abraham. I have worked with Abraham in the past on different quests across the Atlantic and elsewhere. With many of you Christians, I believe there are some things you need to know about him."

Abraham dropped a bag of clothing when he overheard his name. The man looked familiar to him, but he could not remember where he had seen him before.

The light shined brightly on the hardened soil in his chest, and Abraham began to whither. What was growing in him would have to die as Abraham plotted how he could flee. He now recognized Bartholomew.

Where did he come from? How did they find me?

Some of Abraham's secret sins were no longer secret.

He would no longer be going home.

I can't stay here.

The back of William's head moved as he heard and responded to what Bartholomew said. Bartholomew finished after a few minutes and walked back toward town. William's shoulders slumped forward and his head bowed down, as if Adam in the garden had just discovered what happened to his son.

William remained motionless. After a few moments, he paced a short distance away from the ship as well. His head was down like he was deep in prayer, like a son listening to his father for wise counsel.

Abraham put his hand into his pocket and felt his bag of coins. He was safe. At least that was still there. He had enough money to survive for several weeks. He had counted thirty coins. If he left unnoticed, no one would have time to find him, as they had already lost too much time with their unworthy sea vessel.

But he would be apart from Jonathan and his new family. What would happen if he deserted them during the limited time when the king was still allowing some to leave for his profit? He would never be able to return to his family back home in his remaining days. He was not sure he could continue living without Jonathan and the others on the *Mayflower*. There would not be enough time to find another ship before his days ran out.

He remembered his dream of floating on the ocean with all that he owned sinking. All he had was gone.

Someone knew his secret. Dirt seemed to accumulate on him, and he needed a bath more than when he was in prison. Why could he never feel clean? With the familiar trial in his mind and an unknown God as judge, it was a mystery why Abraham was still alive.

The judgment of God is now upon me for what I did.

He was through with that book that killed. He reached back inside the ship and grabbed his few belongings, including that box and its contents within. With the knife secured in the box, he could finish what he should have done before.

Jonathan was distracted by helping the others, and William would explain to Jonathan what had happened. Abraham had to leave quickly and find a place where Jonathan would not find him before the *Mayflower* left.

With his head down and hiding behind others, he moved away from his only way home. William still faced away from Abraham, and if he moved fast enough, William would not see him escape.

When Abraham was the farthest one from the ship, William, with his back still to him, yelled out, "Abraham."

Abraham's hand froze in his pocket. Without turning to Abraham, William said, "Where are you?"

Abraham stopped and covered himself with his oversized coat. He grasped what was in his pocket and his belongings. He did not answer.

William remained looking in the opposite direction. "Abraham? What have you done with the days given to you? Your time is running out."

Abraham could still run away. Even if he could no longer run fast, William would never try to catch him. Like someone who had fallen overboard, Abraham looked upward and imagined William above him holding the only rope. Abraham could choose to ignore it. Or grab it

Let me sink.

At a distance, William turned and walked toward Abraham. Abraham tried to wipe his hands dry. William looked straight at him. Abraham shielded his eyes, as if the sun had moved too close to him.

With a voice just above a whisper, William spoke. "I have inquired of the Lord, and I believe He has spoken. I do not know all the details of your sins. This is not for me to know. That is between you and God. You can try to run from God and fail, or you can enter into His presence and kneel at the hand of the Judge."

Abraham tried to wipe his hands on his belongings but could not let go of the bag of coins. He moved his feet.

Stay away, William, or lightning will strike you too.

He took a few steps away and then paused. William walked closer to him. Abraham took a step closer to William with his head down. William placed his hands on Abraham's shoulders. "You know there is something moving in you. God conceived it. You know it is in you. It needs to be carried. Birthed. Proclaimed."

At the moment, if Abraham could have a father, he would have sounded like William. "We will teach you the way. I have some reading for you to do."

The two walked with William's arm around Abraham's shoulders into the ship.

The *Mayflower* left Plymouth. With the delays, they would be crossing the ravenous great body of sea in its most opportune time. The peak of storm season awaited them with an open, gaping mouth.

And Abraham would soon be judged for what he had done.

CHAPTER 26

PADA

Ndongo, Africa
1619

After the initial stinging in his feet from being slammed to the ground by the fist wrapped around his throat, Pada clenched his hand, pulsating with rage and vengeance. He was ready to unleash the wrath of one resisting a human leash. No one would rule over him.

The other men taunted Pada and hit each other, and they paid no attention to Pada's feet. Pada tried to wiggle his foot back into his sandal. As the strong man held Pada and yelled commands to another man with another captive, Pada readied to free his fist on the strong man's face.

After the strong man finished yelling instructions, he noticed Pada's foot movements. Pada gained some last-moment leverage and swung his fist toward the strong man. Pada's fist struck air several times. Without blinking, with his hand still wrapped around Pada's throat, the strong man pushed Pada downward, forcing Pada's knees to buckle and bend to the force around his throat.

The strong man, looking down from above, raised an eyebrow. He bent to see what was sticking out of Pada's sandal.

He pulled the paper out and read the written note from Goel. He laughed. "Do you know what this book has done?"

One of the Imbangala looked at the strong man holding the paper and ran away screaming. The strong man ignored the runaway and pointed to the paper. "It tells us that slavery is from God. That is why we are doing God's work. Your God commands us to take you as the slave that you are."

"That is not my God. Those are just words that should be buried. Never to rise again."

"Then let's bury them—with you." The strong man shoved Pada face first to the ground. Pada turned his head to breathe.

"I will keep my eyes on you. Until your eyes no longer open."

The strong man let go of his throat and pushed Pada's head back to the ground with the bottom of his shoe.

"Here, read this." The strong man laughed as he straddled over Pada. "I have heard you and your dead friend were given names from the foreigners. You are marked whether you realized it or not. You follow the words of foreigners, and their words oppose us. Those who follow their lies kill us unless we kill them first."

Pada could not respond with the strong man's foot pushing the back of Pada's head to the ground.

The strong man lifted Pada up and guided him westward by the throat. "Those words mean nothing with someone weak like you. You are no threat to me."

Two men put chains on Pada. Unable to resist, he could only stand with his mouth and eyes wide open. He had never seen or heard of chains like these before. They wrapped around him like the hand around his throat.

Maybe I can break these.

Unable to pull them apart, he wanted to scream. He tried to control his breathing, not wanting to let those around him know he was now theirs.

Maybe if I pull harder. His audible grimace sounded like the surrounding moans of other captives gathered around him.

The strong man laughed at the little man trying to yank off his chains and pulled Pada forward. "Every few hours I am going to kick you from behind to remind you of all the terrible things you did behind you as your own people are vomiting you out of their village. You have no home. No friends. You rule over nobody. All your mistakes will always haunt you from behind. You will never escape what you did. Maybe then you will see how I am saving you and taking you to a new beginning." He laughed again.

Leaving the canyon, Pada looked back to the far distance where Amara could still be hidden, if they had not killed her yet. Dozens rounded up from his village now staggered with him. They looked like livestock herded by new owners in preparation for future meals.

They often bumped into each other through blurry vision, unable to wipe their eyes. Some were leaving home for the first time. Some looked back to see homes disappearing over the horizon. Others could only look at their own feet. The weight of others' mistakes and Pada's own made it difficult to raise his head and stand tall.

As he trudged forward, he never had a reason to think much about the dirt under his feet before. Nor the plants and trees in his village and canyon. Or even the sounds of birds flying above him without hindrance. He could only stare at the ground, his hands and feet bound. Was this the last time he would set foot on familiar ground?

They knew where they were going. Many had never seen the ocean before. Some fell upon their knees and begged to be freed. Several attempted to negotiate for their freedom. Husbands offered their own lives for their wives being spared. Mothers for their children. One mother offered her son as a substitute for herself.

The captors silenced them with blows to the head and the body. Two captives refused to walk and heaved with sobbing. They wept more as their captors broke their legs and left them behind as the rest staggered forward. No one answered their cries. Several of the captors laughed as they stated that though they had already eaten, friends coming behind them had not.

One captor smiled. "Stop trying to bargain with me. I don't need your livestock. You are the livestock."

The captor had a deep belly laugh. The strong man kicked Pada from behind. The entire group continued marching. Every few feet the captives would turn and see the two left behind, lying broken. The two tried to sit up but then writhed in pain on the ground, their mouths too dry and their pain too great for them to speak. Their voices joined the others Pada had heard in his dream. Each reached out toward the disappearing group and their captors.

He wanted to strike the captors, but all the captives were attached to each other with chains. Though Pada was still young at age eighteen, they'd bound him to a younger boy who could not be older than ten.

The first ten miles, the boy attached to Pada remained silent. His tear tracks seemed to clear a path through the layers of dust on his face for more tears to come. As the death march continued, the simmering tracks became a boil as the occasional whimpering converted to rage that turned to a constant sobbing.

The young boy looked in all directions, as if searching for someone. His eyes scanned, but the eyes he looked for did not answer his summoning.

Pada did not like the attention the boy's sobbing brought to Pada, as they were one with their chains. With each mile, the boy brought more attention to them. Under his breath, Pada tried to convince the boy that the key to survival was to wait in secret for the right moment. Then they would strike. But the boy could not stop crying.

The strong man kicked Pada from behind. After they walked several more miles, Pada gritted his teeth, as the boy did not listen to Pada's authority. Through his clenched jaw, Pada whispered, "Shut up. Your crying is not going to help you."

Through trembling lips, the boy mumbled something.

The boy spoke again, but Pada still did not understand what he was saying. The boy slowed and tried a third time with a concerted effort.

"I cannot find my family . . . I do not see them here. A few days ago I was late coming home from friends . . . my mother was very disappointed in me . . . and now I have disappointed her again as I am going to be late today . . ."

The strong man kicked Pada from behind. Pada turned his head. Home had disappeared over the horizon.

They were finally allowed to rest and sleep that night, for the captors had to preserve some of their captives to make a profit. Pada could not sit comfortably.

After a restless night's sleep, he remembered the boy's worried words about being late. Though a captive, Pada's thoughts freely wandered. Amara's beautiful face. The last time he'd seen his parents. Goel's last moments. The memories intruded upon any attempts to rest. He lived for Amara's embraces, and he wanted to live to embrace her once again. But had he ended up . . . killing her? Pada tried to massage his aching back.

When his eyes closed, the nightmare descended upon him once again. Or was it already in possession of him and made itself known when his defenses were down?

In the dream, the one of divination once again veiled the people's eyes from seeing the water of the land. The people thought a drought infected the entire region. The one of divination pit every different people group against each other. The rich against the poor. The poor against the rich. Men and women against each other. The oppressors and oppressed. The darker skinned and the lighter skinned. The one of divination hid within each person, pointing a finger of hate toward another. He cloaked himself like a hand within and moved each puppet as he willed.

There were so many voices. Many suffered and died under the spell in the dream. But the one of divination, who caused the apparent drought, offered the dying a beautiful, delicious liquid to satisfy their thirst and hunger. The people united in following and submitting under the authority of the one of divination. But some knew something was not right. They knew the liquid was not the water they needed. Some, even in their thirst and desire to live, refused the liquid. It did not satisfy but caused more thirst for the liquid.

The rebels refused to drink the liquid and sought to find the real life-sustaining water. The one of divination grew furious with the rebels and summoned demons to pursue and hunt down the remnant . . . but someone was on the ocean in a ship . . .

One of the captors hit Pada, and all awakened. The captors did not offer any food. Those who still believed that to live was better than the alternative stood up after the short rest.

But three more chose the alternative. The captors beat the three in rebellion until all heard bones cracked open. As they screamed and writhed in pain, the captors forced the other captives to continue walking. The broken, left behind, remained both chained to each other and to a patient death that knew it only had to wait. Soon the spilled blood with its fingers would crawl to wrap around each throat.

With the short rest and deprivation of food, the remaining staggered forward.

This is not right. Someone has to fight them. If I do not stand up to them, I am complying with them.

He slowed down the death march and then stopped. The strong man approached him. Pada only had the strength to look up to the strong man's neck. He sensed a smile on his captor's face.

"How does it feel to have everything your parents taught you about your God, actually be the cause of what you see before you?" the strong man slurred.

The strong man kicked Pada. A voice within the

midst of the group said, "Your knees will bend, and your tongue will confess the Lord your God."

The strong man's mouth dropped open as he pivoted his head toward the voice.

"Who said that?"

All in the general area looked at each other with wide eyes and opened mouths. No one answered. It was as if they were unable.

"WHO SAID THAT?"

No one answered.

Chapter 27

PADA

Ndongo, Africa
1619

The strong man screamed again, "WHO SAID THAT?"

Pada stood still. Someone whimpered. Everyone looked toward the middle of where the captives stood. They could not have all imagined the voice.

No one answered. The captors beat those in the general vicinity of where they thought the voice came from. As the beating occurred, each face of the beaten proclaimed a different expression than Pada would have expected. It was as if while being beaten, each chose not to be a victim. Though in chains and abused, the voice energized them.

As a captor beat a mother trying to shield her daughter, the captor wielding the stick dropped dead at the feet of the mother. Silence permeated the dead air. One captor bent to check for signs of life in his friend and then quickly retracted his hand, as if avoiding a flame. He shook his head. He walked backward while keeping his eyes on the corpse.

His wide eyes widened as he continued to walk, never turning his back to the corpse. He swatted at the air and swiped at his face, arms, and legs.

"Get off me. Leave me alone—I only did what he told me to do," he pled.

He turned and ran away, flailing his arms, as if on fire.

The captors cast puzzled glances at each other. They looked at the corpse and then their friend almost out of view.

"One of you killed my friend," the strong man yelled. "You caused my worker to die, so someone has to pay. Who shall I kill as payment?"

The strong man's eyes roamed and settled on a mother next to her daughter. He stomped toward her and stared at her daughter. The mother sobbed and fell to her knees at his feet.

She screamed and held her hands clasped together above her head toward him as he glared down at her. He hit her with the back of his hand, and she tumbled to her side. She kicked her feet, trying to get back up. The strong man killed her daughter with one fatal blow.

He pointed toward the west. "It is time to go."

Many shook their heads and closed their eyes as they passed the mother. The strong man pushed and kicked the captives to continue walking. The captors pushed several prisoners and forced them to step on their young friend's corpse. They left the mother behind sobbing.

Pada walked with his eyes closed and wondered if sometimes death was an act of mercy. What purpose was there to continue walking?

The strong man yelled as he kicked Pada from behind. An extra captor was stationed in the back of the group to ensure additional compliance. Only the captors could speak. After several miles, they returned to hitting those who moaned or cried out in pain. If they moaned again, they were hit again.

At about the fifty-mile mark, the entire group stopped when someone in the front fell. No one knew what to do as the woman attached to the one who collapsed yelled out for help.

The men with the sticks beat the girl who fell. They then turned to the woman attached to her and beat her. When one man protested, they beat him as well.

Along the death march, more of the youngest and oldest could no longer move. A few bodies united as one . . . attached . . . broken. Collapsed on the ground.

Every several miles, another captive collapsed. If this occurred around mealtime, some of the captors engorged themselves with a meal.

The captors felt that the "younger meat" made them younger and stronger. They laughed at Pada but did not know that as more vomit left Pada's mouth, more vengeance entered into him. He would rule over the captors one day.

As much as he tried, with his hands chained, he attempted to close his eyes but could not cover his ears. The last pleading words he heard from the ones who had collapsed went into hidden parts of him. It was worse just to hear the murders.

The Imbangala believed that consuming their human prey made their spirits stronger predators. The strong made stronger by eliminating the weak. It worked in the animal kingdom, so they believed it worked with their kingdom of believers. They did not even have to work themselves into selecting evil. To them, it was just natural. When it came to who lived and who died, who could stop the natural selection of the Imbangala?

This is not truth. This is not how we are to live.

Pada swayed as he stood, waiting for some of the Imbangala to complete their meal. His legs trembled. He shifted his weight from one foot to the other as his legs wobbled and began to give out from underneath him. He could not wipe his brows as his vision blurred. His spine bent like he was carrying something heavy on his shoulders. Something splintered into parts of his back and shoulders. Heavy enough to buckle his legs.

The heat and the weight of his chains pulled on him. Clear thinking, for the moment, fled. He collapsed onto his knees. Even on his knees, his legs gave way even more as he fell, pulling on his chains and eliciting a scream from the surprised young captive attached to him.

Several captors paused between bites as they turned their heads toward Pada and the boy attached to him. The captors' eyes narrowed, as someone had disturbed their meal. Two stomped toward Pada.

In his mind, Pada watched his mother bend to pick him up. He lifted his head. Someone in the blurriness stood with arms stretched out wide for him.

My love.

My Amara.

My Amara.

"I am with you . . ." a voice near him said.

He turned his head in all directions, but no one else seemed to hear it. All looked at him with concern.

A few of the Imbangala approached him with their heavy sticks. They stopped. Pada arose.

The captors stopped everything and forced the chained on their death march. Pada wondered where his strength came from.

Why was he still alive?

Though they did not tell them how many more miles they would have to walk, whispers confirmed they were going to where the water met the sand, where greed met the human hand.

Still another hundred miles or so away.

They knew ships awaited for them.

At the start, Pada had counted about 150 captives, but they had to be down to about 120 after a few days. By the time they arrived in the port city of Luanda days later, much crying and many voices had been silenced. They'd left about half of their people behind to die along the way. Many lost mothers and fathers, sisters and brothers, friends, and strangers. The survivors of the death march entered into a fortress designed to take part in trade to other parts of the world.

Human trade.

In the beautiful ocean water, priests baptized each of the captives. When it was Pada's turn, he refused to be baptized in the faith of his parents.

"You do not rule here. It is the law that you are baptized before you leave. Or do you want us to change your baptism into your funeral?" they told Pada.

He looked at his hands, closing into fists. How could a good God force His creation into choosing Him above all others?

Love forced is not love.

Only a human-made god would force people to choose him to then control them.

During his baptism, Pada rejected the words uttered on him. When he refused to go under the ocean water, a man with the priest hurt Pada's back when he forced his head downward toward the ocean floor. His heart almost thumped out of his chest when he remembered flailing in the water in his dream.

He reached for the arms of the one pushing him down as he ran out of air. The hands around his throat were too strong. Through the clear water, he saw the legs of others intervene, and a struggle ensued. The hands around his throat would not let go. Someone else tried to pull the hands off Pada's throat. Before his eyes closed, more legs underwater tried to intervene above the water.

All seemed calm under the surface of the water, but the war for life intensified above his head. Pada could not help but gulp for air underwater. Someone pried away the grip wrapped around his throat and pulled Pada's head upward. He gasped for air as he reached the surface. He bent over, heaving for the lost air he never thought he would find again. He was grateful for life but crushed with disappointment.

Three men pulled away the small man pushing Pada down to the ocean floor. As they pulled him away, and with his back turned toward Pada, he mumbled something in a small voice. He then turned to Pada with a man's voice and much larger in stature, and he spoke with an expression that Pada had never seen before.

"I will find you—I will hunt you down. I will kill you—as I did with your brother. I know what you want to do. You will die before your God can succeed."

Pada looked at him with his head tilted and shook his head. He'd never had a brother.

Does he know about my mother losing a child when she was stabbed? I am no threat while I stagger in these chains.

Would his mother's angry God of the Old Testament allow Pada to live after what he had done? Would the Jesus that his mother talked about have forced baptisms? If he did, then he wanted no part of the "love" of Jesus.

They told those boarding the ship that soon they would be working in the silver mines at Veracruz. They were going to load about 350 people from Pada's village and other villages onto a Portuguese ship, the *San Juan Bautista*. But along with the others in chains, a companion from his childhood still faithfully accompanied him. Pada was already chained to Vengeance even before he'd ever heard of the Imbangala. It grew with Pada over the years, having gone through puberty, and now an adult. The chains were too confining.

When he had the chance, with no regard for his own life, Pada would one day rule by releasing his captive to have its way.

CHAPTER 28

ABRAHAM

On the Mayflower
1620

Abraham bobbed up and down in the ocean, trying to keep his head above water. The voices cried out to him even under water. They were not in him. They came from all the oceans and lands around him. He had only been in the water a few moments but shivered as never before. The storm tossed debris from the broken ships floating around him. No one else could hear his cries as everyone else sank below the surface.

Flailing, he turned his head back and forth between the ship's remains and land far away in the opposite direction. The voices. Voices from the past. Voices from the present. Voices from the future.

Then someone called his name. He heard a whisper above the other voices in the midst of a storm, and the throbbing of his heart pounded in his ears.

Someone . . . something breathed behind him. He turned, and there was a woman! Where did she come from? Even in the midst of the pouring rain, he could tell she was weeping.

The woman's words sliced through the storm. "We don't have much time."

Cuts and gashes lined her face. It appeared she had cuts and bruises from an attack. Her face flashed between that of a young woman and that of an older woman. She had the appearance of an older woman, a mother in pain, when she asked, "Can we save this?"

The hands of the older woman began to lift something that she was hiding underwater. Before she was able to complete the lift, lightning reflected off a piece of metal near her neck.

The woman's face flashed back to that of the younger woman. She pushed what she was holding farther below out of view. A man rose up behind her, holding a large knife at her throat.

A deep ache mixed with longing rose within Abraham. In the throes of something pushing outward from within, he could not help the woman. He could not swim to her.

Abraham awoke from his dream, vomiting as the *Mayflower* yawed and pitched. Seasickness was one of the greatest challenges for all on board the first few weeks of their journey. Starting with a full account of hopes and dreams, the storms created hourly withdrawals with debt approaching.

The angry sea made claims on their lives as payment for passage and attempted to pull them down into her abyss. Abraham winced each time he gripped parts of the ship. The ocean was an unforgiving judge of his sins, demanding payment at its convenience.

Abraham wiped his mouth as another storm started. He grabbed his sore neck. There were no fine goose-down pillows or Dutch linen here. He protected himself on the floor of the ship as people slid around and over him across the slippery surface. Something tightened around his throat. Or was it a large knife? He reached for his throat to free himself. There was nothing there. The storms hounded all aboard, and Abraham panicked, trying to breathe while feeling suffocated with water coming down from topside. He took several deep breaths, trying to return to a normal pattern of inhaling and exhaling.

Staring at Abraham, Jonathan's eyes focused with concern. Jonathan held his friend and allowed him to rock back and forth with the ship rhythmically.

Like a horseman of death from Abraham's youth, it seemingly galloped and closed in to prepare to execute judgment. Abraham avoided the secrets that dwelled in a forgotten closet in a room within him for most of his life. He would not wander into that hidden room's closet where it stowed away secrets. For years he indulged in distractions or drink to prevent himself from remembering that room with that closet. But in quiet times, when he wandered off leash, something in permanent shadow pulled at him toward that closet.

In the dim lighting, all aboard the *Mayflower* fought against being broken into two and sinking into the ocean. Amid the thunder and pitching of the ship, in his mind he ran into the forbidden closet with its horrors.

Kids who knew his mother as a mistress of a man of the king, told young Abraham his father's name was Alexander. He would have otherwise never learned his father's name.

Alexander was a stranger. Absent. Missing. As a child, Abraham learned to be adept at denying his struggles with his father's absence. How could a young child truly know something was missing if it had never been present? But yet, even at a young age, something was vacant inside of him.

His mother's empty presence haunted him even more.

Eleanor.

He remembered again how he had never heard someone say her name to her in friendly conversation. He only knew her name because a person shamed her one time because of her matted hair and wrinkled clothing and what people said behind her back.

She was distant, though she lived with Abraham. Perhaps "lived" was too strong a word. She lived hidden away from Abraham to prevent him from seeing her torment. She said this was better for him.

One night she took young Abraham to the beach. With tearful kisses above his left eye, she caressed him and carried him in her loving arms into hip-deep water. Abraham remembered a lovely kiss on his forehead. The next moment, she pushed him and held him underwater. As Abraham kicked and attempted to scream, he could only swallow water. He remembered the beautiful moonlit sky through the cold and blurry water. The grip around his neck seemed to be from a strong man, well beyond his mother's strength.

But . . . I love you, Mother.

His heart stopped in mid-beat with complete horror.

He awoke on the beach, holding his throat and coughing out water, shaking and shivering in the nighttime air. Searching for his mother.

Where are you?

A cold panic set in as the only light was from a partial moon reflecting upon the crashing waves. His heart pounded and seemed to push outward in his chest, as if reaching for an embrace or a hand. He did not want to be without both a father and his mother.

In the chaos, he ran without direction, his heart hurting. His chest heaved, trying to find air. Was he now an orphan? Where was she? Did she kill herself this time?

There she was. At a distance sitting on the beach with her back to him. Her arms wrapped around her bent knees. Rocking back and forth.

The *Mayflower* rocked Abraham back into the present. Against all orders from the crew, Abraham broke away from the closet he'd run into. He ran through Jonathan's embrace and broke through multiple attempts from several friends, and he escaped in the middle of another storm.

Topside, the crew cursed at him and attacked him while trying to push him down below. Abraham inhaled when he broke free topside to the stern of the ship.

While flailing his arms to keep the crew away, Abraham yelled, "Look over there. I knew we were not alone. Do you not see someone following us? Hunting me?"

The crew looked in the direction he pointed. One of them spoke with angry spit and teeth prepared for tearing through the storm on his way to Abraham, when Jonathan arrived.

The crew member's lips barely parted when he said, "There are no ships. There have been no ships—we will push you over, and then your life will depend on your other ship saving you."

The leader of the crew stepped toward Abraham. He hit Abraham in the face as Jonathan attempted to pull Abraham back to safety down below. Jonathan then stepped between Abraham and his assailant and attacked the leader. Several from above and below separated them.

The leader swung wildly. "I will turn this around if you are insubordinate! I will turn this around!"

If Abraham stayed topside, they would turn around. But he could not go below with water from above suffocating him.

Jonathan whispered in his ear. "Together we can get through this. I do not think anyone is hunting us. I will tell you why when we get below."

The leader taunted Abraham and Jonathan. "Stay up here so I have an excuse to be rid of you . . ."

Abraham looked at Jonathan and knew they were thinking the same thing. It was a trap. They needed to walk away from the trap.

The storm raged and worsened after they stepped below. Both Abraham and Jonathan clenched their fists as they sought the face of the taunting leader of the crew. They could still hear him and his crew above.

"He will pay for that," Abraham said. "Will you help me in vengeance?"

"He will pay for what he did to you."

They settled each other down to prevent one of them from stepping into the trap above. Jonathan, with a look of remorse, spoke. "Abraham, you know I have always wanted what was best for you."

Nodding, Abraham prepared for what was coming next.

"On one of our last nights back home, I awoke hearing someone going through the house. I saw someone taking some of your things. I chased him down the street, and I punished him. He was following you. I can assure you he will not be following you anymore. That is why you are now safe."

Like a heavy burden lifted off him, Abraham exhaled. Perhaps the king and his men were not going to push Abraham to the bottom of the ocean. He inhaled deeply but then held his breath as he asked, "Jonathan, what did you do to him?"

Jonathan turned his head away.

As if to awaken him from his slumber, Abraham

shook him. "The man who was in our home. What did you do to him?"

Looking away over his own shoulder, Jonathan whispered, "You don't have to worry. I did not allow anyone to follow you."

Abraham would not get an answer.

My God. Did Jonathan kill a man? Will they chase us down for murder as well as treason? Will there be ships after us for what my friend has done?

Abraham put his hand on Jonathan's shoulder. "We will get through this."

Each wave of water raining down from topside was another reminder of how little control they possessed in the ark below. Verbal violence exposed the worst of their hearts as passengers sometimes turned on each other.

They resisted the takeover with turns at prayer while Abraham also took turns with vomiting. Someone stated that God was building a new temple for Himself. A living temple. They were the living stones, stepping stones for future generations, to construct God's plan from the other side of the Atlantic to the nations.

Because Abraham's days were disappearing, he would not be able to join them. Yet his future was tied with theirs and future generations. He still had a waking dream for them. Even if it took hundreds of years . . . a dream. A dream with a future promise to be fulfilled. A dream where the gentle would be exalted and the proud laid low. Truth would be seen and crooked hearts made straight. Anyone, male or female, rich or poor, saint or stranger, from every tribe, tongue, and nation, would be free to love and serve each other and their God.

He had a dream.

While slipping in the messes in the dark and tight quarters, the call of judgment from the ocean abyss pulled on Abraham.

It would not be denied.

CHAPTER 29

JONATHAN

On the Mayflower
1620

Judging from everyone else sleeping within his limited view, Jonathan assumed it was nighttime.

Jonathan turned toward Abraham, who lay with his hands covering his chest in a deep sleep. Jonathan held his breath as he leaned closer to see if Abraham was still breathing. Jonathan exhaled, remembering the silent sound of his dying sister waking him just moments before.

As he stared at Abraham, the memory invaded him. Eight-year-old Jonathan knelt with his heart racing and his body shaking over his injured sister. He looked at his trembling hand dripping with blood, and dropped the knife. He fisted his hands with a new rage for the first time.

He pointed a finger toward her. "Why didn't you listen to me? I was trying to help you and . . . Mother and Father."

She did not answer him as he stood. She was not safe. He could not control the bleeding. He needed to find someone who had control over life and death.

"I will be right back—just lie and rest like Mother and Father always need to do."

His chest pounded. Everything was blurry. Jonathan wiped his eyes. "I will go get the man of the king a few houses down."

Jonathan ran like never before. The man of the king was leaving his home. Jonathan yelled, "Stop! Stop! You need to save my sister."

As Jonathan wiped his hands on his breeches, he told the man of the king what had happened. The man of the king saw the blood on Jonathan and went ahead of him. He ran into Jonathan's home and interrupted his parents' midmorning alcoholic haze.

In the commotion, Jonathan's mother awoke after Jonathan's father pushed her out of a chair. Jonathan's parents staggered trying to keep up with Jonathan and the man of the king into the backyard.

You better be sitting up, or I am going to be angry.

When they all arrived with his sister still lying down without movement, his father awoke from his stupor, horrified to see his daughter's life fading away. He picked up the weapon that minutes earlier had been sticking out of her side.

Jonathan's father waved the knife in front of Jonathan's face. "You did this?"

Through tears and quivering lips, Jonathan said to the man of the king, "You can save her, right? You have control. I have seen people seek you for both life and death."

Without a word, his father struck Jonathan on his face with an alcohol-infused back of his hand. Jonathan lay on the ground, holding the cut on his face next to his sister. All eyes ignored Jonathan's sobbing.

Jonathan covered his face with his trembling hands and mumbled through his wet fingers, "Why didn't she listen . . . I didn't protect her . . ."

Jonathan's father, with his back to Jonathan, turned toward him and uttered words through gritted teeth. "Her blood will always be on your hands."

Jonathan tried again to wipe his hands. His father was not finished.

"The king should take your life for hers."

Jonathan lay with life spilling out of him, next to his dying sister's blood spilling out of her. No one could see hidden in a far corner of his heart the longing of a forgotten orphan crying for a home. No one knew the pain in his chest hurt more than any cut on his face ever could.

Jonathan's uncle raised him after they buried his sister. Jonathan mourned the loss of his family.

He grew up watching his uncle, a devout Christian for a few hours on Sunday, consumed by the devout alcoholic occupying him every other hour of the week. Jonathan had horrific dreams of his uncle's angry God coming to kill Jonathan for killing his sister. One night, after having such a dream, he ran to the man of the king's house for help. He stood at the other side of the closed door and deemed himself not worthy of disturbing the holy man. He walked away.

As an adult, Jonathan married his lovely Elizabeth. Elizabeth was a gift from God, and God gifted Jonathan and Elizabeth with a son. But Elizabeth died after the delivery of their boy. There was no consoling Jonathan. He held his newborn son with one hand and his dying wife's hand with the other. He said goodbye to his love and tried to comfort his new love.

He remained standing with life in one hand and death in the other as he stood in the crossfire of both. Who could control both life and death?

With no sense of control but desiring it, Jonathan sought another good woman who could ease his pain of loss. Jonathan found comfort in consoling another who needed help. He later married a woman whose husband had died under mysterious circumstances.

During their first year of marriage, his second wife claimed that Satan was haunting her life with the spirit of Jonathan's first wife. She said that Elizabeth cursed her from the grave and that Elizabeth's spirit did not approve of her. His second wife fought to end all reminders of Jonathan's first wife. She said it was the only way she could save her family from the ghost of Jonathan's first wife.

Every time she looked at her stepson's face, she saw Elizabeth. One morning Jonathan awoke to find both his son and his wife gone. He never found them. They both disappeared, and rumors said they left to start a new life away from Jonathan's reign. He could never find a way to forgive himself for his wife and son leaving.

And now, in the ship sailing away from the king, Jonathan dwelled with people living under an unknown King. Through flawed natures, he saw them live the life prescribed by this other King. He had never heard or seen this kind of life before.

Weeks before, when Jonathan heard someone at night rummaging through his and Abraham's home, he'd chased down the man of the king. It was the man who'd run out of their secret meeting with the Separatists. The man had succumbed to the need for the security and control of the king, for his own safety. Jonathan pinned the man down to the ground. Jonathan's controlling grip wrapped around the man's throat. All the rage he possessed coursed in the blood pounding though his shaking hands.

"Why are you following us?"

The man on the ground motioned for Jonathan to ease his grip so he could breathe and speak. Jonathan kept both hands on his throat but relaxed his grip.

"They know about the gathering of some of the Separatists. Not all were at the meeting, and we need to know about the leaders."

"Leave Abraham alone."

"I only follow the commands of my king."

If Jonathan let him go, his life as well as Abraham's would be threatened. If he killed him, they would both live life on the run.

Then he thought of the temptation of every man of the king. He took out money he held for both him and Abraham as he kept the man on the ground.

"Here, take this. But on your word, you must tell the king that Abraham is not a threat."

The man took the money. Jonathan searched the man's pockets. He took out papers belonging to Abraham and papers belonging to several others who were at the meeting that the traitor left.

With the pounding rage, Jonathan saw his grip tighten again on the man's throat—

A sudden jolt returned Jonathan back to the *Mayflower*. He studied his hands.

His hands.

Jonathan wiped his hands on his clothing.

He could not wipe his hands clean.

It was Jonathan's fault that Abraham was going to die on the *Mayflower*.

Why didn't he listen to me?

The storms were not the only thing hunting them down. Though they left home because of death living among them, Jonathan could feel life and death opposing each other inside their ark. The conflict followed him. It was a battle of faith between two kings within each person and between them.

But there was more. There were things that their eyes could not see. It was cloaked. He could feel it as the forces assembled.

And Abraham was in the middle of both sides.

It was Jonathan's fault that Abraham's life was in

the crossfire between life and death.

My dear Abraham, I should not be alive. I have ended lives.

Jonathan turned toward Abraham and trembled and wiped his hands on his shirt, as he feared there would soon be more blood on his hands.

CHAPTER 30

AMARA AND HUMILITY

Ndongo, Africa
May 1619

"Amara . . . I did this for us . . . please forgive me . . ."

Amara awoke predawn, hearing Pada's voice. He'd left her after he let a new friend of his take her away two days before. All she had left was his voice calling and echoing in her head. And the prayer stick from under the baobab tree he'd given her to remind her of him. She squeezed the prayer stick, convinced that hidden behind his words, he cried for help.

Why did he have me taken away to come here?

Enough light from the moon infiltrated inside for Amara, and everyone else in the hidden hut with her still slept. Pada told her that she needed to hide with his new friend and his family until he could return to come take her away for good.

It's been two days. He should have found our parents by now. Where is he?

Pada had been hiding her in different locations even before their parents left together. Their parents must have been angry when they had to put their lives on hold to find their son and daughter, who'd disobeyed their orders not to be together. Their parents thought they were getting too serious too soon. Perhaps their parents had enough of their rebellion and searched for them to separate them once and for all.

She loved Pada. She loved her parents. When Pada found them and both families were reunited, she was convinced she could charm everyone into getting along. Yes, the bones in her body often broke, but she could break any hardened heart. When she and Pada married, they would all be one family, so they might as well work toward that now.

Have I been guilty of ignorant and blind trust in Pada for even hiding me in the first place? Maybe Pada is right—this was the only way we could be together.

The family she now stayed with assured Pada she would be hidden and protected. Overprotected was a better word. Very few people knew about the isolated and hidden hut among trees, east of the canyon near their village.

Demonstrated by food and water stored, the family was prepared for several weeks if necessary. Did something happen back home in her village? Pada, and the family she stayed with, did not tell her why they hid.

They are all hiding something from me. It must be safe now to go back home to my family.

As the family slept, it was time to move. More light would soon be rising, but the veil of darkness was still over the land. If she had her way, she would soon pierce this present darkness.

Amara grabbed the hidden food she had gathered the previous days, along with some extra clothes. She stood at the entrance of the secret hut and, small in frame, bent forward, ready to face the unknown outside. Her heart raced, and her legs seemed harder to move. She took in a deep breath. She took out her prayer stick and smiled.

She turned her head behind her. Though it was difficult to realize key moments in life when one was only sixteen, she knew that if she took one more step, one single step outside, her life would not be her own anymore. Life would be out of her full control, and she would be in the hand of her God.

She thought of her previous years in the world. Her mother carried her when she refused to walk and be ridiculed by other kids. As a teenager, mom still tucked her in at night with kisses on her forehead. Pada hugged her whenever he knew she was scared. How would things be different if she left the safety of the hut? She lifted one foot and then recoiled her leg when she thought of what could happen outside.

She could never outrun trouble.

What traps would be awaiting her?

She would be at the mercy of the God she could not control. With the fate of the world seemingly resting on her foot, she lifted it just above the ground and stepped outside.

With one foot outside, she kept the other safe inside. She turned to look at the sleeping family one more time. She then saw a quick flash of her mother, of Abeni's face. She stopped in her tracks. Her mother's face disappeared.

The mother of the family in the hut, still lying down, opened her eyes. With the look of what only a mother could have, she whispered, "I will not stop you, Amara. Do this with prayers from Chinasa and Abeni. Be careful. I will pray for you . . ."

With her hand on her chest, Amara mouthed *Thank you* and limped outside. With the long hike back to her village ahead, she prayed for no broken bones.

I have to watch my step. I cannot fall.

With her village a long and slow walk away, and with darkness still roaming the land, she moved as fast as she could. If the danger she was protected from was still present, her life depended on being in the safety of her family and friends back home before daylight exposed her vulnerability.

After a short time, she tripped over a rock when her foot did not clear it. She fell and landed on her left side.

No! . . . I think it's okay . . . I didn't hear anything crack . . . Can I stand up okay?

What was she to do if she could not bear weight again on her left leg? Scream out for help? Crawl back to the hut and not know what happened to her family—or Pada?

With a groan, she pushed off and put all her weight on her right leg. She stood upright, afraid to put weight on her other leg. She looked down. Her leg wasn't bent sideways like last time. Now she needed to shift her weight onto her left leg to see if it was only sore or broken. She felt a new expression on her face as she smiled and grimaced at the same time. She thought she could walk. She took a step. Not too much pain.

She walked faster to make up for lost time but tried to be more careful. She could not risk another fall or an unknown enemy spotting her.

On the outskirts of her village, she took a deep breath, trying to find comfort in the ordinary.

There are no familiar smells of morning meals wafting through the air.

Was it too early for hearing the older folks in their early morning conversations? Where were the barking dogs? No one was out and about starting the day's activities.

As she reached her village, the early morning light exposed a new day. A few older members of her village moved about as if looking for someone or something.

Pada and others had told her she needed to be hidden for several more days before returning to the village. Ignoring their counsel, she moved toward Pada's home.

Where is everyone?

The villagers she passed did not look up at her.

When she reached Pada's home, she was surprised his parents did not stop her from seeing Pada.

Where was his family? Their home was empty. Someone had burned the back part of their hut.

What will Pada do with another one of his homes burned down?

Her hands and feet froze. She stepped back and looked more closely around her. How did she not notice?

In the distance, huts were burned to the ground.

Amara's heart pounded as she stumbled to his neighbors. They were also gone.

She ran with her limp toward her home. *Where are Mom and Dad?* No one had burned her home down, but her parents were still missing.

An older neighbor hobbled outside with her walking stick, looking for something.

"Amara, they are gone. Many are gone."

Amara wiped her eyes. "Where have they gone? They can't all be gone."

The neighbor looked down and said, "Only us old folk are left. I am so sorry."

Amara's voice raised and broke. "What happened?"

The woman turned her back toward her and swiveled her head back and forth, as if trying to continue her search. "The Imbangala worked with the government. They took about three hundred to the ships. I do not think we will see them again."

The older woman walked away, seeming to have aged another five years.

Amara put her head into her hands and wept. *Is this my punishment? Please forgive me. Despite my many sins, despite our many sins, move for my people's sake. I have heard of Your great name. I have heard of Your mighty acts. You are ruler. You are King. Only You can save. Save us. Free us.*

Many were taken away. Days later, older family members left behind still wandered in a daze and in shock. Several approached Amara, seeking help.

"Amara, I have not seen my son. Do you know where he went? Where was your God?"

"My daughter is gone. They took her away. I have heard what they have been doing. I pray to God, but He does not answer."

"Have you found your family?"

She could only wipe the tears of others, and then her own. She had nothing left and only herself to give.

Could Pada be with her parents on their way back home? The same parents she was angry with days before, for no longer letting her see Pada, were now the even more cherished ones she loved and missed. As an only child, she had no one else who could console her. Her one love, family, and friends—gone.

What was she to do? She needed to save people if she could. If she stayed, what would she live for?

God has also left me.

If she left her village, where would she go? To another village to then be abducted or to find more friends abducted? Even if she wanted to go to the port city, her legs would not allow her to make the long trip. What could she possibly do even if she made it there?

Amara decided to make the long and difficult walk to the place where the love of her life, and the love of her parents, were taken. Her fellow villagers gave her supplies when she ignored their pleas not to go.

She heard about a secret route and began her slow march to the port city of Luanda. Years ago, her mother, Abeni, told her they used to visit a friend in Luanda, and that was where her mother had met Pada's mother, Chinasa. Not too soon afterward, Chinasa, Okoro, and their son, Pada, moved near to Amara and her family. Thankfulness for the random meeting between her mother and Chinasa soothed Amara's heart.

Maybe all of this is not random.

Soon others joined her on her rescue mission at the ocean. An older man spoke as he walked alongside her and the others.

"I walk to get my grandson. I have nothing to lose. I have lived a long life, and I am not afraid to lose my life for my grandson's, who was just beginning his."

An older woman spoke. "I do not want war. I want my daughter."

A friend of her parents then asked her, "Amara, why do you think they did not take you away or kill you?"

A chill went down Amara's body, like a criminal discovering that the authorities took away the innocents for her crimes.

Did my sins cause a curse to my village?

Amara looked away from the searching eyes toward the rising sun attempting to overcome the cloud-engulfed sky.

Could not the God who executes judgment also execute grace?

A lone bird flew above. It swooped and then soared, leading others. Amara needed to stay strong for the survivors of her village. She wept and covered her face with her hands. "I don't know. Pada and I hid from our parents—so we could get married."

The older woman marching for her daughter wept, then flared her lips. "Why did he not hide all of us? Why did he only save you?"

There was only silence.

I should not be alive when it is better to be dead.

They slept hidden from the secret path. Some took turns being awake for protection, but there were no disturbances. Walking with a small group of refugees brought a sense of false security. They welcomed any sense of security.

Confidence that the Imbangala were content with their plundering and pillaging in their region filled Amara and the others. The Imbangala had likely moved on to other areas farther away.

She walked for days with the small group of survivors. Her fellow travelers refused to wait at home for the slight chance of family and friends returning. Those traveling with Amara knew the Imbangala had left them because they were too old.

They had little time left to waste if the refugees were to free the captives.

She gazed at the light rising high above the clouds. How much better it was to die pursuing and rescuing loved ones than to live without them.

Amara tried to keep up with the group but moved too slowly. People would alternate staying back with her as the older walked at a faster pace. She caught up when the group stopped and rested, as she refused rest so as not to slow everyone else down.

At times the weather did not cooperate. It was now June, and the days hit the extreme temperatures at night and midday. Several in the group had never traveled away from the village in their lifetimes. Most had lived their entire lives in the village of their birth. Some walked toward the coast for the first time. Some had never wet their feet in the ocean.

Several brought food for themselves to share with others. But after several days, they had to ration their food. Whenever it looked like they would have to skip meals, generous people from nearby villages gave them food.

As they approached the port city, they avoided any common paths and took lesser-known routes. They arrived at a cliff above the area where the ships entered and left. A common peer pressure existed to continue conversing and sharing their hopes and dreams for families and friends along the entire journey. But upon the cliff looking down, silence spoke for each of them.

Birds swooped up and down below them. Someone on the outer perimeter below lay on the ground, dying from a gaping wound to the side. The thief of life hovered over the area, waiting patiently to steal the last breath.

Amara and her friends agreed that death swallowed life and spat out corpses in the enemy fortress below them. In one corner, humans herded fellow humans into another section. From there, the captors pushed their herd into another area. Amara covered her ears, and others turned their heads away from the beatings occurring at several different parts of the fortress. Captors tossed live bodies, and dead bodies, in random directions. Most of those thrown no longer moved.

Upon the cliff, Amara and the others searched and pointed for loved ones down below. What would they do even if someone spotted them?

Amara placed her hand over her chest, looking for Pada and her family. She and Pada had hid to escape their parents and to marry. The visual evidence below confirmed that Pada had saved her life by hiding her.

Memories of love entered and filled her heart. Then regret followed and subdued it. Guilt reminded her that anger was the last emotion she expressed to her family and Pada. At the time, how could she have known that it was the last time she would see them?

She'd yelled at her parents when they told her she could no longer see Pada. She'd yelled at Pada as his new friend had carried her away to hide one last time.

Pada hid her so they could get formally married, against their parents' wishes of waiting for a better time. *Our mothers talked about an attack that was coming. Did our parents want our families to escape together before Pada and I got married and left their protection?*

Pada then had left her with that family to find their parents after their parents had left looking for her and Pada. Days later he did not come back. Her parents never found her.

She looked for them down below in the fortress but could not find them. Could they have all escaped and now waited for her back home? Had the captors below already taken them away on one of the ships, or were they mixed in with the tossed corpses, mercifully saved by death?

Amara shook her head, thinking how she both loved Pada and was also filled with anger toward him for leaving her. For what purpose would God spare the life of a young girl with deformities and allow the healthy to be killed or enslaved? She feared that her deformities from birth would prevent her from ever being productive in life, let alone saving those below. Her brokenness used to make her doubt God. Now she had new doubts.

Loved ones were taken away against their will from their homes and into a cursed world elsewhere. And they left Amara alone to be cursed in the world they left.

In the quiet, apart from the others, Amara stepped closer to the edge of the cliff. She listened to death serenading her from the world beyond. It waited down below with open arms.

Perhaps someone called her to the edge of the cliff. The edge between life and death. There had to be a reason.

Step forward.

***

Jamestown, Virginia
August 1619

Humility shivered in the warm morning air as she stood outside her front door, waiting. *Where are you, Abraham?*

Could her missing husband now be walking down the dirt path back home? It had been months since Abraham had disappeared on the ship the *Treasurer*. Life in Jamestown for a wife with two children, without a husband, had proven difficult.

A neighborhood girl arrived again at the door, ready to help Humility.

Humility smiled at her. "Good morning. Another ship from Point Comfort should be arriving today. Like the times before, I hope to be gone for a short time. Caleb and Rebekah miss their father but think he will be back soon. When I told them you were coming, in between their moments of sorrow, they are still excited to continue playing their games with you."

The girl smiled. "I'll take good care while you are gone. You just do what you need to do . . . I hope your husband is returning this time."

Humility nodded. She grabbed some paper that she had been writing on. She hugged her kids and began to walk away, when she stopped at the doorway. She stood still with the path ahead of her while thinking of what was behind her.

Why did you leave us?

She closed her eyes.

What did I do wrong?

She turned, and her heart ached more as her children waited with wide eyes and opened arms. Both lined up side to side and facing her. Trying to be brave and trying to keep tears from escaping.

"Children . . . I will be back. Do not worry. I will come back. Your father will come back as well . . ."

She went back to her children as they jumped into her arms. They gathered into one large hug, with each deciding not to let the others sink. When they pulled apart, each of them wiped the tears of the others.

Humility left, and partway through her walk, she stopped to write as the Lord spoke to her. She was unsure why the Lord had her write His message, but she held on to it as one would keep a treasured letter from a faithful lover across the ocean.

She walked and carried her letter like a soldier carrying a secret message, protecting it against an unseen force that wanted to stop the letter from reaching its destination. She held it even more firmly.

She walked carrying the secret battle plan up against the left side of her chest. Tears escaped as they rebelled against all her efforts to restrain them.

A person walking in the opposite direction asked, "Humility, are you all right? Is there something I can do?"

Humility was unable to answer and could only shake her head no as she continued walking.

Her right hand gripped harder . . . into a fist.

Another person along the way with a look of concern said, "Perhaps Abraham will be on the next arriving ship?"

Humility pulled her sweater tighter and nodded with a "Thank you."

Another person saw her and said, "Perhaps you pushed him away? You and Abraham could be irrational at times."

As she continued walking, Humility's fist clenched harder and required extra effort from her left hand not to release a hand of justice. Her right hand tried to hold what was in her thumping chest from breaking apart. It felt like a gentle fist on the left side of her chest tried to lunge through her right hand to search for and save the missing.

Up ahead was her destination with a bare path. Her beginning and end seemingly meeting where the ocean met the sand. She heaved with wave after wave of sobbing.

Just a little farther.

She reached the port under the beautiful morning light in the sky before her. She walked toward the water. She removed her shoes and put her bare feet into the water. Such beautiful, calm water. A single ship was arriving on the horizon. She remembered the severe storms coming here. How dangerous that same beautiful water could be.

She walked into the water and saw a bird of the sea diving and hunting. Perhaps to feed its young.

For the next generation.

When the water was about knee deep, she fell onto her knees.

With arms pleading, she said, "My God, I know You are here, but why do I feel that You have deserted me? Abraham, why? I love you . . . please come home . . ."

***

It was August of 1619, and Amara had spent a few months going home and then returning back to the port of Luanda. She sometimes looked out at the sea like a soldier's wife waiting for her lover's return.

Where the water met the sand, she met with God.

She walked into the water and fell to her knees. She spoke as if her audience of one was right there with her.

"Where are you, God? Mother? Father? Will you ever come back to me, my Pada? I love you . . ."

Another ship left with her people.

Arise, O God!

***

This was to be a significant day. It was August of 1619, and Humility studied the ship arriving at Jamestown. She took in a deep breath of ocean air and rested, knowing she could stay here for as long as she needed. She could trust the neighborhood girl to continue watching her children.

The ship was called the *White Lion*, and she sensed Abraham was not on the ship, but she felt compelled to pray for those who were. A wave of nausea knotted her stomach as an evil committed elsewhere approached.

With more light from the parting of clouds, she looked down at her note from God that she had written. Why did He speak in a single word?

"Africa."

Arise, O God!

"I can feel it. The tide of prayer is rising onto these shores from distant shores. Even with the darkest of nights arriving today, may the greater light of your presence foreshadow the new life. New liberty. Help us cross the Jordan."

Chapter 31

ABRAHAM

On the Mayflower
1620

With Abraham, and many on the *Mayflower*, the leash pulled harder the farther they moved from their homeland. The almost constant storms plotted against any stable foothold. The tyranny raining down from topside to those below attempted to pit each against each other from within and without. Comforts of familiarity pulled from one end of the leash, and the dream of life away from the king pulled on the other.

Abraham and Jonathan were two friends together on a massive ocean, sharing stories and Scripture readings. At times finding humor in their miseries. At times finding hope in the ark with their remaining days aboard the *Mayflower*.

They lived each day with incessant fleas and lice. The daily seasickness afflicted most. It was impossible to stay dry below deck because of the almost constant storm conditions above. The crew taunted and mocked them with spitting words of violent vulgarity.

Their supply of food reserves dwindled daily because they'd had to eat much of their reserves before setting sail. Food fatigue set in as they grew tired of the rock-hard biscuits, dried beef, and salted fish. Small critters were known to frequent their food. Some of the passengers delayed eating until it was dark enough not to see all that was being consumed.

Jonathan, with a weakened sigh, put his head into his hands. "I do not know if I can withstand the dying inside me. Is what I smell a result of not being able to bathe, or is it the death in me that surfaces from my inner depths? I grow weary of the endless scratching. Some of us are in the same clothing as when we left."

He turned his head closer to Abraham. "When can we cook a real meal? Where is a wooden trencher full of the finest hog roast? Mutton pie? Even a bite of a cheese tart. Or milk with nutmeg and honey? How about even a taste of cold stew with mutton and barley?" He laughed. "Even if we could eat, the children would vomit their food minutes later!"

Abraham's body shook, and his chest throbbed with each heartbeat. The walls were closing in. His throat was tightening. How can one escape what was inside of him?

He thrust his hands back toward the inner wall, trying to push the wall away. There was fear with a two-handed grip on his throat. Panic had one hand over his mouth, and the other was trying to rip out Abraham's hope from his insides.

Is it . . . is it too late to turn back? To return to our previous lives, safe at home on land, without drowning, safe with our king?

Abraham was not like most of the others. At the moment he desired to return to the king, who determined his life. Abraham reached to his side, as Jonathan focused elsewhere. The box with the weapon was still underneath his belongings.

It was difficult to tell the time of day from down below. Jonathan stood up in what room was available and tried to stretch to help ease his back pain. As Abraham lay on the floor, he tried to keep his belongings bundled to protect his things and his box.

A gentleman by the name of Thomas, a quiet, tall, and lean man, with his young boy Moses, came behind Abraham. Abraham covered his belongings.

"Abraham, we have something for you," Thomas said. "God sometimes does some amazing things with my six-year-old. He is a good boy, and he loves to serve his God. I do not understand where this comes from, for I was never that way in my youth. This is not from me."

Moses then stepped out from behind his father, reached into his pocket, pulled something out, and offered it to Abraham. Abraham studied the boy's eyes as he took the object. There was a joy in his eyes, and yet a sense of sacrifice. Abraham looked at the object the best he could in what light was present. He was unsure what it was, but it appeared to be an incomplete piece of metal? There were raised markings on it. The material was a mystery. It was not wood, and it was not of a metal he was familiar with.

"Thank you, Moses. What is this?"

"I do not really know. It was given to me." Moses shrugged.

"About a year ago, there was a young boy at Steven's. The boy asked for prayers for a future relative—a relative who was not born yet," Thomas said, shaking his head. "The boy then gave Moses this . . . thing. He said Moses was to protect it and then give it away at the right time. We don't know exactly what it is. We don't even know what it is made of, or how it was made, or even why it was made. But there is something special about it. It has been Moses' most prized possession."

"I am supposed to give it to you," Moses said as he placed both his hands over his heart.

Abraham fought to restrain any tears, as his hand warmed holding it. Something unlocked inside him. He took a deep breath. He wanted to eliminate his box and what was inside it. The box that was to determine his future. His final judgment.

Who is this little boy?

"Thank you very much. I know this took a great love and sacrifice. I am honored to receive this gift."

The boy smiled with a wonderful light. There was something different in his eyes. *What a special boy.*

Moses had an unusual impact on Abraham. During evening prayers, Abraham asked a question of all those present.

"Something happened to me earlier. Tell me more about this God. Can you speak of a time in your history when your God intervened in your life?"

For the next couple of hours, many spoke of transformative moments in their lives. A shift occurred in the attitude of every person. Many proclaimed the love of their Lord. There were stories of people being freed and saved from alcohol. Saved from overwhelming anger toward a spouse or children. Marriages were saved. Someone saw a person years before raised from the dead! Spirits were lifted. The singing of praises of their God sprang up.

A few members of the crew stomped down from topside, like guards ready to punish captured rebel prisoners. They heard the singing and loud prayers and were in a foul mood.

The leader turned toward his crew and yelled, "I still cannot believe we are carrying subversives."

He pointed to his cowering crew members and then toward the passengers rebelling against his authority. He looked down at those below him. He made a fist. "Even with the storm, we can still hear you from topside. It pierces the storm. Enough! Be silent!!"

The ones from above reinforced their control by reminding those below of the fear of their law. There was to be no going topside with each storm. Though the entire crew mocked them daily, the leader was the worst. Every day, while red in face and spitting with violence, he had a particular fondness for two words in describing the passengers aboard.

After mumbling some obscenities, he raised his fisted hands. Through clenched teeth, and with veins pulsating on his neck and forehead, after saying "puke" and before he could finish with "stockings," he dropped dead.

Multiple gasps filled the deck. A crew member checked on the fallen leader as someone from the back yelled out a "Hallelujah" but was quickly quieted.

"Lord God, have mercy on his soul," a passenger prayed.

"He has no defense," a woman in the back said.

The crew remained still while looking down at their leader. They could not seem to move or speak. Abraham turned his head toward Jonathan, whose mouth was wide open. Fear and an awe and a reverence presided in their midst.

There was no sound as death had abducted life and all thoughts. Members of the crew flinched when someone finally yelled, "Be right with your God. The same power from the same God that ended this life, is the same power from the same God who can save your life."

Abraham did not have the vocabulary to describe what was before him. Was it the presence and fear of their God that enacted justice and ended life before his eyes?

Abraham grabbed his throat.

I am next.

The avenger was searching the sea and coming

after him next. *Their God is the avenger. Their Judge killed the man slumped before me, and He knows all my secrets.*

Where could he hide? He deserved to drop dead more than the man who once inhabited the corpse before him.

After the storm, the crew and passengers ambled topside into the late hours with a sadness over their loss. The crew joined them in prayer, and they prepared the ocean burial. Behind the large group, Abraham brought his box over the edge of the stern above the water.

The sight of the corpse at the starboard edge above the sea brought complete silence.

An inner pull urged Abraham to open the box in his hands. To hold what was in it for a while.

Just one more time.

He thought of the little boy Moses and the object given to Abraham. Unknown to the others, he held Moses' object in one hand and dropped that box with the knife into the sea.

In days I will die, but I am not going to make it easier for the avenger.

Abraham watched the box float away and then turned to see them drop the body into the ocean. With sore and tired hands, Abraham held on to the ship.

It was day fifty of seventy-six days left. There was still a pull on him.

Where can I run?

Abraham hoped that dropping the box and the body of the crew leader into the sea would satisfy the mouth of the abyss.

Abraham felt the pull on his shoulder.

The Judge wanted more.

CHAPTER 32

JAMES

England
1620

James awoke with another nightmare and left his slowly dying Anne alone in bed. He stumbled to his garden to sleep under the light of the moon behind dark cloud cover.

Changing the location of where he slept that night could save his life. In his garden there was no self-exiled wife. No slithering noises under his bed. No waking up checking his neck for wounds. In his garden there were still reminders of the lovers' paradise he'd had—and would one day restore.

James awoke in the morning, gazing at his right hand opening and closing. Though bereft of sleep, he was still full of joy and confidence that more subversives had been found and rounded up. There were now fewer goats and wandering sheep. But yet others were hiding. And they hid the murderer.

He, and the others in generations before him, had obeyed the voice of the Dark Light. The voice with its great commission to spread its power to control and help the weak. During the length of his rule, it begat success with the king, adding disciples of different peoples from different nations into the kingdom. More were coming to know the security of his power.

But something was still missing.

He took bites from his favorite garden fruits. He forgot to care that juices dripped down his neck as he walked back to assume control upon his throne.

The blessings of God have always followed after I have obeyed. The kingdom is spreading. My kingdom. The New World will also be mine, and it will shine a light to those blinded in darkness and living in fear for their lives. But I—

One of the king's pawns entered into the throne room with permission and spoke with his head and knees bowed.

"My lord, your servant that you commanded is seeking permission to submit to the throne."

The king smiled and stared down at him. "Wonderful. More reports of the spread of my kingdom. Bring him forth."

The king's servant entered, turning his head from side to side, as if planning an escape. He bowed his head and knees in obedience at a safe distance in front of the king.

The king almost winced at the scar on the left side of the man's face.

"As commanded . . . we have extracted information from prisoners suspected of rebelling against your church and its practices. We continue to eliminate those deemed a threat and . . . release those deemed not a serious threat back to the community to remind the people of their fear of their God."

While chewing, the king's chin dripped with juices. He waved his hand toward the one below him. "Continue."

The pawn protecting his king closed his eyes and inhaled deeply. "We recently released one who was blind in one eye and six others afterward."

You released the murderer.

James pounded his fist. It echoed throughout.

The man grimaced and lowered his head and voice. "The one you have been seeking may have been released."

"And what shall I do with the remaining idiots like you who serve their perfect king?" James yelled.

The man paused. The king enjoyed watching the man suffer under his penetrating eyes. No one ever looked him in the eye when they knew their king was angry.

After savoring the trembling servant drowning in silence, the king asked, "How old was the one you released?"

"He was in his thirties. Longer hair and beard than anyone else. I do not know his name."

Is he too old to be the boy?

After several moments, the man spoke with his head bowed down. "I take full responsibility. It was as if someone shielded him from my eyes until it was too late."

The king leaned toward him as if to propel his words forward with more force. "Your life is not shielded from *my* eyes. My people are in danger. Left to themselves, they will destroy themselves. The king saves lives. I can see your arrogance unhindered. In your pride, you let your guard down, and now your prideful act has affected *my* kingdom. You have one week to find the murderer, or you will pay for your sin of pride with your life."

The man dared not turn his back to the king and walked several steps backward. He spun and left.

James threw a nearby bowl of his fruit. He cursed at how close he was to saving his crown for eternity. He drew blood with his talons as he closed his fists.

A voice from within James surfaced and spoke inside his thoughts. *The hand of covering will move away, and I will see him. I will find him. You will find the murderer . . .*

As if held under the surface of a vast ocean, James was then allowed to surface his head above the water to breathe and speak.

His eyes widened. "You know I despise you. What do you want me to do?"

Silence.

The king needed to find the coming assassin before the assassin found him.

I am going mad looking for him.

The king clutched his chest and spoke to him who was near. "You have always helped me in the past. But is this what you want? Do you *want* me to go mad? I do desire peace, but do you *want* there to be warring factions in my kingdom?"

After several moments of silence, the Dark Light spoke. "The murderer wants you *and* your son."

CHAPTER 33

ABRAHAM

On the Mayflower
1620

Over many days, the stench in closed quarters continued to be debilitating. With the severe storms, they were all trapped and unable to go topside.

Young man Peter sat crouched in front of Abraham and Jonathan with a look of concern. Abraham felt tightening around his throat. Peter reached toward Abraham to help. Abraham found a breath when Peter then reached for his own throat and collapsed. His eyes and his mouth opened, and he seemed surprised that what was around Abraham's throat was now around his. His eyes were stuck wide open. Peter heaved and searched for the breath that seemed to elude him.

He sprang up as Jonathan tried to keep him on the floor to rest. Young man Peter broke through Jonathan's arms and ran topside with his hands around his throat.

No one could respond fast enough to stop him. Who could judge him when he did what each person wanted to do? The ones who saw him run waited below to catch him when he was thrown back down. After several minutes, something was not right, as he had still not returned.

Jonathan ran topside. Abraham soon followed when Jonathan did not return.

Abraham popped his head above to see several running in different directions. "What is wrong?"

"They have not seen him," Jonathan yelled between quick breaths and scanning the ocean.

Abraham went topside against the storm. Sensing a crisis, others followed him. They searched every part of the ship topside. All eyes turned to the water. Men at the bow and starboard side yelled that they could not see him. Abraham ran to the stern and port side looking out at sea, and those there just shook their heads in silence when their eyes met Abraham's plea.

"He is not here," someone yelled.

The ship moved violently, and visibility was limited. With a tenuous faith with tenuous footing, they searched for their brother during another storm. With the freezing temperature of the water, time was running out.

Where are you?

Then Jonathan yelled and pointed near the stern. "Peter! There he is! I think I saw his arm!"

All held on to the sides and each other and moved toward Jonathan.

"There he is," someone yelled. "He is holding on to one of the lines!"

"He must have fallen and been able to grab one of the ship's lines!" someone else yelled.

Young Peter still had enough strength to grab on to a rope thrown over for him. Several men pulled the rope in the race against the freezing water and Peter letting go.

He already looked dead as they pulled him nearer, but they knew he had to be alive, as he was still holding on to the rope. His eyes never opened.

"Pull! Pull! We don't have much time."

"Peter, just hold on a little longer!

"We almost have you!"

When he was within arm's reach, he collapsed and let go. Several hands caught him before he fell back into the water. After pulling him aboard, shivering was his only movement. His chest was not moving. They found the least wet blanket to try to keep him warm.

Abraham covered his face with his hands. Peter was blue. The crew bent their knees and bowed down but did not know what to say. They looked like family members hoping their brother would awaken at his own hastily arranged funeral.

From bent knees, the crew looked upward, as if needing help from the surrounding saints and strangers.

Peter was still not breathing. Death was consuming him.

Jonathan then pierced the sky with a short prayer. "Father, save my brother, Your child."

With the wet wind swirling around him, Jonathan wiped his face. "I know my brother's heart. Young Peter is like each of us. He wants to live—to then truly live."

The wind calmed. Abraham saw the blue fade as young Peter coughed out water and began to breathe.

Death is roaming to and fro. It will not be satisfied until it consumes me.

Abraham stepped away, as all were distracted with the celebration of young Peter's return. Abraham put his hand on his own throat for protection. There was now nowhere to hide. Someone or something knew he was on board.

CHAPTER 34

PADA

Ndongo, Africa
June 1619

Pada and the other captives knew things would worsen if the captors herded them from land into a ship.

At least on land they could run away after attacking their foes. But on a ship in the open sea, a sea that many of the captives had never experienced before, where could they run?

Would anyone know how to sail and navigate a ship? Even if only a short distance offshore, they could not swim home, as most did not know how to swim. Someone needed to lead an attack before they set foot on a ship.

Pada tried to communicate to the others using his eyes and expressions.

Someone is communicating to me through my dreams. If I could share my thoughts into their thoughts . . .

Pada wanted to rule, but his people staggered to survive the next step.

People, rise up.

Most eyes were too tired to lift up. Closed eyes were a respite from the surrounding evil and a chance to search inward for any remaining vestiges of hope. He could not find a single pair of eyes to lock on to.

Attached to each other, they all took steps toward the ship.

A crew member of one of the ships smiled at Pada as he spoke to the those standing at the entrance of the *San Juan Bautista*.

"Even though you are less than human, you will be highly esteemed workers in the silver mines of Veracruz. You will be wealthy beyond your dreams. You will be the envy of all those left back at home."

He smiled a crooked smile. "I do envy you as you enjoy an extended holiday."

The captors forced them to march forward, when Pada stopped to make his stand. This was his last chance. One more step onto the ship, and he would not return. With the abrupt stop, the person behind him bumped into him. A captor turned his head and narrowed his eyes in Pada's direction. Pada did not move forward.

Two captors looked at Pada. One rolled his eyes as the other complained about having to move again. The captor cursed and stomped toward Pada. A woman in chains nearby locked eyes with Pada's and mouthed, *Your role must yet come.*

When he was a little boy, Pada's mother had told him that God created Pada for His own purpose.

Goel died so that Pada would live. Amara always had great hope for his future. She said he was going to save the world one day.

The piece of paper Goel gave me. In the beginning God created the heavens and the earth. If there is a God, He created. There is order. There is purpose. Somebody created Amara.

The captor raised his fist and prepared to punish Pada. With eyes focused on the woman, Pada stepped forward.

The captor shoved Pada into those in front of him. He then kicked him in the back. Pada yelped in pain and fell into the others. The captor walked away, letting Pada and those ahead of him struggle back onto their feet.

When Pada's foot hit the deck of the ship, Pada knew his life would never be the same. How could he ever see Amara or his family again? On board were stains of body excrement. Bloodstains. There were deep marks, as if someone had attacked the ship. Or had attacked what was inside the ship. Even with his eyes closed, Pada could feel, could see, a small settlement of hell on a floating vessel. If death had a favored place of residence, it stayed here at times to rest from the daily roaming. And it waited with extending fingers as they entered its floating neighborhood.

Chained and shackled together, a few resisted and then were punished. After the extended death march, little to no food, some away from home for the first time, most were already crushed and chained even before new chains were applied.

Pada closed his eyes to block out what was before him. He tried to delay the inevitable. He paused to remember the sounds of the birds and ocean, above the sounds of humans turning on each other. He thought of Amara and her beautiful face as the ocean kissed the shore every few moments. The predictable pattern of the ocean waves meeting the shore reminded him that there must be some order to the chaos surrounding and consuming him. There must be a Creator of that order. There must be right that can defeat wrong.

Can there be a God in this place?

As Pada stood near the end of the broken line entering the bowels of the ship, he took one last time to memorize everything above. He knew he would be below for a long time—until he died.

It was a beautiful day full of sunshine. The birds. The breeze on his face. The taste of salt in the air. From where he stood, there did not appear to be any light down below where he was being herded. He had no idea what awaited below.

But there was no mistaking the sounds of men and women below reverting to their childhoods, pleading for their mommies. Lost children cried and screamed worse than if trapped by childhood monsters returning to haunt them in the dark. He had never heard grown men and women cry like that before.

For the moment, he blocked out what was happening before him. For the last time, for the first time, he focused on the birds. New sounds he hadn't noticed before the chains. The birds seemed to create their own winds as the gust of the wings whooshed nearby in several parts of the ship. Sometimes they swooped above him as they flew down and back up as they pleased. Sounds of the birds scraping the creaking wooden deck with their claws seemed to surround Pada and the others. The birds gathered at different locations on the ship, as several picked at food on a pile of clothing near Pada.

Was someone naked somewhere? Then the pile of clothes moved! Someone had collapsed. The person was a small adult who probably weighed no more than a little girl. The person under the clothing tried to move his arms to swat at the birds picking at him. The birds tore away some parts of his clothing and now picked at his now exposed skin. The little man tried to hit the birds, but there were too many.

The captors walked around and over the moving bones. They stepped on him and kicked him when he got in the way. After several minutes, a small captor picked him up and threw him overboard. The birds followed.

What could Pada do? Pada turned his head in all directions to determine the best place to throw up without drawing attention or laughter from the captors. He clenched his teeth and swallowed.

He only had a few moments left of life up above

what waited below. *Is it possible that I can feel Amara nearby?* Pada turned his head one more time to study and memorize life beyond the cries of his people—toward the bluffs above the fortress. The captors pushed them forward, and the chains pulled Pada below. Light from above dissipated after a few steps below. Most of the captives already inside were lying down, chained to each other.

There was already a sickening smell that permeated through and out all parts of the ship.

I can smell death from every splintered beam.

CHAPTER 35

PADA

On the San Juan Bautista
June 1619

Down below in the *San Juan Bautista*, many vomited from the offensive odor. Pada gagged and tried to think of the beauty of the ocean above as the wave of nausea abated, until the next wave.

They forced Pada to the bottom deck chained to two others. Many still winced and moaned with muscle cramps from the prolonged standing and walking to the port city. Now the only movement allowed while lying down was periodic readjustments with what their chains permitted.

They had not set out for sea yet. Some of the chained yelled at their captors. The one chained to Pada's left did not speak and only groaned in pain. Or perhaps he tried to talk but could not be understood through the whimpering. His trembling was strong enough to hurt Pada as his chains pulled on Pada's wrist and ankles.

Chained to Pada's right side was a young man who looked to be in his twenties. The captors renamed him "Christian" when they learned of his beliefs.

"Where is your God? People die because of belief in your God," Pada said.

"It has always been our liberty to die for the God of our choice. You are no different from me. Creator or creation. I have chosen. Who have you chosen?" Christian asked.

Pada did not answer. As if he could feel someone looking, the right side of Pada's face burned.

Christian raised an arm upward. "Do not be deceived by these chains. The visible is not always representative of the invisible. I cannot run. But I am free. You know why the Imbangala captured you. You know why you had that dream, don't you?"

Pada clenched his fists while twisting his head away, making sure Christian could not see his face. He turned away from the annoying question toward the annoying whimpering noises to his left. Pada checked himself to make sure he was not the one making the noises of weakness.

Pada could not answer him.

"There is a reason Satan wants to stop you. There is a reason he wants to kill you. Do you realize the threat that you are?" Christian asked.

"I cannot be a threat when I am in chains," Pada said as he tried to raise his arms.

"Your body is in chains, but your spirit and soul can still be free."

Pada kept his head turned away with the lone tear falling down the left side of his face.

"Even in these chains, He can still free you," Christian said above the whimpering.

"I was not free before these chains."

"I don't know exactly what God will do with us in the next few moments, let alone the next several weeks or months. But I am trying to trust Him."

The creaking of wood warned of footsteps approaching. They stopped talking. The footsteps moved next to them. The feet belonged to the leader of the captors on their deck. Pada turned his head to the leader. The leader was missing an ear. It looked like it had been cut off. The man grunted and laughed as he inspected his prisoners.

The leader stood tall with his hands on his hips and his chest pushed outward. "It is hard to see you in the dark with your dark skin. Perhaps if you smiled for me, you could make my work easier," he said as he laughed.

He walked as if inspecting the goods in his market. "I am glad some of you still have some clothing. Your bodies disgust me. But the women and the children we have elsewhere . . . they are different." He laughed again.

His feet moved and stopped next to Pada's head. He crouched down to get a closer look at Pada. "Your god dwells within me and through me. For all intents, I am your king. Your god. My realm is above. Down below, where I allow you to dwell, is also mine. You will only dwell below. You will not go above. I will tell you the weather. I will tell you when we reach our destination. I will tell you what you can say. You live if I decide that you should live."

He walked away from Pada and scanned his kingdom and smiled as he nodded. The smile seemed to be of joy as he turned his head back and forth before his loyal subjects. He then ran toward Pada and kicked him in the ribs. Pada yelled and cursed at the man. The man laughed with pure joy and kicked him in the same place again.

Pada did not say a word the second time.

The man positioned himself with his feet next to Pada's head. He swung his leg back and then quickly forward and gently tapped Pada's head with the front of his shoe. He tapped his foot several times against Pada's head as Pada squinted and winced each time in anticipation. The man laughed again and turned to walk away. He then spun and kicked Pada one more time on the same left side of his ribs.

Pada turned his head toward Christian, and Christian returned a concerned stare. The leader looked down at Pada like a man beating his misbehaving dog.

"I have been watching you. I will make sure there is no rest, as you will be working the mines for me. You are mine. You will make me rich—or maybe I will sell you for something better." The man walked away.

"He is not your master," Christian whispered.

Pada could not control the flood of tears and heaved for the next breath.

Over the next several days, sickness spread through Pada and the others. Pada was unsure whether it was because of the unsanitary conditions, seasickness, homesickness, or a mix of all. They developed painful sores, as they could not change positions from lying down while chained. Bodily fluids dripped from other decks above and from those beside with the ship's movement, which did not help the sores or nausea.

The captors alternated between protecting their cargo for economic reasons and not caring about the suffering and lost lives. At their convenience and whims, the captors would feed their human cargo yams and rice. Some captives refused to eat to quicken their eventual destiny in their own timing and on their own terms. The captors sometimes force fed their profits to stay alive a few more weeks.

Every few days, the captors would douse them with seawater to rinse them off, likely more out of a concern for the odor and loss of possible future profits than for their hygiene.

After Pada had recovered a few days later, Pada and Christian continued their discussion.

"God is Father, Son, Spirt," Christian said. "You are spirit, soul, body. You are made in His image, so you are three parts as well. On this ship, Satan probably believes that if he can rule over your body, through chains visible or invisible, he can rule over your soul and spirit."

He raised his arm to lift Pada's. "That is why he is killing you. You are a threat. It is not your body. What you have inside of you, that is what he wants. That is the real threat."

Pada's eyes widened. "How do you know about my dream?"

"Now you are figuring it out. I only know parts of it, and I did not want to bring it up until you were ready."

"I will be ready later," Pada said as he shook his head. "They gave you a new name. Christian. I know that is not your name. What is your real name?"

"God is the one who gives me my name. He is the only one left who knows my real name." He paused as his voice cracked. "I am a Christian. Their name for me is not a threat to me, but strengthens me."

Christian smiled. "I overheard you tell the young man next to you your name. You must know that you have a Hebrew name?" Christian asked as he turned his head farther toward Pada.

"Do you know Hebrew?"

"I learned a few words with Christians from Portugal. Your parents must be strong Christians to use a Hebrew word for a name."

"Many know my parents. Okoro and Chinasa. Especially my mother. She is . . . was . . . a Christian. My parents are friends with another family, and they named their son with another Hebrew word. Goel died before they captured me."

"I am sure you know that it is not unusual for God

to name his children with names that describe, or will describe, them, right?"

"I am not sure He knew what he was doing with my name. Pada. To deliver? Goel. Redeemer? I don't think those prophecies turned out too well. Goel got killed, delaying me from becoming a slave. Now *that* is a God who is all powerful."

"Do not mock God. He is not done with you yet. The story is unfinished. You will come to know more as you know Him better."

They stopped talking as a captor walked near them.

As the days and the odors on the ocean multiplied, the captors often did not remain with the abducted.

Pada slept a restless sleep. In his recurring nightmare, all the people were drinking the liquid given to them to answer their thirst. They united with the one of divination. A remnant of the people attempted to convince the thirsty that it was not water they were drinking and that God had provided the real water with His baobab trees. That drinking the liquid from the one of divination was a trap. In response, the people attacked the small remnant who resisted the one of divination.

As many drank the liquid, they soon became more thirsty and more dependent on the one of divination. Soon, most were either dead or dying. Their eyes were not clear, and their vision clouded. They could not see the real water. How could one know when they were being deceived? Many continued drinking the liquid. Many did not think it was a trap until it was too late.

In the midst of the one of divination's deception, some were captured and taken against their will onto a ship to sail elsewhere. They were forced to spread the kingdom of the one of divination.

But a remnant escaped the land of the one of divination. They sailed in another ship, with something illegal, and endured many difficulties. The one of divination knew that the remnant in the escaping ship could free the ones taken in the other ship against their will. The one of divination attacked the remnant in their ship, as its power extended beyond its land and into the sea. It broke the remnant's ship into two, and the spirits and lives of many broke at the bottom of the sea.

Pada then moved from observing to being in the dream.

He flailed in the water and began sinking because he could not swim, and no one could help him. As he dropped below the surface, Pada's feet lifted up in the water from underneath. It was as if someone was holding him in the water so he would not sink. He focused on his surroundings. A power entered into him. He prayed a powerful prayer for those in the two ships and those in the water. Even within the storm, he heard someone breathing. He turned to see . . .

Pada awoke to the sounds of the captors yelling and screaming above them. He felt burdened to pray again for those escaping Pharaoh in the other ship in his dream. He prayed for the ones in the ship escaping with the illegal contraband so they could help the ones in the other ship taken against their will. Perhaps even in chains, there could be a power in his prayers.

How can that be?

The sounds above his deck differed from the previous days. Those below could not see what was happening above. Something significant was occurring.

The main captor came running toward Pada's area. He ran like someone chased him and he was out of time. He kicked Pada in the head. Christian yelled at him to stop, as Pada did not make a sound after the first kick.

"Stop! God will strike you dead if you do not stop! Your life is cursed, and you will be struck down! Stop!"

He continued kicking Pada. When he tired, he crumpled onto his knees, heaving, trying to breathe. He flailed at Pada's head.

While staring at the dazed Pada, the captor yelled, "You will not stop us . . . We know who you are . . . We know what you carry . . ."

Only Pada's chest moved with shallow movements.

Christian then yelled, "Be gone! In the name of Jesus, who frees all slaves, I command you to be gone."

The main captor hit Pada in the face and prepared for another hit while pleading, "Do not torment us . . . Leave us be . . ."

"Be gone! I command you to leave!"

The ship jerked like it was hit or had run aground. The main captor screamed and ran as if attacked by a ghost.

CHAPTER 36

ABRAHAM

On the Mayflower
1620

It roamed and found young man Peter. It was looking for Abraham. If Abraham was hidden before, death was hovering near him on the *Mayflower*. Who could ever escape death? How many days did Abraham have left with his days disappearing?

Abraham imagined running up to his wife, Humility, waiting outside their front door. At least the others on the *Mayflower* had hope beyond his remaining allotted days.

But during another breaking storm, some broken spirits, and the creaking of wood, the sounds reminded him of how life could be broken into two.

I have cursed those on this journey with my life. Would lives not be saved by ending mine?

Abraham had rid himself of the weapon and that box. But the sea was still present, and it held him trapped in a giant wooden box gripped in its hand. All death needed was a crack in the ark door, in the floating coffin, to sink it for a perfect burial at sea.

Death always won. Had anyone ever outlasted death? It was day sixty of seventy-six. The inevitable was coming.

What could he do?

Abraham's body trembled. His legs buckled, and he collapsed like a lawbreaker waiting to be hung. He put his hands to his throat. His time was approaching. It was getting more difficult to breathe.

Jonathan put his hand on Abraham's shoulder. Abraham and Jonathan looked at each other as they watched two women, Elizabeth and Susanna, debate a few feet from them.

Conflicting emotions moved through the people. After seeing life ended and saved right before their eyes, some were in awe. Some in fear. Some slept better. Some lost sleep.

The saints were strong, and most did not waver in their faith and what God asked of them. There was a near-unanimous sense of unity among the saints. But there was debate among the strangers and between the two groups.

And then there were the two mothers before them. Elizabeth and Susanna had debated in the past, but their arguments intensified after they'd dropped the body of a man struck dead by God into the ocean.

Their husbands looked uncomfortable with the rising tension between their wives. Yet they also desired to let the women resolve their differences among themselves. Though the debates were civil, all were growing weary.

Susanna was pregnant and made sure her children were under the watchful care of their father as she spoke.

"Elizabeth, I understand how you feel. We saw someone die, and it reminds us that our lives are not our own. You are right. We are not safe here. Our future *is* uncertain. But I do know God is certain. In times of trouble, I believe our God has His plans already figured out. He would have us remember Him and continually converse with Him in prayer and through His holy Scriptures. He has provided in all previous times of trouble. We must remember His history. This will help us help each other in the present and future."

Elizabeth was also pregnant and clutched on to her children and would not let them be with their father as she spoke.

"Every storm reminds us that there is danger here and more coming. We are not safe. This is not a safe place. We need to appoint a leader that we can trust to protect us."

She then whispered and moved closer to Susanna. "What we need is not found in the men who lead us now. Because of the fault of our leaders, we are minus one person. We almost lost another. We are all ill and hungry. They ineptly guided us, and now we are running out of food. And we are not even halfway yet. We need a leader who will lead us back home. Then we can pray."

"Back home? God is leading us away from a

counterfeit king who resists God, and you want us to return—"

"Being alive to care for and protect the future of our children is not under the care of a counterfeit king."

"We should follow what God wants and not bow down to comfort and safety. We—"

"We are not yet halfway. We have enough food and fewer storms if we turn back now. Where is the leader we can follow and who is courageous enough to do what is right for all of us?"

Elizabeth looked at Susanna and tried to lead Susanna's eyes toward Elizabeth's husband. "We need a leader to decide for us. He needs to do what is right for all of us. It is not about individuals—it is about what is best for all of us as one."

Both women stepped in front of their children. It was then that the husbands intervened.

Elizabeth's husband stepped in between Elizabeth and Susanna and spoke to Susanna.

"I don't like this conflict. Our children need to know they are safe. They need more of our protection. A safe space away from your ideas. We need to go home. That you don't think of the safety of the children first is offensive to me."

Susanna's husband then stepped between Susanna and Elizabeth's husband. "Sometimes we need our conscience pricked. The God we serve does not serve our comforts. God is calling us to move forward in obedience. Even when it is uncomfortable and inconvenient. Seek not comfort but the Comforter."

Others nearby turned their heads toward the conversation and shifted themselves either away or toward the small group gathering. But it was Abraham who was most uncomfortable. Abraham waited and then stepped between the men.

Did it even matter what Abraham said or did, for he had just a few days left to live? Should a hypocrite speak? He could speak without fear of offending anyone, for he was going to die soon anyway.

Abraham stepped closer to Elizabeth and her husband to speak to them. Sharp pain on the right side of his head, along with his left leg buckling, brought him to the floor. Someone screamed, and another said, "Not again!"

Several gathered above him to see if he was still alive.

Am I dead? He found me . . .

He tried to speak, but it was difficult to form words. Jonathan shoved aside the men surrounding Abraham to give him space to breathe. "Abraham, please speak to me. Are you okay?"

O God, not yet . . . not yet . . . not yet . . . give truth a voice before You take me.

The prayers moved in his heart. After several minutes, he sat up holding his head. With help, he rose.

He hobbled to Elizabeth and her husband, paused, practiced with a few words, then spoke. "Inside the walls of your heart, your home, you have replaced the truth given to you with comfortable soft furniture of your own convenient making. You locked your doors to escape from the God you cannot tame. You are teaching your children to do the same."

All stood with their mouths open. Abraham had tears in his eyes as he shook his head.

To where does a hypocrite run away from the God who is going to kill him?

The pain in his head lessened. He stood on his leg with more stability. He turned his head from side to side, as no one was speaking. The surrounding men caught him and helped him back to the floor.

The ship creaked like the bones of an older man. From the floor level, Elizabeth's stomach stood out. Abraham covered his face with his hand as images passed before his eye. Even with his eye closed, he could not remove the images inside his head. In mere moments the child in Elizabeth's stomach grew, had children, those children had children, and soon there were many generations. He saw soft children in the future trying to put their hands over the mouth of God as they lounged on their soft and expensive furniture with doors closed to God. They tried to ignore Him. They accepted sexual sin. They complied with infanticide! He saw what started as a soft tyranny turn into a hard tyranny. Then the images stopped.

We must stop her!

Abraham wanted to stop Elizabeth. He had to tell the others what he saw. Even if Abraham was not going to be alive, he could not allow her to take what she was carrying to the New World!

It's on the Mayflower *too! What is in the king is cloaked within our midst!*

Abraham sat with his mouth wide open. Others stared at him. They must have thought he was a madman.

Abraham wanted to do something. What, he was not sure. Sitting down and not doing anything would not stop the evil. But Abraham could not move.

Elizabeth and her family all stood stiffly. Offended. Among the pair of parents nearby, two hearts looked softened. Two hearts looked hardened. The children followed.

The four adults then whispered and took their eyes off Abraham. There seemed to be a mutual agreement for the two sides not to speak to each other. Each couple, with their respective children, walked in separate directions within the small confines of the ship.

Abraham became lost in thought as he looked at the pregnant women's stomachs.

What will become of these two children to be born?

Abraham watched as each family moved farther apart and went to opposite sides.

He squeezed both of his hands together and noticed his strength was like that of two different people in the same body.

It was harder to breathe. He knew what was seeking him was on board. It would find him. He would die.

It cloaked itself within and among any survivors to the New World.

CHAPTER 37

JONATHAN

On the Mayflower
1620

Lying on the wet floor of the *Mayflower*, several images passed through Jonathan's mind.

His sister lying lifeless on bloodstained dirt.

The last dying words of his beloved wife after she gave birth to their son.

The last threatening words from his second wife before she took his son away.

And then the image that shook him at his core. Abraham, seemingly broken in two, dying at the bottom of the sea.

It was only a dream.

As Abraham slept, recovering from his pain and weakness, Jonathan rose to seek peace. He collapsed in private apart from Abraham. For just this one time, he wanted to live without the burden of what was best for Abraham.

Maybe it was a prophetic vision?

In the dream, he saw Abraham resisting his efforts back in Southampton to save him from the ocean's judgment. Abraham insisted on crossing the Atlantic. He did not listen to advice and forced Jonathan to find a way to bring Abraham on the *Mayflower*.

Why didn't he listen to me?

He then saw the *Mayflower*. Broken. Disjointed. Out of place. In two. In an abrupt change in the dream, Jonathan was then swimming among parts of a ship. He turned his head in every direction, looking through distorted vision. He wiped his eyes. His cries for Abraham went unanswered.

He then dove into the open mouth of the grave. Abraham could not swim, and he only had seconds to find Abraham and then extract him back to the surface. Somehow, light penetrated from the top enough for him to see underwater. The storm was strong above the surface, but below it was quiet and calm.

Abraham lay broken at the bottom of the sea. His eyes were stuck open. Something dark swirled in the water above his head. It contrasted with the beams of light penetrating through the ocean water from above. It moved above and then around Abraham's head. As it moved above him, Abraham was unable to breathe. It was as if the swirling object was taking the life out of Abraham.

Abraham's eye blinked. He was still alive!

Jonathan reached down to pick him up. Abraham could not try and help. Jonathan tried again to pull him up with all the power and control he could gather. Abraham did not move.

Why didn't he listen to me?

Jonathan remembered the final moments of his sister's life. He'd stood above her with his hands on his hips. Then for the first time in years, he remembered the voice he'd heard when his sister was dying.

That voice. That voice. No one else was around. It was only him and his dying sister. He heard a voice.

A prolonged dark whisper.

Each word elongated and said slowly, with intent.

"A n o t h e r   w i l l   d i e   b e c a u s e   o f   y o u ."

Jonathan stopped thinking of his dream and covered his mouth. He tried not to let his emotions escape from behind the wall built over decades. Could he hold it in? If he could not contain his scream, he would have to explain to the others.

He coughed to cover his sobbing.

There she was. She gave up her last breath. I wanted to hold her hand. There was so much blood.

The beams around him creaked as water dripped down with more pitching of the ark. The ordinary sounds of the ship and its surroundings overtook the cry he could not contain.

He curled up on the floor and tried to close his eyes and sleep a restful sleep with his trembling. Jonathan would not allow his friend to die at the bottom of the ocean. If a storm broke the *Mayflower*, or if it was attacked, he would be at Abraham's side at all times to ward off death.

But what if Abraham was correct and would soon

die on day seventy-six? Would his friend then finally find peace from the torment of life?

During another storm, Jonathan slid with the ship's movement and tried to control his descent by gripping whatever did not move.

His hands. In the wet dark, it looked like his hands were dripping. So much blood dripping down upon Abraham.

Chapter 38

JAMES

England
1620

James pulled the covers of his bed over his head as the flies hovered above him. His enemies were trying to break him in half, and now his son.

The murderer was still out there somewhere.

My people. My sheep need me.

He sat up and checked for a deep cut on his throat. His throat was uncut, and there was no visible wound to his chest.

People told him while he was growing up that nightmares had plagued his mother and father when they were alive. And now King James sat on his bed worrying about the dark power. He needed it. He was scared of the demons and witches.

With her back turned to him in bed, his wife, Queen Anne, asked, "Are you all right?"

James did not answer.

She was dying, and yet she had concern for him.

"You must stop your heart's wandering. You know who torments you night and day."

He snarled. "Go ahead and die. Get it over with. I know what I am doing. What would a wife, existing solely for the convenience of appearance for the sheep, know?"

There were no wounds on his throat, but for just a moment, his heart was heavy with the cuts that his words inflicted. She didn't cry like she used to. The silence cut him—there were no more tears that Anne could cry. Even in her final days, she tried to love the husband she married by proxy.

No more time to think of the past. *Focus on the present.* The Shepherd needed to eliminate the wandering sheep leading others astray. He needed to eliminate the wolves hiding among his sheep. Having thoughts and emotions that impaired the rule of the kingdom was dangerous. Conforming was a virtue. Insurrections must be suppressed. Even when they were within him.

He sprang up from the edge of his bed. Even with her back turned toward him, he knew once again that his wife had closed her dry eyes, pleading for an earlier death to serenade her to permanent sleep.

But he survived another night. The sheep still had their Shepherd.

His eyes scanned part of his kingdom. Everything in his bedroom was his. The queen with her back to him. The memories of him with his lovers. But the group of flies moving about his room reminded him of something or someone else.

Where was the cloaked presence hiding? The one that made the hairs on his neck and arms stand up.

Even with the ever-present loneliness that accompanied him and his wife, there was always another in his bedroom.

It was there.

It was somewhere in the room.

He just could not see it. His heart raced, thinking about what was under his bed again.

With his fists clenched, he yelled, "They cannot stop me."

Anne flinched as his voice echoed in the room.

With trembling hands of fury, he stormed out of his bedroom and slammed the door shut. He walked to his room, where only those he approved of were allowed to enter.

His feet pounded. He screamed.

"When can I rest?"

There was no one around as he reached his den. Soon he would be safe in the room of refuge away from the refuse. He proclaimed his superiority on the shelves and in piles that filled the room. He displayed all his books to remind him and others of his vast knowledge. So much knowledge. So many philosophies. This was his religion. With, of course, the assistance from the Dark Light. It was here that he gave over his life and was filled with so much power.

He ran to a table with piles of books and paper. One by one he slid each item off the table. He threw them onto the floor when he decided they did not serve his purpose. He ran to the next area within the room.

It has to be here.

He had no concern as he cluttered his floor with the discarded during his hunt. He bent forward and clenched his fists over his head and screamed, "Where is it?"

Many flies gathered on one side of his room.

He swatted at some of the flies that hovered over him on that side. His eyes opened farther to the other side of the room. "It must be on the opposite side!"

He stomped to the opposite side of the room and found that book buried beneath greater desires. He grabbed the Geneva Bible that one of his men had ripped from the hand of a rebellious corpse. He tore it into two, which he then multiplied into many more pieces. He threw all the subversive lies on the floor. The lies that separated them from their King.

With a smile he stood over the pieces that looked like remnant parts of ship debris floating on the ocean. He put his hands on his hips. Looking down his nose, his lips parted into a snarl. With a storm building within, he spat on the subversive propaganda. He pointed a finger at the floating debris and wondered how they dared to divide his church against him.

Let them all die.

"I will break you before you break me."

His right hand, as heavy as iron, clenched and pounded the table before him like a clap of thunder. The burden of the divine right of king buckled his knees. He pulled out a chair and collapsed into it. The chair was not his permanent throne, but only he could will his throne to follow and obey him.

A cold heaviness engulfed him.

Memory of the nightmare entered into him again.

In the nightmare, he was at the site of broken ships on the ocean. Debris was strewn across a wide area. He searched for the survivors.

But not to save.

He moved his eyes to and fro, like a little boy looking for the monster that chased him. But James was a man now. He was strong now. His head darted in quick chaotic directions. He heard himself saying, "Where is he?"

Through the storm-enraged waves and the dark-engulfed sea, two adult males flailed in the water. One older and the other one younger. Then, as if a hand blocked his vision, he could not see any other clues.

Move away, hand. Which is the murderer?

The king trembled, remembering the booming voice coming from the abyss under the ocean. "I will kill the younger one. His kind must be stopped. You will kill the older one."

Then the voice from below changed to one of fear and concern. "No, someone is preventing me from seeing . . . someone else is here . . ."

Then a hand surfaced from the ocean, searching with a knife.

Everything in the dream moved faster. Compelled to move to another area, James now trod water in another part of the surrounding debris. He dove underwater. He could not find another person. There was no one else.

"I killed Tyndale. Rogers. Cranmer. Many others. It must be destroyed," the voice then said.

James' chest hurt, and he could not control his trembling. His body shook as power entered into him.

The voice spoke again. "I stopped the others, and I will attack the ones on the ships. You must not fail."

Do I follow a voice that kills, or disobey it and be killed?

He stopped thinking of the nightmare and whispered to himself, "I know someone is coming after my son and me. I will not allow the bad seed to destroy my family line. For the sake of God and His kings."

Power through the generations came to dwell in James, even before his birth. Before the beginning, he was born to be king. There were only sheep and shepherds. His intellect reflected the divine advantage of not being raised by sheep but by the most gifted teachers of his time. Someone had to be lifted up to shepherd all the lost sheep.

But what recourse did a mighty king have when the ignorant resisted truth? Left to themselves, they would sin against God and destroy each other. What could the Shepherd do when the sheep resisted the source of their faith?

"Where is he?"

"He is now closer to you and your son. A wolf among your sheep."

He listened to the god who hid in the Dark Light for counsel. The same one who'd told him that he had appeared to and counseled his ancestors. Even with resistance against the king, the Shepherd remained steadfast.

The rebels against God were becoming more of an annoyance to him, like the many flies that followed his appetite. They had forced his lovers to leave the country. James was only happy to return the favor. He would hunt his enemies down. Especially the ones in the nightmare. He would continue to imprison them. Force them to obey. For James, to fail was to fail God.

He'd gained power multiple times in the past by stepping into and savoring the bloodied bellies of the deer he'd hunted. But to have more control, he needed to gain more power from the god who hid in the Dark Light. Soon he would manipulate this god in all His glory to give James more strength to save others. Though there were bloodstains on James' hands that sometimes kept him awake at night, it was time to gain more from the giver of power. The living power that used James as a tool in its hand.

He stepped outside onto a patio of the top floor of his fortress. He scanned his kingdom below and before him. He walked to the edge of the balcony and raised his hand. He pointed and summoned the living power toward the Atlantic Ocean.

The living power that would soon turn into a fist that would break the dreams of an enemy into two.

CHAPTER 39

ABRAHAM

On the Mayflower
1620

It was day sixty-five of seventy-six. There was no line from a ship for Abraham's rescue. He yearned for home and the security and comfort of the king determining his days for him.

There was something hidden in another part of his heart home, underneath where the closet was. Tucked away in a hidden basement.

Will my secret sins haunt me during my final breath? O beautiful bride, I prayed that I could have lived long enough to say to you how I am sorry. My children, how I wish I could gather you up and relive those lost days and live as if brand new. This, I shall dream.

Abraham looked up from his Bible reading, his candle flickering beside him. The wick was short. The light still burned. The candles of the others would continue beyond the life of his. A renewed hope and perseverance spread through all in the ark. Word spread they would be at the halfway mark of their travel within a few days. Susanna and Elizabeth had resolved that they would carry differing viewpoints to new shores. If they remained disciplined, they would have enough food. For the first time, a sense that they were all going to make it united them.

With the good news, many prayed to their God in a song of thankfulness. Abraham and Jonathan smiled at each other and tried to sing along with them. With a sincere joy for the others, Abraham laughed, as no one could have convinced him that he would one day be on a ship going back to the New World.

With a sudden jolt mid-song, without gradual warning, the most powerful storm yet started. This one was different from the others. Within moments the *Mayflower* pitched and almost rolled completely from side to side. Abraham held his chest and throat as Jonathan looked like he had seen the corpse of a best friend. Jonathan then gathered himself to help Abraham.

The singing turned to screaming. Most fought to remain upright. Others accepted the power and rule of the ocean and remained lying on the ship's floor, trying not to slide into hard objects. Pain pierced Abraham's chest as he heaved for a breath.

Jonathan tried to hold Abraham with an arm wrapped around his back and shoulder. All were tossed and tumbled when the sound of a crack broke through and silenced the screaming. It sounded like a mighty tree breaking in half after refusing to bow down before the more mighty wind. The resounding crack echoed like a clap of thunder crossing an entire ocean ahead of them.

They were not alone.

It has found me. Spare the others. Take me.

This thunder was different from all others before.

This thunder was among them.

It was within the ship.

All heads turned to where the sound came from. Several staggered and stood underneath the origin of the crack, and gasps spread through those nearby. The main beam of the ship had broken, like a thin twig broken within an iron fist. Abraham could not move. They gathered underneath the broken beam like soldiers around a beloved comrade who had fallen in battle. The storm jolted the ship again. Trying to stay upright, they looked without hope at the main beam of the broken *Mayflower*. Disjointed. Out of its proper place. Their brokenness in full display. The vessel's life now sacrificed and punished for them. The splintered beam was separated and broken into two main pieces.

This was the end. The attack disabled the old ship, and it would soon sink with all aboard.

Abraham put his hands around his throat to help free it for breathing. Jonathan was not moving on the floor and unable to help.

No one could join the two pieces together. How could they possibly continue on their journey and survive the storms and the lengthy distance still in front of them? With the main support beam of the ship now broken into two?

They could not.

In the mad commotion of panic, several trampled over Abraham and Jonathan on the floor. Some ran topside so as not to be trapped by the water coming to sink their hope. Many of Abraham's letters were gone. Laboring for each breath, he was unable to stand. As he fumbled for his letters, something else was missing. His wedding ring had slipped off. His heart raced as he groped to find his belongings.

His ring was gone. Gone. A righteous fire burned through his veins. Though he knew no one on board had taken it, he clenched his fists, ready to find the invisible thief who had stolen his ring.

The same one who had stolen his days.

Abraham jumped up and walked over to where death resided over them. He pushed those in his way aside and moved to the center of the circle of onlookers.

His hands unlocked from fists. He looked up at the broken beam. Like God and man, there was no way to reconnect them.

While thinking of Samson's story in the Bible, he grabbed each part of the broken beam, for once trying to put things together. With all his strength and the storm calmer, he pushed the two pieces toward each other. He screamed in pain from the cuts inflicted by the splintered beam as he used all his strength.

The pieces of the beam did not move. With all his power, he could not unite the two parts.

Several tried to help Abraham, but the beam did not move. Others checked to see if the ship was taking on water yet. Children were crying. Somebody sobbed from the back of the circle surrounding the fallen comrade.

"Is this it? Are we done?"

A mother holding her crying child asked, "Did freedom die for my son and my daughter?"

A weary-looking father said, "Perhaps Elizabeth is right. We are not yet halfway. We may not be able to make it to the New World, but we might still have enough time to go back home, as it is a shorter distance."

Jonathan remained on the floor, still appearing to have seen a ghost. On one side, a few yelled that they should return home. On the other side, the majority cried that they could not go back.

Abraham pivoted his head between both sides while holding the two parts of the beam. William moved from the back of the gathering to the front. The formerly mocking crew rushed down, with some who had run topside, and examined the broken. By the look of dire death dominating their countenance, the situation was without hope. Hope was abducted, and death was now the tyrannical ruler.

Abraham collapsed, as he had used all his strength and could not stand. He crawled next to William and pulled on his breeches for reassurance.

I can see death in their eyes. I can see through the windows of their eyes death's image within them looking and snarling back at me. It is both residing beside me and inside of me! I see death! Its multiple fists have multiple death grips wrapped around each of our spirits. It will not let go until we are on the ocean bottom of our watery graves. God, spare them and take me. Remove the curse. Like Jonah in the Bible, throw me overboard.

Abraham's chest pounded so hard that he winced. His last bond with his bride had slipped away from his hand. It was gone. With his life. With his hope.

"This cannot be the end," Abraham said to William, searching for any sign of hope.

William did not look him in the eye.

The ship yawed around a new abnormal axis. It creaked in a different way, like an old broken branch still bending in a strong wind. The crew, like battle-worn witnesses of many horrors, looked like they had said goodbye to a dying comrade broken in half.

Abraham stood up, looking for hope. A large amount of water splashed down below from above. His ring finger was bare. The *Mayflower* was broken. His last chance to see Humility was gone. The God that most on board worshiped had shown Abraham that his sins permanently separated him from his love. They could not be reconnected. Whatever slivers of marriage remained were broken in two.

It was all gone.

Abraham collapsed to his knees. He wiped his face. Could anyone help? Some had withdrawn and left to die unseen. Where was Jonathan behind the sea of legs? Could William, his teacher of all the verses, give a splinter of hope one last time?

Abraham could see a fire arising in William. A narrow beam of light. He stood firm as the ship swayed back and forth with the still-present but almost-forgotten storm.

"Enough! We shall pray to the God who has faithfully brought us this far."

A mother holding her children yelled with her fist clenched, "Yet, Lord, Thou canst save!"

Several lay facedown next to Abraham. In pure desperation, many laid their hands in prayer upon the splintered beam. With pleading and broken hearts, they begged God to heal their broken vessel.

As they prayed, Abraham had the strange sense that a memory was placed into his mind. The Geneva Bible he'd taken from Steven's house. Steven's written message in the Bible for Abraham. He remembered reading, "Imprinted at London by the Deputies of Christopher Barker 1599."

Abraham held his breath.

Imprinted.

The printing press.

The printing press!

"The great iron screw from the printing press!" Abraham proclaimed.

"The great iron screw!" someone else yelled.

With death accelerating the hourglass, they quickly searched with what lighting was available. There it was. Stored away to help the illegal rebel voice in the New World.

Many screamed and pleaded for help. A few yelled

their doubts. They moved with little time to spare.

"Hurry!"

"How can this work?"

"Only God can save!"

They carried the great iron screw with a hush among the gathered and lifted it up. Several screamed prayers of desperation. Was this it? Their last hope?

Abraham helped lift it to the point where the beam was broken. They gripped the great iron screw and turned it. It stopped turning when it encountered the resistance of the wood. More hands helped support it. They held it more firmly. They twisted it harder into the wood. It pierced the two separate pieces. They turned it more. Were the broken parts moving together?

"Push harder!"

"We can't lift it up by ourselves!"

More entered into deeper prayer.

The sea raged as if trying to stop them. A few men holding the screw fell. The remaining staggering men yelled as they held it for their friends.

"God, show us Your power."

Those who fell recovered and staggered back up. Stronger.

Abraham closed his eyes with the sound of wood cracking. Would the two pieces hold up?

God, please don't kill me. Don't kill us.

With a powerful thunder crack, the two beams united into one.

It was finished.

The attack was thwarted.

The *Mayflower* jolted one more time as all fell down.

The storm. The screaming. The pleading ceased.

There was a deathly silence.

The last light went out.

In the quiet, reverent darkness, a single person could be heard sobbing. Soon another. The floodgates opened as many wept in unison with heads bowed down with bended knees.

All released a simultaneous eruption of shouts and laughter in joy. They screamed and sang with the tongues of angels as they celebrated the unexpected rising of their fallen friend at his funeral.

Abraham stood and scanned the area. There was enough light to see every knee was bent.

The hand that had them in its grip was stayed but still present somewhere nearby.

Still searching and gathering strength.

CHAPTER 40

ABRAHAM

On the Mayflower
1620

Dear Humility,

My friends were saved from certain death a few days ago. It is day seventy of seventy-six for me, and I regret that I was born. For what purpose am I? I have run as far as possible with my life tethered to the king and the hound of death stalking me. They will soon find me. Like an escaped prisoner, God will find me and throw me into hell. Or He is an unjust God.

Those saved days ago on this ship left their familiar king and lives for another King. They live in a dangerous world. They feel freed from the security of a tyrannical parent to a life with faith in a future that is unsafe and unknown.

I acclimated my life to the king's desires over my own. I now struggle with how shall I live with my last few days?

At this moment, we are not in the midst of another storm, so I can record my thoughts and studies. William has taught me much about Scripture. I must pass this along to you to make amends for my past denials. Please teach the children the story.

Then Pharaoh gave this order to all his people: "Every Hebrew boy that is born you must throw into the Nile, but let every girl live." —Exodus 1:22

The ancient hunt continues today.

After the flood, over the course of many generations, the children of this God multiplied in great numbers living in Egypt. Soon the Egyptians feared their numbers and were consumed with terror that they would join their enemies and overtake them.

I believe that Satan was trying to prevent the birth of the seed that would end Satan's rule promised in the garden with Adam and Eve. Pharaoh, the Egyptian leader, became a living vessel for Satan. In a violent response, Pharaoh enslaved the Hebrews. He killed all the young boys to murder any possibility of the prophecy of the Savior coming true.

There was much wailing and weeping as Pharaoh slaughtered the Hebrew children. Survivors cried out, for they believed there was one who was prophesied to save them.

As I read through Scripture, I learned that though God did not crush those killing His children immediately, he did something else. Despite the king's murdering of many of the young boys his age, Moses was born and escaped immediate murder outside the womb. The deliverer was delivered.

After his birth, Moses, protected by God, was sent adrift in a vessel of protection on the Nile to escape the murderers hunting for him. Pharaoh's daughter saved him! She took God's deliverer of the slaves into the home of the slave master, Pharaoh! What would happen next with Moses, God's possible seed, or at least a helper for the seed? He was now in the home of the vessel of Satan that was seeking to destroy the prophesied Savior.

What will become of us in this vessel floating on our Nile while Satan roams the earth? Can the king not see that my friends will be raised, right under his reign, across the Atlantic? Or is the king pursuing us to kill us in the open sea, where we have no recourse? Is there someone on board who is to betray us?

On this ship, no one has sinned as I have sinned. The ocean opens its mouth, expecting to be fed. I pray that your God would hunt me down for what I did, and not the others. I have cursed this ship with my presence.

I deserve death at the bottom of the sea for my sins.

But yet I live for a few more days.

I will not see a day past my allotted number, and I will not be able to see you again. Please know that I greatly desired to be with you and the children. Just one more time. I have heard of the grace of your God, but I do not deserve. Your forgiveness of me would be the greatest miracle of all. I am sorry I ruled like the king and prevented you and the children from reading the full Story because it threatened my own.

I must share with you one last thing. I sense that it means something, and I want the content of the dream known beyond my limited days. Please take these words and spread them.

I have had a repeating maddening dream in the past, but last night I had a new dream.

I dreamed I was feeling very ill, and I had a terrible stomach ailment that pained me. The pain came in wave after wave. I was carrying something. It was dwelling inside me and pushed outward. I looked down, and I was birthing a baby! I was suffering with great pain when I saw a small head coming out from me, screaming and calling out, as she looked upward to the heavens. She reached with a hand upward, as she could not free her other hand. It was as though she called out for assistance. This baby struggled and cried out to be birthed. Then a hand from someone above us came down and began pulling her out of me. I wailed in convulsive pain with the spilling of much blood, then met with great relief.

All three of us wept at her birth. Such beauty to behold! She was so new and beautifully different from any previous child I had ever laid eyes upon. It was as if she was the first one born of her kind! Such joy and grand hope for the future as we celebrated her birth! Such a beautiful reward for the pain and sacrifice in suffering.

But shortly afterward, minutes turned into generations. The baby in our hands then herself began giving birth to another baby. How can this be? But this second baby birthed from the first baby did not cry out. This baby stared at herself, as if gazing into a mirror. Can a baby marvel at herself? She looked at her arms and her hands, like a hunter examining his finest weapons. She attempted to care for herself independently of the hand, the first child, and myself. This second baby became agitated and began to strike me, the other child, and even drew blood on the hand reaching out to help her.

I shared this dream with the others, now convinced that their God used me to speak to others. What kind of God is this? They believed that the dream was for the sole purpose of praying for the future. We are to pray for the children of the future and give a warning to the children of the blessing.

Children of the future, are William and the others correct that you must choose between two paths, Creator or creation, the King or a king?

My desire is that my writings will document my days remaining in this life and proclaim the hope and the warning of my struggles with the two pathways. I pray that you, my love, and the others are correct. That there is another King, a God, who can, with almighty power and love, take what we meant for evil and turn it into good.

Child of the future, as you are reading this, I am from years in the distant past speaking to you now. Son and daughter of liberty, will you listen to the burden placed into me from years past to the present, for your future?

Though I do not know this God, and I do not know you, I pray for you as you read this from the distant past. My voice calls out to you, my future brothers and sisters. Do you hear me calling you in my final days? Though many voices crying in pain haunt me, do you hear my voice echoing from the mountain top through the open fields, the cities, and into each home? Calling you to return home to the Father of those I dwell with. I can only pass along what I have learned from the others around me. In their imperfections manifested daily, they say they can only place their faith in this God of theirs. I tap you on the walls of your heart to open up and remember their God and the love, or you will remember the tyranny of Satan.

Perhaps William is correct. Is it not a trap to fight for the belief that creation can set you free from the slavery that creation itself has created? Should we not want the Creator over His creation?

Listen to the Author as He converses His story.

Do not forget.

Remember my chains!

Acknowledge yours.

Who can possibly pay the cost to free the slaves?

Though I cannot be with you, know that I loved you, Beautiful Bride. Beautiful Caleb and Rebekah.

Children, remember your Father.

I love you,

Abraham

CHAPTER 41

JAMES

England
1620

King James studied the priest and his assistant as they prepared for his son's baptism. The assistant surprised James, as he was younger than most of the other men who worked with the priests.

James's son cooed in the king's arms. His son already wooed many, as all at the ceremony locked eyes on him and paid no attention to the king or the men of religion. James shielded his son's eyes from the sun halfway up the sky.

The priest's assistant opened his arms to take the king's son.

James moved his son forward but then retracted him back to himself. The religious man's exposed and extended arms reminded James of his previous cutting rituals with another priest. *I remember what entered into me. I was never the same afterward. I remember what the Dark Light told me. The murderer was a wolf among my sheep. The murderer was coming after my son and me.*

The king pointed to one of his men, and the servant moved the priest and his assistant to the side.

James gazed at his reflection in his son's eyes. He whispered a prayer into his ear and lifted him up to the heavens. King James continued the ceremony alongside one lover to his right and another to his left.

His dying Anne stood, with help, behind them. She tried to smile.

The king pointed to the priest's assistant. One lover grabbed the assistant's sleeve and pulled him farther to the side. The king dismissed all in attendance except his lovers, the religious man's assistant, and Anne.

As he gazed at his son lifted up, King James closed his eyes. He savored the wielding of a new power in his hands that he had long waited for. He waited for God to give him a premonition.

In the daytime vision, images passed through his mind. A man of religion assaulted a young boy in a different era, sometime in the future. The boy grew, and years later the boy watched the murder of his father on the floor. The king saw a house church opposing him and his son.

The images stopped. The power beyond his own pulsated through his body. Once upon a time, he was alone. But since his cutting-ritual pact made with the Dark Light in his youth, he always felt the presence with him, executing its own desires.

The power coursed through him like a cold ocean wind destroying ships and shaping the land. It was as if the king had been pulled away from the scene with his body still standing. With one hand, the body held his son, and the other clenched in a fist. He spoke with a new voice inside the old body that had been waiting for this moment.

"You will not be hunted down," he promised the baby. "I now give to you the power that was in the garden, through the ages, through kings and queens. I now pass this into you. I will be cloaked within mine as I set my enemies against themselves."

Just as quickly, the cloaked one disappeared, and the king returned to his standing body. He wiped his eyes. With trembling lips, he cleared his throat and cleared the path for his voice to return as a steward.

Sometimes James did not like it when the voice took over him, and other times he sought it. Who should rule over the king?

"I am a voice in the wilderness. I proclaim these truths. No one will hurt you, my son. I oppose those who oppose us. I prepared the path for you and your offspring as we live eternally. New life is now released through you and your offspring. We will cause all to submit to the kingdom, and the light of the kingdom will be from shore to shore."

He held his son closer as he searched for any assassins. His heart broke as he looked at the innocence of regality in his arms. A teardrop fell upon his boy as he remembered there were two families at war.

So many have died. So many more will die.

He knew there were offspring of sedition in hiding. It did not escape him that a ship was carrying members of the opposing family to his New World. They were tools in his hands to bring prosperity and expand the kingdom. But God told him that enemy life would be running its course through the hourglass. Even if they made it to the distant shore, the king would still be with them.

He let the rebels believe they escaped, when in reality they were simply given a longer leash to plant and spread the seeds of his kingdom to another land. He was expanding his garden to overcome the Resistance. If he decided to let them live, the king would use those who survived the journey to create a land to his liking.

In his image.

The Dark Light fed upon his rage and summoned James to seek more.

He held the assistant without a voice. *He appears to be in his early twenties. He could be the boy I was told about who would one day come to kill me. Is this the murderer, the wolf hidden as a sheep? The one also after my son?*

King James continued his prayer.

"It is finished. By the hand of God, the seed is now in both of us to pass on to the future family and our kingdom. We will overcome the weaker family."

The king, fully engaged with his son, watched with the corner of one eye. Anne walked away a few feet with assistance.

She stopped and turned toward the gathering. Her fists clenched and then opened. She whispered a prayer. "Out from Israel, England, Africa, and the natives already there, and from every tribe, tongue, and nation, may there be a new land."

The king ignored his wife and walked with his son toward the young man of religion. The man trembled and mumbled a sentence under his breath—only part of "revolution" could be heard.

The king pointed to one of his guards, and the guard pulled out a knife hidden under the clothing of the young man. The guard used the man's blade and stabbed the young man of religion in the back. The man of the king pulled out the knife from the corpse and held it for the king. The king smeared the blood on the blade onto his hand and cut his finger on the blade. He ordered his servant to take the knife away to hide.

What have I done? Did I just kill the assassin? I never wanted to cause problems with the religious fanatics. Have I just made things worse?

The king raised his glistening hand to the sky. He looked at his son in his left hand and the blood on his right hand.

The voice returned and spoke through the king. "Another one dead. Now to find the murderer."

CHAPTER 42

PADA

On the San Juan Bautista
July Going into August 1619

Through Pada's blurry vision, Christian looked puzzled as the main captor ran away after kicking Pada in the head. The main captor fled for his life, yet no visible person chased him. Limited by his chains, Christian moved closer to see Pada better.

Christian's face went pale. "Pada, are you okay? Speak to me."

Pada could not move.

"Lord, please give him more time. Free us. Heal us. Perfect God, use the broken to bring at least a shadow of your freedom, even a glimpse, to all shores," Christian prayed.

With yelling and banging topside, Pada tried to blink his eyes several times. Christian turned his head frantically from side to side as the sound of water entered their deck.

More yelling and sounds of additional feet moved above them. Someone threw things, and then feet moved, as if a fight had broken out. If they had run aground, that would not explain the sounds of people running and fighting.

Pada could feel his body involuntarily jerk and shake. He vomited on himself and then gagged and coughed.

"Turn your head so you don't choke!" Christian pleaded.

Pada opened his right eye farther upon hearing Christian's voice. He coughed again as the shade of blue in his arms began to disappear.

Pada spoke between breaths. "I know . . ." Cough. ". . . .In is with me . . ." Cough. Cough. ". . . .Who the dream . . ." He turned his head to vomit again.

He opened his eye, now fully awake. "Where was I? What happened?"

"He attacked you. And I believe someone attacked our ship. Are you okay?"

Pada squinted. "I cannot see out of my left eye—I cannot see. And I cannot see as well as I used to out of my other eye . . . my head hurts." He tried to hold his head but could not free his hands.

"I prayed for you, my friend. Your role in prayer is not done yet." Christian's voice cracked.

"My left eye is not working. I don't think I can hear out of my left ear."

Tears ran down his eyes as Pada blinked his eyes to clear his vision. "I believe God spoke to me. He gave me the dream again. Each time I see more, and I saw more this time."

Christian shook his head. "I think we are sinking. Do you hear the water coming in?"

They turned their heads to see water entering. Pada told him an abbreviated version of his dream until they both heard more yelling and more fighting. Footsteps moved into other parts of the ship. Fast and heavy stomps moved closer.

They glanced toward each other with wide eyes. What was going to happen to them in the next few moments?

Somewhere, they heard the sound of water entering the ship getting louder.

"I don't know how much time we have," Christian said. "We may drown before they free us from our chains. The pirates are probably seeking treasures and things for stealing and trading. Our captors were not prepared to fight and die for us. If we do not sink and drown first, I do not know how the pirates will respond to finding us here."

Pada spoke while trying to catch his breath. "I saw a woman. But not clearly. She was in the water with me—in my dream. Someone was going to attack her, and I was told to pray for her. My purpose was to pray for this woman. But she was not alone—someone else was with her. Someone else was with both of us and . . . God wanted me to pray."

He stopped talking to breathe. *God, this is Your story, not mine. You are the Author. Thank You for my role.* Multiple feet neared with the sound of water entering.

Two English privateering ships working together, the *Treasurer* and the *White Lion*, attacked the *San Juan Bautista* as it headed to Veracruz, looking for silver and gold. After several minutes, the fighting stopped. Only new voices yelling and demanding things from the captors could be heard.

Pada turned his head, and the first man to step down from topside covered his nose with his forearm and elbow and then slipped and fell on the fluids on the floor. He cursed aloud as another man following him also stumbled. The rest of the group of men following laughed at the sight of their fallen brethren. They laughed even harder when the men who slipped stood, their clothing a darker, smellier shade than moments before. The two men who'd slipped looked down at themselves and then at each other. They both shoved and pointed at each other and laughed.

The men who had not slipped exercised extra caution with each step as they tried to maneuver themselves onto the lower deck. They stepped firmly as they held on to any immobile part of the ship, and they continued laughing.

Then . . . silence.

Audible gasps ended the laughing as they discovered the chained cargo. Their wide eyes screamed of shock with terror. Some extended the coverage of their noses to their eyes. Another gasp escaped when the cargo moved.

Someone lying down moaned for help. Several

men stood motionless. Others shook their heads. Some bent forward and involuntarily added to the bodily fluids on the floor.

The ship leaned sideways, and water gushed in and covered the lowest part of the deck. The leaders of the new men staggered and arrived on their deck and yelled at the other men to free those in the water quickly. The men tripped over themselves and the captives. More water cascaded in. The ship listed. They loosened the chains on the prisoners in the water, but a few of the freed men and women did not move. The men tried to help them up—it was too late.

Pada shook his head. *Perhaps they are free now.*

More water rushed in, and the new men took off the chains and released the captives—those still alive. The new men pulled them upright and steadied them as each captive's legs buckled and swayed, like a foal walking for the first time. Cries of pain echoed through the ship as stiff limbs moved for the first time in weeks toward the blinding light above.

Though not all the captives spoke English, they all understood "Move! Move!"

With each step, Pada's head hurt more. He moaned in pain as the men pushed the captives topside.

Unable to cover their eyes when exposed to the light of the day, the prisoners moaned. Pada wanted to lie down and hold his head, as it pounded with each heartbeat. He still could not see out of his left eye or hear out of his left ear. Something dripped down the side of his head.

Pada's head pounded harder. The right side of his body was weaker and more difficult to control. His heart burned with betrayal as one side of his body fought to live, while the other side wanted to stop fighting. He straddled a wall, with one side in living light and the other in a dead shadow.

He could not stay on the wall forever. He would fall to one side, and if he tried to remain where he was, his inaction would choose for him.

After adjusting to the light, Pada tried to turn his head in all directions. The *San Juan Bautista* gently rocked, blackened from fire and attack. Captors he had not seen in weeks from other parts of the ship lay motionless. The new men ignored a small fire on the bow. They yelled at others below, and Pada thought that some of the men had slowed down the amount of water entering. How was it still floating? On his right side, even through blurry vision, a large hole on the top part of the ship made itself known.

Something caught his eye through the large hole. The main captor who'd attacked him stood. The last time, the captor ran for his life. Now he stood with a strange expression on his face—impaled with a beam from the ship that had broken and splintered, the man was now motionless, suspended in the air.

The new men reapplied the captives' chains. Two men, each a captain of their respective attacking vessels, scanned the human cargo topside and then separated themselves from the others to converse in private. One of the captains, whom the others called Abe, was older than the other captain and had long hair and a beard, and the other was shorter and clean shaven. Their heads moved up and down and then side to side. After several moments, it appeared they struck an agreement.

The sound of water entered below at a slower rate. The ship listed to the port side, and several lost their balance. Banging below echoed as workers tried to save the ship from sinking. They quickly divided the captives into two groups, with each going into a separate attacking ship. Because many had already died, they placed about twenty prisoners into the ship they called the *White Lion*, including Pada and Christian.

Somebody needed to save them before they were taken captive into another ship. Pada took an interest in the older of the two captains, pulling on his long hair and beard with his left hand. Pada had never seen a left-handed white man before. Could he free them? The captain turned his back to the captives. He put his hands into his now fuller pockets and stared at the distant sea.

After distributing their newfound wealth, the new captors kept Pada and Christian joined to each other.

What was I thinking? No one will save us. The left-handed older captain went onto the other ship and left Pada and some of the others to depart on the *White Lion*.

On the *White Lion*, they did not tell the captives their destination. They did tell them that when they reached their next stop, they would serve their new masters for seven to ten years, depending on their master. Down below, the mentality of their new captors differed from the captors in the previous ship. But they were still taken against their will to another land, away from home and apart from their families.

They took the twenty-odd in a ship not designed to be a slave ship, but the chains were the same.

"Where do you believe they will take us?" Pada asked Christian.

"I do not know if we are like the Hebrews leaving Egypt to a promised land. Or are we like the Hebrews to be enslaved in Egypt? Is it both? I do not know. Perhaps we will play a role like the Hebrews crossing the Jordan? What has God told you?"

"You know that God has spoken to me—you tell me."

"I will be the first to tell you that most of the time, I do not know what God is doing. But He is not idle. Only a good God can turn what was meant as evil into a good that can save. I don't understand it, but at a later tomorrow, I know that He will have His way."

Pada could not respond and turned his head away from Christian.

Christian prayed with his voice cracking. "Father, I am so weak. I do not know if I can go any farther. But I know You have a role for each of us. Give me the faith to know that You have all things under Your control. Do not forsake us."

In the silence, Pada pivoted toward his friend.

Christian tried to blink the tears away as his hands clenched next to Pada's. He then continued. "And, Father, give Pada the strength to trust Your rulership and not his own. Show him that he cannot rule on his own. It has to be Your way and not his. Give him new eyes to see and new ears to hear."

Pada closed his eye. Thoughts flooded his mind. Amara. His parents. His village. Luanda. The ocean. The sun shining with the birds flying above him.

The beautiful birds.

Pada was fading away.

CHAPTER 43

ABRAHAM

On the Mayflower
1620

His sins permanently separated him from his love. His ring was gone. His eye was gone. He would not see his love again.

She was gone.

According to Abraham's calculations, it was the eve of his death.

How do I live when my life is down to my final hours? It was late at night approaching the later months of 1620, as the patience of death waiting over Abraham was expiring. As he scanned those around him, what was all this suffering for? Each would eventually die. What then was gained?

With his stomach grumbling for hope, Abraham turned to Jonathan. "I was never this hungry with the king. We are running out of food. It is even more difficult for me to see food withheld from the crying children."

"We must save our food. We don't know for sure how much longer we have to go."

"Is it selfish to want what I once had? Will anyone remember our suffering, or will we end up being forgotten history?"

Abraham closed his eyes to summon more strength. "We had food. Water for drinking and bathing. No scratching until our skin bled. A dry place to live. Were we better off dying back home?"

He moved a long strand of hair out of his face with his left hand, rubbed his beard, and thought about his life before he stepped aboard the *Mayflower*. "I remember hunting months ago in a remote area, when I observed a beautiful eagle. What a lovely and powerful sight. It was resting on a large, vertical piece of wood, a beam someone stuck into the ground."

He paused to collect his thoughts. "The eagle would fly in every direction but always returned to find its rest back on its perch on the old splintered beam. What a wonderful majestic sight to see this beautiful eagle soar and fly through its sky. One time after it had returned to its beam, other birds sharply veered downward toward the eagle to dislodge it from its perch. They tried to attack the eagle."

Jonathan arched his eyebrows. "What happened to the eagle?"

"When under attack, it did not move. It was as though this eagle could not be moved. It stood without any fear and continued its undisturbed rest. What a sight to behold as I witnessed the birds swooping down toward the eagle on several different occasions, and it did not move! The attacking birds dared not touch the eagle. When the birds eventually left with only failures, I then saw the eagle fly proudly away, and it left its rest. It flew down into the valley where the hunters lay in wait. When it was out of my view, several hunters below fired their weapons. I could not see the result. I left wondering what happened to the eagle."

William overheard Abraham and stood next to Jonathan. He asked Abraham to write down what William was about to pray with the others.

"Lord, forgive us of our pride," he prayed. "It is only with You that we live and breathe. Children of the future, you must heed the right voice to get back to where you once were. You are no more virtuous or possess any more wisdom than your flawed ancestors. We are the ones who will suffer to plant the liberty of God, and we will have less to gain of the fruit of liberty that we will be planting for you to consume. This fruit was grown and fertilized with the blood and tears of those before you. What many will die for, you will hold in your hands. You will have the freedom to choose that which your heart desires. Learn from history, and choose better than the fruit of Adam and Eve. Return to your Father." William sat back down.

Jonathan rubbed his chin. "Even if we are successful, there will be a day when many will tear us out of the pages of history. Many will choose to forget what we have done and will only remember our imperfections and our transgressions."

William shook his head. "I must ask—will they remember the truth when faith in the false gods of money and kings collapses? Will they remember the truth when the fear of the people turns to the false security of the same leaders that purposed the fall?"

The ship jerked with the beginning of another violent storm. The sea sickness was a rising tide within Abraham's mouth. Many became ill again, and several slipped and fell on the mixture of fluids. The odor of the sickness in small, dimly lit quarters seemed to be more troubling this time for everyone.

Abraham had done his calculations. Was this to be his last memory on his last day?

William watched him. Jonathan had somehow fallen asleep. Abraham needed a place to close both eyes for the last time.

There was only one place of refuge. A separate location from the rest of the ark. The small part of the cube-shaped food-storage area that only a few people accessed. Spacious enough to lie like a large unborn in a small womb surrounded by stormy waters. A good place to die before William and Jonathan took his body away to drop to the bottom of the sea.

He had avoided the food-storage area for a reason. Would he find evidence of someone on board smuggling stolen goods for profit? Would there be stolen goods, like the other times he'd sailed? Or would he find evidence of someone stealing the depleting supply of food, as he feared?

The thought that someone was stealing food for their selfish hunger haunted him. Or worse, someone was working for the king with the sole purpose of aborting the birth within the womb and sending them into a hungry ocean grave? Even if they made it to the New World, were there some on board who would transform all his friends' efforts into the image of the king?

Death had finally cornered him. He had hours left to live, and he did not want to live waiting for death in the midst of his friends.

Abraham turned to William. "On this slippery deathbed, I do not lament that I am dying. No. I regret that I did not live. I did not treasure the days I was given. Death quietly ruled over me with both my compliance and without my knowledge. With living to die, there was both no life for me to live, nor life to give."

Abraham reached into his pocket and gathered his remaining belongings. He handed William his writings. William bent his head down and closed his eyes. "Tell my family that I love them and that I am sorry for what I have done. Can you pray to your Lord that he would not torment me for eternity? I fear entering the throne room and kneeling before him with all my sins fully exposed. I would bring lightning strikes upon this ship. I know there is a God I am accountable to."

He wiped his face. "Tell my lovely bride and my children of my mistakes, how I miss them, and my love for them."

Why did you ever love me? Goodbye, my love.

"What about your dream?" William asked as he lifted his head toward him.

Abraham's mouth opened and stayed open. He hesitated. "Did I tell you of my dream?"

With searching side-to-side eye movements, William paused and stood unmoved. "No. But the One who gave you the dream did."

Silence. Abraham turned his head away from William.

"All those verses. The stories. We have talked about them. The Author of Scripture is the same Author of your faith—and your dreams. He is the same God," William said.

"I was trying to stay afloat. As I looked to one side, I saw my ship sinking. When I looked to the other side, I saw land and my family," Abraham replied.

"But there were others with you . . ."

"I heard a multitude of voices coming from all around me. Coming from all the lands. All the waters. There were two other people with me in the water. And maybe one more? There was a young man and a young woman. Darker in color than me. They seemed to have a deep love for each other. It seemed like they had been apart for some time. Then hands from the abyss reached up from under the ocean surface and placed a knife at the woman's throat. The young man was initially concerned with saving himself but then saw the woman in a new light as the hands from below tried to kill her. Even with the storm and all the water from the ocean and the rain, it could not remove the bloodstains from the hand holding the knife. I could hear countless voices crying out! And I heard the young man praying."

Abraham placed his hands on his chest as it rose and fell with rapid succession, like he was running a great race. He took three deep breaths. "I heard many voices. They were in my language and many other languages I have not heard before. Voices from the past and present. Even voices from the future. The voices came from the hands. The voices cried out from the bloodstains on the hands from the abyss! The blood of Abel multiplied!"

He wiped his face. "But the hands felt a fear. They felt threatened. The hands could not see that the young woman was carrying something hidden under the surface of the water. I could not see it. It was in her grip. It was a weapon."

Abraham remembered more details as he described the dream. "But something distracted the hands away from the woman. There were prayers that were answered. The hands shifted focus to the life of the young man and many others like him. The young man closed his eyes as if he was praying—but now not for himself. The hands were distracted by the young man and his powerful prayers, and let go of the young woman."

"But there is more."

"I do not know what happened to the young woman . . . and the hands. I had the sense that I, too, was carrying something. Throughout my life, those hands from down below in the abyss have tried to end my life as well. I have felt them wrapped around my throat multiple times. But I saw something . . ."

Abraham finished with a whisper. "We were each sent with different roles. Each of us creatures of prey for the hunter. But distracted with his desire for blood, someone smuggled something past the hunter. I was there, along with the young man, to fulfill our roles. To pray for the will of God, for all in the water, and those to follow. Many others were also sent. Though the king tried, the king was distracted and could not stop all of us."

The ship jerked with a yaw and a pitch. Abraham crashed with force, facedown upon the floor. A strong downward pull yanked upon his depleting strength.

He saw no purpose in standing anymore, no match for the power of the ocean. Jonathan slept with a large handful of food—food that did not belong to him—falling out of his pocket.

Abraham lowered his head to the floor.

Where are you?

Tears fled his eyes. He rolled onto his back and put one hand on his chest and the other on his face.

Where is my box? I need my box.

He rolled onto his stomach and gently pounded his forehead on the floor.

Jonathan never grew past believing the king was his god. Jonathan did not try to kill himself. He was waiting for me to kill myself. He was the one informing the men of the king of our plans and whereabouts. How else did they know where I was all of those times? How else did they know about Steven being a threat to the crown? How did they know I was becoming a threat to the monarch, though I did not fully realize it myself? Where was Jonathan when they searched through my belongings at home? My friend did not take care of the man following me but made a deal with him—out of guilt over me or to prolong my life for more information. The possibility of a spy on board . . . the disappearing food . . . my eye . . . people killed . . . he is working for the king . . .

Abraham lifted and turned his head toward William for answers. William's face told him that he also saw the food spilling out of Jonathan's pocket.

Abraham stood and lunged toward the sleeping Jonathan. William thwarted him before he could connect with a swing.

"Do not be deceived. He is not the one you are fighting," William said sternly.

He looked around, then leaned toward Abraham. "Do not lose your vision. Satan always pulls on puppet strings and pits individuals and groups against each other as the puppet master smiles. Your hands are not clean either before your hour of death."

I used Jonathan to get me aboard the Mayflower. I was ready to leave Jonathan behind when we landed. My sins.

Abraham collapsed to the floor.

William stepped toward Abraham, bent, and returned Abraham's writings and Bible next to him. Abraham tilted his head away in the throes of sobbing.

He could not lift his head. What was he to do with the friend he loved? Should he kill Jonathan because of the innocents who died? Should he wake him up, confront him, and then strike him? Should he remain on the floor and just wait for his own coming death?

Jonathan betrayed me and sold me for pieces of silver.

Then Abraham remembered the silver and gold in his pocket.

With all his strength, he lifted his head partway toward William, who knelt beside him.

"Left to himself, Jonathan will eventually kill the traitor. Perhaps with your death, you will save him?" William asked as he placed his hand on Abraham's head. "Jonathan believes that doing the will of the king is the answer. But there is another King."

With faltering strength, and after William wiped the tears from Abraham's face, Abraham spoke with trembling lips and downcast eyes. "What does a man do after a betrayal with a kiss?"

"He gets up."

Ahead was the small cube space where he would die. Abraham struggled to his feet, pushed William aside, and limped forward with his book and writings. He staggered, with his world rocking underneath him. He dragged his leg and shoved away all living barriers between him and his remaining time.

Chased by generations of death, he could not out-run it. He was finally hunted down.

But he could confront it.

He groped for his final destination. From life within the space of his mother's womb to life outside of the womb, he crawled into the beating heart of the womb of the *Mayflower* to make his final stand.

CHAPTER 44

PADA

On the White Lion
August 1619

Pada tried to stay alive. Somehow there had to be time for someone to save him or help him. Pada and Christian shared much of their stories as days passed. Even in chains, Pada had moments of gratefulness for Goel sacrificing his life for him. Goel had been a great friend and had known what he was doing. If God was going to use Pada for His purposes, then God used Goel's life to help fulfill that.

Even in the dark moonlit night, he remembered the light in Goel as he attacked his attacker. The light attacked the dark. Goel had known something. He'd fulfilled a duty out of his love to assure more days of life for his friend. The light picked a fight with the dark.

Pada was told they would land first at Point Comfort and then at Jamestown. He was awake for the first landing but fell asleep before the *White Lion* landed at Jamestown. Pada was asleep and attacking an unseen attacker. Though asleep in one world, he also knew he shook his head from side to side and pulled on Christian's limbs in the other world.

He could not leave the dream world yet but heard his own voice mumbling in the other world. A warmth in his heart told him Christian was praying for him as he struggled, stuck between worlds. Something flowed over him. Like water rinsing him. Cleansing him.

He awoke. "I cannot fight any longer. Stop your praying. You win."

Christian laughed. "If you submit unto God, *you* win."

Pada closed his eyes. He tried to forget about the worsening headache. "I already told you about the first part of the dream with the one of divination. I will clarify the second part."

He readjusted his position with a moan to temporarily relieve pressure on his back. "There were two ships. There was a group taken away against their will in one, and a group that escaped in the other. The ships sank, and I was in the water. An unseen hand held me up. I heard someone breathing behind me. Here is what I know now . . ."

He opened his eyes. "I now know that the person behind me in the water—was Amara! It was Amara! She had left as well. Some of us freely chose to leave, and others were forcefully taken against their will. Their skins were a mix of various shades of dark and light. They spoke different languages. The one of divination had attempted to pit them against each other the whole time. But all wanted the same free-dom. What would they end up drinking? Life-giving water or the inferior substitute that never satisfied? I wept, knowing they took Amara away against her will. Or was she taken against her will?"

He blinked to clear his eye. "They took her away, but they could not see what I saw in her eyes. I saw something in her eyes! I saw a reflection of my hopes and dreams in her eyes, reflecting back to me. They did not defeat her. She was not dead. She still had life inside her. She had not given up. They could not take that away. While we were in the ocean amongst the pieces of the ships, she held on to a piece of a ship with one hand, and with her other hand . . . she held my hand again, as if we had just finished saying our marriage vows. She thanked me for the prayers that prepared the way for her in the future."

"My heart aches for what you have been through. There is so much more."

Pada closed his eye, trying to hold back the tears. "Now what I am about to say is not part of the dream. Several months ago, before the Imbangala attacked, God told me the Imbangala were coming."

"Did you think they were coming for your punishment?"

Still adjusting to seeing with one eye, Pada nodded and squinted to better his right eye. "We disobeyed our parents. Both sets of our parents did not allow us to see each other. They thought we were too young. Her parents thought I was trying to turn Amara against them. That I was trying to be her family and seducing her to run away and escape with me."

"But somebody found out about one of your secrets."

Pada sobbed. Christian waited until he gathered himself. "That is when the Judas approached me. He had been looking for us, as Amara and I were good at hiding from our parents. I wanted us to leave." Pada shook his head. "Me and Amara . . . we shamed our families with what we did. We should have waited until we got married. We then decided we were going to formally marry against our parents' wishes. Our parents thought we were moving too fast. Somehow, the Judas had found out about our secrets and threatened to tell our parents what we had done and what we were going to do. For the Judas' own profit, and for his own promised safety, he informed the Imbangala about whom to specifically take away before they attacked, to instill fear among the people."

"The Imbangala desire young people, especially young girls."

A calm rested on Pada. He spoke much slower, measuring each word. "If I did not tell him where I hid Amara, he would tell our parents what we had done. I could see a dark joy in him, and he wanted me to suffer. If I refused to tell him where she was, he would also inform the Imbangala about our parents, and they would take our parents away."

"I do not know what I would have done in your position. What did you do?"

Pada spoke even more slowly. "I refused to hand over Amara. I allowed them to take our parents away. I could not tell Amara what I had done. If I still did not tell him where she was after they took our parents away, the Judas told me that when they found her, he would tell her I helped the Imbangala take away her parents. Then they would eat her in front of me and allow me to live with what I had done."

He turned his head away from Christian as his face warmed. "I waited to see what they would do. After they took our parents away, I then tried to kill the Judas. To stop him from finding Amara."

A wave of sorrow and regret swept over him. "He may have found her. Amara is dead." Pada waited for the trembling to subside. "I should have stopped him from taking our parents, but I was too busy hiding and protecting Amara. I rebelled against our parents not wanting us to be together. I must confess—a part of me wanted our parents out of the picture so Amara and I could be together out of the reach of God. I thought with her parents out of the way, I could then protect her from what God had told me He was going to do with her."

His friend remained staring upward. Pada laughed. "Did you hear me? I tried to hide her from God. I lied to Amara. I allowed them to take away our parents for selfish reasons."

Pada cringed. "Did I kill them? The great Chinasa, Okoro, Abeni, Amara's father—all taken away. I took her away from her father, and I tried to take her from her heavenly Father! I thought I could rule over the Ruler of all creation! But she is not mine. She belongs to her Creator. My God, I give up—You win. You have rightfully punished me for what I did. Please forgive me. I give my life to you."

"Do you know what the dream is about?"

"God is punishing me for what I have done."

"No. Kings, the Imbangala, slave traders, Satan himself, cannot stop dreams from God placed into people's minds. God speaks first in His Word and also through His creation. Sometimes in His creation's dreams."

"No! He is punishing us."

"He has His own language, and He speaks how He wants to speak to draw us closer to Him. If He only wanted to punish you, He could have killed you a long time ago. He wants you. Like a lover courting us, we learn more as our hearts seek His. But He has to reveal His language for us to understand."

One of the captors walked by, as if looking for the source of a sound above the groaning and creaking of the wood. The man stopped, twisted, and walked toward Pada and Christian. He stopped next to them. Pada tried not to flinch with the captor's foot next to his head. The man looked down at Christian and Pada sleeping. The captor then turned away to continue his search among the others.

Pada and Christian opened their eyes.

Christian smiled. "They can try, but they can't stop God. Enemies don't understand Him. They don't know His language. His code is hidden in His Word.

His code is hidden in His children. They can't stop Him, and they can't stop His message, so they try to stop God's children. I do not know how much longer we will be on this side of home."

"Why am I here? Of what use is a sinner to God?"

"You confessed your sins and accepted God's payment for your sins. You are no longer condemned. God kept you alive so that you would be saved, to pray for Amara, and know He is with you. Pray to pave the way for how He is going to turn evil into good."

He paused again and looked around. When he knew it was safe, he whispered, "God will have His way with or without your help or interference. You will play a role in freeing slaves. But His enemies do not know—it is not just you they should fear."

"I was distracted. I believed my enemies were many. My parents, Amara's parents, our corrupt leaders, the Imbangala, our captors, even God above all others. In my head I was pitted against each."

"That's what the one of divination wants you to believe. To deceive you into drinking the lie that we can have power and control over God and then wield that power and control over different groups of people at our convenience and profit. The truth is that we can never have enough, and we come back to the one of divination thirsting for more."

Christian raised his chains again. "I refuse to take the bait. Ultimately, our battle is not against our captors. It is not against the competing powers. An adversary is hiding behind and within his puppets and groups of puppets."

He rattled the chains. "In God, no matter what happens to you, you eventually win."

Men from topside came below and removed some chains and kept some in place. They took the remaining few above, those still alive from the death march to the port city.

Even with half his vision gone, Pada smiled at the beautiful day up above. Such a beautiful land. A much different port than the one he'd left. The sounds pleased him. Waves gently crashed on the shore. People talked topside and on shore. Birds swooped up and down toward the ship. He saw other people, besides captors and captives, for the first time in weeks. They gathered at the waiting dock.

He made up stories in his head about those waiting at the shore for the crew on the ship. Focusing on their stories distracted him from the pain in his head. Wives, sons and daughters, mothers, and fathers perhaps waiting to see their loved ones for the first time in weeks. Members of the crew waved to waiting loved ones.

Where is my Amara? My family and home?

He dreamed of a place where he could be free in a new land. A new land of the free. A land where all could love and serve God and each other. Could there ever be such a heaven on earth? Yes. He had a dream.

But it was still not home.

He sensed the weight of Christian's stare, mixed with concern and prayers. This time he welcomed them as the pounding in his head worsened. He still could not see with his left eye. His legs nearly buckled. He did not know how much longer he could stand as the captors prepared for them to step off the ship.

Someone said it was now August of the year 1619 and that they were in Jamestown, but it seemed like one long day that did not stop to Pada. His head pounded more. The faces of people lining the dock at Jamestown became clearer. A large group waited at the pier, and a single person stood on shore apart from the others, closer to the dock. Even from a distance, his right eye locked with the woman standing off to the side.

In the beginning God created the heavens and the earth.

She was beautiful. If the Creator created her in His own image, He was beautiful. *Even when we try and destroy His beauty in His creation, He is still beautiful.*

She stood alone, wiping her eyes. The fine details of her face were not clear, but the color of her skin was different from his. Was she just watching the unloading of the darker-skinned people, or was she waiting for someone?

As they stood looking at each other, something entered into him. It was as if he received something from a stranger living a world away, but now near. A new inner strength supported his wobbling legs as the men pushed him toward the dock. Christian pulled up on their shared chains to help prop Pada up.

Pada remembered waiting as a child to be picked up at a friend's home. He remembered, he'd waited to be picked to play childhood games. He remembered his father one day saving him in the middle of a fight with a much larger foe.

The captives lined up.

And now his life was not his own. Maybe it was all a bad dream? Could his father somehow come to take him home to play again in the canyon? Could Mother finish her prayers under the baobab tree and then come and hug him and wipe away his tears? Could Amara greet him with a kiss and then walk hand in hand back home with their parents seeing them?

He remembered one of the last things his mother said: "I love you, and I have prayed that you would one day be as free as when you were running in the canyon as a little boy."

The other captives stood without noises. There was no crying. No more pleading for mercy. They all seemed related by blood, as they each had the same blank stare.

Pada tried to keep it all within but could not keep the sorrow captive. He heaved in heavy sobbing and tried to breathe to say one more thing.

"Mother . . . Father . . . please forgive me."

He shook his head to try to make his eye clear. Through blurry vision, he looked up and down at the lineup of human cargo. He wondered what he was worth to his captors. What was the value of a human being?

Who would pay for broken me? Who would pay for me after what I have done?

With one eye blind and the other seeing, he remained on the wall that divided him from the light and the darkening shadow. He could not remain straddling the wall.

In his mind, Pada jumped off.

He squinted and opened his eye fully. He prayed for all the voices that he heard cry out. For the beautiful woman off to the side. She would need new strength. He prayed for the love and liberty of God and for all those walking onto the shores of this new land.

Eyes scanned over them. Eyes stopped on him. His head pounded more.

Christian told me I am forgiven, yet I do not feel forgiven. Who would want me for what I did to You, God, and my parents, to Amara's parents, and for what I did to Amara?

Pada took one more step. He felt a gentle tap on the top of his head, like an invisible hand or sword, and collapsed. The last thing he saw was a seagull swoop down and then fly away.

CHAPTER 45

THE ASSEMBLED

On the Mayflower
1620

Abraham crawled into the small space on the *Mayflower*, like moving through the opening of a giant torn veil.

This can't be happening. What is this?

Before him, a grand room. His chest hurt, as if awakened in the middle of heart surgery. He arose with clenched fists and pushed forward with another step. "I do not want to die," he yelled.

On the other side of an opening ahead of him, a distant sliver of light.

This could not be. This was not the *Mayflower*.

He was outside of the *Mayflower* as he knew it. Before him lay a room big enough for a large table with several available chairs. And much open space.

Where did this come from? How can this be?

Entombed in the Dark Light, his throat tightened. His chest ached. Pain appeared where his eye used to be. The expanding sliver of light ahead moved toward him.

He was not alone.

As the brightness approached, Abraham could only gaze downward with a partially opened right eye.

He stood bent forward in the large room, and the only opening was closing. Someone, or something was inside with him and was squeezing his throat. It was difficult to breathe. With a downcast eye and trembling lips, Abraham swung his fists. "Stay away, Death. Stay your hand! I want to live!"

His throat tightened further. The shining sliver moved closer. He could not make a noise. It was as if he was sinking as something pulled him down.

My sins! My sins! My days are to end now as I am judged for all my transgressions. There is no place for me to hide. The eyes of my heart are ripped open for me to see inside myself. My sins!

As the glowing neared, the floor trembled. Abraham shook more as powerful, invisible waves crashed over him.

No more secrets! I am fully exposed!

His legs buckled. The last thing he saw was the Dark Light swoop down over him before he collapsed.

I loved you, my bride.

Above him, the Dark Light that seduced him his entire life and the approaching expanding sliver of Light. The room quaked from what moved above and around him.

The last remnants of life began to flee from him. He became a hollowing corpse.

I feel heat. I do not want to go to hell!

With a last burst of life, Abraham swung at what was moving above and around him.

"I want to live!"

The shining sliver turned into a hand of Light and violently opposed what was moving over him. Abraham was fading away. The hands of the Dark Light moved from the familiar grip around his throat to reaching inside his throat. Abraham raised his hand upward like a drowning man waving for help.

Please, God, save me!

The darkness circled above, preparing to enter into him fully. The hand of brightness swirled above him and lifted him up to his knees.

Last breath. Eye closed. Unclear speech. "My God! My God! My . . . God! I confess! I confess . . . You know my every deed. I wanted to be different from my father, but yet I left my wife and children at Jamestown. I betrayed and left my family unprotected to feed my lust and hunger for riches. I left them for the illusion of riches on the sea. I traded my family for greed, and I have not returned. I am a coward."

He could hear what sounded like fire splashing on flesh above him as the Dark Light tried to enter him. The room quaked more as the swords of the Light and the Dark Light clanged above him.

He tried a hard swallow. "I was with the *Treasurer* and the *White Lion* . . . We attacked the *San Juan Bautista* . . . We took their slaves. The *White Lion* went back home . . . I went on the *Treasurer* with full pockets and boarded another ship to England. I left them . . . I left them . . . yes . . . I have blood from my African brothers and sisters on my hands because I lusted for riches."

He heaved for air. "I know the *White Lion* took them to the New World! I know in my heart that they became slaves, and I profited from that! I am the Judas who traded what was of God for silver. I did it. It was I. I conceived self-deceit, and I believed I could flee from my sins and guilt."

The fire splashed around him. Abraham wiped his face and shielded his eye from the expanding bright light.

"What can I do to stop the injustice that I helped midwife into the New World? I am guilty. God, I confess that I have sinned against you. I committed a great sin against my family and my brothers and sisters. I am undone before you. Who can undo what I have done?"

For the first time, he looked up, and he could clearly see the Dark Light. His good eye was opened. He gained strength. He looked at his left hand. He was no longer a victim or off to the side of the battle.

He was now swinging a blade within it.

On her death bed, he remembered his mother's final words about her final months.

In my weaknesses, I failed you. I could not see Him in you. In my weaknesses, I cried out, and He entered my hardened and fearful heart to love you and protect you.

A new strength coursed through his veins as he swung the sword around and above him. Could someone else, committed to victory for him, be inside him? Fighting through him? Fighting for him?

Sounds of fire splashing and singeing from his sword echoed as the sparks landed on the Dark Light. The air was filled with clanging until it became consuming. Yelling. Screaming. Clanging. More fire. The Dark Light paused after the sound of something being cut.

Abraham tired. More strength came. His strength emptied. He was filled more. He swung more. More rage slithered at him. He swung more. Several minutes. Tired hands. The grip around his throat loosened.

His hand froze with the sword. He swung more.

He laughed when the Dark Light screamed at him and fled. Death passed over him.

His heart was at rest. No more gasping for air. No longer being pulled in multiple directions.

He then swung some more.

Heaving for air, he opened his eye to see through the new elements surrounding him.

He was not alone.

Voices. Many voices. These voices were not crying out in pain. He heard the multitude of voices singing a new song in the room. Partially covering his eye from the glowing brightness, the veil lifted. There were seven figures seated at a table. Voices of many tongues from many nations filled the expanding room. Their faces were not clear through the bright light. He realized someone transported him to a place where he could no longer feel the ship pitching and yawing. No more sounds from the severe storm. No crying. No longer scratching his head and his body from the incessant lice and fleas.

This smells beautiful.

Abraham thought he saw a quick flash of someone else. A young woman appeared and then disappeared off to the side.

Then the voices stopped. He collapsed again. A voice of majesty shook the room. Like mighty thunder above massive waters.

"Arise. Remove your shoes, for you are standing on holy ground."

Heart pounding, Abraham complied.

"I have heard the cries of my children. The Spirit has moved you. You have sought my face and forgiveness. You are forgiven of your transgressions."

That voice. It is the voice that awoke me from the dead. It stayed my hand. He called my name. It was with me in the empty church!

Seven figures sat before Abraham. He could not formulate words that did not even exist in his vocabulary to describe what was before him.

A Light with other lights.

The figure to his far left spoke. "The King called you out from a nation and appointed you to become part of a new great nation. You will be part of the light blazing in the darkness. A flawed nation in the shadow of the perfect Light. It will help bring the one true King's light to other nations dwelling in darkness."

One within a light next to the first figure spoke. "You are leaving a pharaoh and are part of a journey to a new land and new freedom. The King is ahead of you, leading, behind you protecting, and is dwelling with you and in you to sustain and give you His vision. Know that the Light of the world will shine His light and many will be freed from the tyranny of this world. A pharaoh will attempt to bring them back to their chains. But the one true King will act with signs and wonders to intervene and save His people."

The next figure in another light from left to right spoke. "You must be holy. The children who possess the light of liberty will sin against their own brothers and sisters. Leaders freed from slavery will become slave masters, and this sin will affect the generations. If sin and unforgiveness reigns, all will be enslaved. Those who abuse their liberty shall lose it. But the Father will not forsake His children. The kingdom will rise in all parts of the world, and many slaves will be delivered."

The next figure seated to Abraham's right of the center figure spoke with a lovely voice. "Your heart will be pierced. You will proclaim, 'If the Son sets you free, you will be free indeed.' The very Son of God who conquered death is the same God who conquered the tyranny of creation. You will play a part in expanding the kingdom of God. You will serve the

King whom you love with the gratitude and thankfulness of one whose friend gave his life for yours."

Then the next one from left to right spoke within another light. "You will be given the signs and wonders of God to proclaim the good news of the Savior who opposes tyranny. Many will be prideful and sin against their own brothers and sisters, yet you will live with a thorn of the flesh as you suffer alongside the native people of the land. With suffering, the prayers of some of the natives will assist in the birthing of liberty. Some who suffer injustice will find their hope in the God who will bring justice. Many will pray effective prayers that will help set the course of a nation. You will gladly live the truth of the love and liberty of the King while you will take on the chains with and for your brothers and sisters."

There was a pause as Abraham waited for the last figure to his right to speak. The glowing light pulsated like a beating heart. It vibrated at an increasing rate, seemingly in rhythm with Abraham's beating heart. Abraham's vision in his right eye improved. The final figure to his right remained still, with his eyes closed.

I know this one. He was one of the chained that went on the White Lion!

The figure illuminated through the light. Even with closed eyes, he had a wounded left eye and ear. There were marks, like scars from chains, wrapped around his arms. Then only his right eye opened. Then his left eye opened, and all the wounds disappeared.

"You have been bought. Saved. Redeemed. Paid for. You were once called slave. The chains once upon you are now broken through the suffering of God and His children. Those of tyranny and eternal debt of sin tremble at the Name, as all will bow down before the King. Only love can pay the price that frees. Only love can pay for the release of the captives. Only love is worth the cost."

Abraham fell to his knees.

Someone planted an image from his repeating dream into Abraham's mind.

A new final scene.

He was in the water, and only the woman remained. The hands from the abyss and the young man had vanished. The woman's face flashed from an older woman into the face of a younger woman. The small young woman looked around herself, as if looking for help among the remnants of the broken ship. Her face glistened with torrential tears and waves of sobbing with gentle seizures. Would she submit to the pull of the ocean or fight to stay alive?

Then the young man surfaced from underneath the water. He had been holding her above the surface and preventing her from being pulled down. As he held her up by her hand, he moved between the young woman and Abraham with a fist raised, as if having defeated one foe and ready for the next. The young man pulled Abraham closer, and they all embraced. The young woman lifted her hands from below toward the water's surface, preparing to show something to Abraham. Then a voice. A voice from another King, came through the mouths and voices of the young man and young woman . . .

Then all went silent.

The figures in an upper room of the City Cubed bowed down.

The seventh figure in the middle of the assembly spoke. A gentle power emanated and wafted in the room.

"The cries for justice have met their measure. From death comes life. You will arrive upon the land, and written covenants and proclamations will be made, as this land will be dedicated to my Name. There will be a day when my people will once again forget their first love and attempt to raise up prideful kings who will deceive many back into slavery. What will become of the prodigal son?"

A hand reached down and lifted Abraham to his feet. Without veiling, Abraham looked at His hand under Abraham's chin.

The blood . . . the blood . . . this hand created and nourished the beautiful tree that would one day be used to kill Him. This hand is different from any other hand of any other king . . . this King's hand is stained . . . with His own blood.

The hand lifted Abraham's chin toward His face.

Those eyes! No king but King Jesus.

Abraham put his hand in his pocket and dropped the bag of coins at His feet. Abraham knelt with his head bowed down. He felt a tap upon his head.

The sword . . . I will know this grip . . .

Abraham thought of the contents of the womb afloat on the Atlantic he'd lived in minutes ago. Soon to give illegal birth to a stronghold of the Kingdom.

He had come to fight on his last day of life. He remembered the suicide pact with Jonathan to pay off the debt of his sins.

I cannot pay that debt. It was already paid in full for me.

And now, day seventy-seven and beyond was no longer his. It was to be given away.

In his pocket, a warmth and movement from the object that the boy Moses gave to him. The door in the City Cubed then veiled again. The Light relocated into him.

Will you also heal my vision? Will you also heal me so I can walk as I should?

Abraham shook his head and smiled. There would be another day he would enter into the City.

As he stood, the ship moved under him. He knew where he was. With a new strength, he lifted his head.

He adjusted the new ring. He put his shoes back on. He picked up the book and held it firmly against his chest and crawled out of the space. He failed to brace himself to stay upright as the ship pitched. He fell. Rose. With a limp and vision in his right eye only, he entered back into the awaiting storms and took one step toward his family . . . and Jonathan.

***

On the other side of the Atlantic, the Dark Light roamed with concentrated power alongside and within the king. The king paid no attention to the blood on his hand and now on his son that he held. He cursed and shook his head and fixed his gaze both upon his bloody right hand and his son raised with his left hand.

He smiled at his son's beautiful face. A face that had already attracted many. Cooing the sweetest sounds that would entice any ear. A face and a voice to shepherd the masses.

The power in his son's hand, now bloodstained as he squeezed his father's finger, already possessed a strong grip.

The cloaked one hid within his vessels. Lies. Power and control. Pride. Deception. Division. Unforgiveness. Hate. There was much fertilizer to feed the thorns in the cursed garden.

The king placed his shaking head into his shaking empty hand. He pulled his hair. He screamed. He made his son cry.

Murderer.

"WHERE ARE YOU?"

***

Continents away, after trips between what was left at home and back to Luanda, captors behind Amara stomped toward her. Amara stood small, bent forward, as if carrying something, with her back to her captors. Before her, at the top of the cliff, the fortress below continued with death overcoming life. Behind her, she waited for the captors to enter the trap.

What do I have to offer You, my God? I have nothing to deliver for You.

She raised open arms. Her open hands turned into fists as her voice lifted upward in song. She felt a tap on her head. With a gentle power, like a distant rolling thunder moving from the distant past to the present, from one continent to another, she opened her fists.

A sliver of the surrounding Light cut through the thick cloud. She turned her body toward them. She stood taller and stared at the approaching captors. She placed the prayer stick Pada had given her between her and the coming captors. The object Chinasa had given her years before from Chinasa's favorite baobab tree near Luanda, warmed in Amara's hidden pocket.

A gentle yet powerful wind caressed her face. In her mind's eye, Amara saw something planted in trampled hard soil. It was still alive. Surrounded by awakened, growing thorns alerted to what was implanted. She placed her hands on her stomach as she felt something move within her.

A seed.

Like a small, gentle, powerful fist, trying to get out.

The "Mayflower Compact"

In the name of God, Amen. We whose names are underwritten, the loyal subjects of our dread Sovereign Lord King James, by the Grace of God of Great Britain, France, and Ireland King, Defender of the Faith, etc. Having undertaken for the Glory of God and advancement of the Christian Faith and Honour of our King and Country, a Voyage to plant the First Colony in the Northern Parts of Virginia, do by these presents solemnly and mutually in the presence of God and one of another, Covenant and Combine ourselves together in a Civil Body Politic, for our better ordering and preservation and furtherance of the ends aforesaid; and by virtue hereof to enact, constitute and frame such just and equal Laws, Ordinances, Acts, Constitutions and Offices from time to time, as shall be thought most meet and convenient for the general good of the Colony, unto which we promise all due submission and obedience. In witness whereof we have hereunder subscribed our names at Cape Cod, the 11th of November, in the year of the reign of our Sovereign Lord King James, of England, France and Ireland the eighteenth, and of Scotland the fifty-fourth. Anno Domini 1620

Modern version
www.plimoth.org

ACKNOWLEDGMENTS

As one of many scribes, I give thanks to the Author of our Story. Thank you to my wife and family for the support and challenges. Thank you to Dori, Patrick, Adam, Dara, and all others who helped bring about more of the *New Seed* Story.

SOURCES
OF INSPIRATION

The Light and the Glory, Peter Marshall and David Manuel
Wikipedia for *Imbangala, Slavery in Angola*

blackthen.com for *The Imbangala:Death and War Culture*

britanica.com for *Imbangala*

NIV and NASB Bibles

history.com for *What happened to the "Lost Colony" of Roanoke, Jamestown Colony*

brighthubeducation.com for *The Difference Between the Geneva and King James Bible*

ABOUT THE AUTHOR

As a storyteller and a physical therapist, Charles Anthony Solorio works with people who are physically and sometimes emotionally broken. He believes that stories can confront the raw side of our brokenness and bring about healing by seeing our own lives through the lenses of both faith and a faithfulness woven into our history. *The Splintered Beam* is Charles' second novel. Charles lives in Southern California with his wife and adult children. You can meet Charlie at charlesanthonysolorio.com